About

James E Mack was born in S
childhood abroad, gaining a
and wildlife. He became a Commando in the late [illegible] and a member of a Special Operations unit, with a 22-year career serving in many of the world's troubled hotspots. James subsequently specialised as a Counter-Terrorism adviser and assisted in capacity building operations in support of UK and US Government initiatives.

His passion for wildlife led James to assist in the development of counter-poaching programs in Africa. This passion remains and James spends much of his leisure time photographing the very animals that he strives to protect.

When time allowed, James began writing novels based upon his experiences in Special Operations and conflict zones around the globe. His first novel, *Only the Dead*, was very well-received and attracted interest from several screenwriters.

James lives in Northern Scotland where he enjoys the surfing and the mountains nearby.

This is a work of fiction. Names, characters, businesses, places, events and incidents are either the products of the author's imagination or used in a fictitious manner. Any resemblance to actual persons, living or dead, or actual events is purely coincidental.

Published by Achnacarry Press

ISBN: 978-1096360865

THE KILLING AGENT

JAMES E MACK

Once again, I must thank everyone who has supported me throughout the writing process. For me, being a writer is the culmination of a dream I'd harboured for many years but just didn't have the time, or the confidence, to put pen to paper. So, to everyone who has been behind me, thank you once again. I might write the books, but you help me make them the best possible stories that I can produce. And to the Readers *must also go my heartfelt gratitude: Without you, I'm just a guy in a quiet room typing furiously on a lap-top. And finally, to my partner* Teresa; *thank you for your support and advice in both writing and life itself.*

James E Mack

Also by James E Mack:

Only the Dead

Fear of the Dark

'Men are not punished for their sins, but by them'

Unknown

LONDON

He moved through the crowd with his customary smile and took care not to bump into people. It amused him to see the stress and strain of the morning commuters as they poured out of the underground exits of Tottenham Court Road, the weight of the world on the shoulders of people without any real problems to speak of. The steady stream continued unabated as rumbling trains below the street disgorged the hordes. Men and women, young and old, black and white, suits and dresses. Some in shorts to counter the warmth of summer. Taxi horns and bus engines clashed with emergency vehicle sirens, the background accompaniment to the migration of the masses on a sunny London morning. The taste of exhaust fumes thick on the stifling air.

Safi was sweating heavily under his thick jacket but fought the urge to scratch at the irritations. As a Police Community Support Officer there were standards to maintain. People had to look up to him. He had to be trusted and respected, an acknowledged representative of the forces of law and order. And life was good. He'd kissed his wife Alisha and young son Naji before leaving home, determined, as always, to make them proud of him, to be an example for the boy.

So, Safi smiled and nodded at anyone who caught his eye as they brushed past. The heat was becoming uncomfortable. Licking his lips, he imagined a cool drink of water slaking his thirst but pushed the notion to one side for the time being. Side-stepping a persistent Big Issue seller, he glanced at his watch, and had just looked up when the huge explosion rocked him. Screams of fear roused him from his catatonic state of shock and looking towards the sound of the blast, he saw thick, roiling clouds of smoke billowing out of the junction of Great Portland Street. People were now running away from the blast area and he could see bodies staggering from the depths of the cloud, clothes shredded, white dust lending their features a macabre, spectral appearance. Safi shook his head and struggled to stay on his feet as he was buffeted by the panicked mob. Another huge blast somewhere behind him brought a further cacophony of screams and shrieks and halted the movement of the crowd.

The fear was contagious, with people sprinting away in every direction and Safi knew he had to take control. He pulled a whistle from his webbing vest and began blowing a series of short sharp bursts to get people's attention. Seeing some of the pale, tear-streaked faces turn towards him, he pointed at the entrance to the underground. 'GET

INTO COVER. GET INTO COVER. NOW. NOW. NOW. GET OFF THE STREET.' His voice hoarse from the shouting, he began pushing those nearest him towards the underground entrance. Grabbing, thrusting, bullying anyone he came into contact with to get them moving. He could see it was starting to work. There was now a general flow of panicking people, hunched and sobbing, faces pale with shock, heading into the Underground. Safi continued to direct the mob, his eyes stinging from the acrid smoke that was drifting into the street. He coughed and rubbed his eyes but maintained his stoic management of the crowd. There were hundreds of people in the station now and he knew he had to make his own way there soon or he would pass out from smoke inhalation. He took a final look at the street around him, a post-apocalyptic vision of thick, black smoke, and stumbling wounded people as alarms and sirens pierced the poisonous air.

Dry-retching after inhaling another lungful of the acrid smoke, Safi knew he had to move. Staggering down the steps of the station, coughing and spluttering, he found some clearer air and took several deep breaths. The sound caught his attention first; a miasma of wailing, sobbing and crying multiplied by the echoing acoustics of the station's curved walls. As he watched, he could see many of the crowd talking into their telephones, hands covering ears to block out the din of suffering around them.

Safi made his way into the crowd, pushing people gently aside, his uniform lending him the authority to those who questioned him with their glassy stares. He patted shoulders with a reassuring firmness, nodded at people with confidence to show them it was all going to be okay.

He couldn't believe it; there were hundreds of people down here. People *he* had brought here. His chest swelled with emotion. Today, Alisha and Naji would be very proud of him. The press of the bodies against him grew tighter as he made his way to the centre of the crowd to make his announcement. Sweat beaded his forehead as he found himself pushing harder against the close-knit bodies, flashing his smile to calm the irate stares and frowns.

He stopped and created a small space around him by gently manoeuvring bodies with his hands. Looking around he tapped a tall man on the shoulder and then another. The men turned to him and Safi took them by an arm each. Leaning in to be heard over the wailing and crying, he shouted. 'Lift me up so I can address the crowd please. We need to calm these people down.' The taller of the two pushed his wire-rimmed glasses up on his nose and nodded, glancing at the other man who was also nodding as he wiped tears from his eyes. Safi waited as they stepped in close, then put his arms around their necks and braced his legs as they raised him onto their shoulders. He patted each man's head and looked out over the huddled mob. Suddenly, he found himself at a loss for what to say. *No*. He knew *what* to say, it was just how to say it clearly and without causing confusion. Frowning, he shook his head to dispel the distractions. Clearing his throat, he looked out over the throng and wondered if everyone would hear him. He reached into a webbing pocket and pulled out his radio, turning the volume dial and activating the power. He took a final breath before lifting the radio above his head and yelling at the top of his lungs.

'ALLAHU AKBAR'.

EDINBURGH

The concourse was heaving as the platform for the London train was announced on the digital display board. The scrum of people and luggage surged towards the turnstiles as one, jostling and vying for position to breach the chrome barrier control. The rush was halted by the impediment of a group of scruffy backpackers who struggled to squeeze their array of packs and baggage through the confines of the turnstiles. One of them turned to the crowd as he wrestled with his large pack that was jammed fast between the barrier and the floor. His handsome features broke into a wide smile as he swept his blond fringe away from his tanned forehead, the beads of sweat apparent as he attempted to shift the dead weight.

Curses and tutting were audible from within the crowd as the throng pressed against each other, and one of the station staff approached the barriers from the platform side. Shaking his head, John Mackay gave a small smile to the pretty brunette who had managed to sling her pack over the barrier and was squeezing a smaller rucksack through. She returned the smile with a silent, mouthed apology and he waved his hand in dismissal. This time of year, with the

Fringe festival in full swing, the city and the station in particular, was a madhouse of tourists from every corner of the globe. He'd seen it all in his twenty-odd years working at the station, and a wee kerfuffle at the entry turnstiles was pretty small beer. And he was looking forward to a beer later with some of the Cross-Country crew he was friends with. One of the drivers he knew was retiring and John had been asked along. Nothing fancy, a curry down Leith Walk and then a few pints at Hoagies before tottering home.

He'd reached the brunette's turnstile and was just about to speak when she pulled something from the backpack and pointed it at him. He struggled to process the image that he was confronted with and the look of puzzlement was the last expression that John Mackay's face ever held. The burst of gunfire from the AK 47 split the air and tore chunks from John's face and skull as his body was propelled backward by the kinetic energy of the bullets. His lifeless corpse slammed onto the marbled flooring of the platform and slid several feet before coming to a halt against an iron column, a crimson pool colonising the white slabs beneath him as his body was finally at rest. Another burst of loud shots echoed through the cavernous interior of the station as the brunette turned her weapon against the crowd. The screams started and masked a lot of the shots until the blonde backpacker turned his Uzi towards the running mass of people and opened up, the lethal hail of bullets emptying the magazine in mere seconds. The third backpacker, a girl in her late teens with a fashionable bobbed hairstyle, followed the carnage with several well-aimed throws of the fragmentation grenades that she had retrieved from her small rucksack. The sound of the explosions was not as loud as she had anticipated, possibly as a result of them detonating among the throng of tightly-packed bodies. She shrugged and fished another couple of the grenades from her pack and began pulling the pins.

The crowd's screams and wails of terror filled the entire concourse of Waverley Station with most of them running into the shelter of the food court and shops. Herd mentality kicked in, with those straggling individuals at the back of the crowd following those in front in the belief that they were running to safety. A giant explosion shook the floor and even the backpackers were knocked over by the concussive effect of the bomb in the food court, timed to perfection to detonate when the hall was filled to its maximum capacity. Large slabs of glass, concrete and structural beams tumbled from the high roof, slamming into those already wounded or incapacitated with a terrifying finality.

The brunette backpacker picked herself off the floor and shook her head in a vain attempt to clear the ringing in her ears. She looked towards the food court and was pleased with what she saw. The billowing clouds were settling and a slow-moving fog of dust and smoke was creeping towards her. She glanced at her companions who were also rousing themselves from the floor and then pulled a small pistol from the small of her back. In three quick strides she reached the handsome blonde boy, thrust the pistol against his head and pulled the trigger. Without even the slightest pause she stepped over his body and put the gun against the head of the grenade thrower, who looked her in the eye, smiled and nodded. The shot and the jerking back of the head were simultaneous and the brunette nodded with satisfaction before taking a final look at the carnage around her. With a beatific smile and an undisguised glow of pride at a job well done, she put the pistol to her own temple and pulled the trigger a final time.

CARDIFF

Billy hated shopping with his mum. She never went into any interesting shops, it was always Dorothy bloody Perkins, River Island or, on particularly shit days, New Look. While his mum *oohed* and *ahhed* over whatever tat now passed for female fashion, Billy endured the humiliation of following her around while having to occasionally look interested when asked what he thought of a particular garment.

On one level he knew it was his own fault; since he'd been caught shoplifting, she'd refused to let him out of her sight whenever they came to the mall. He hadn't even wanted the stuff he'd been caught with but he'd just got in with Kai Evans and his gang and he'd been doing it to fit in. Life at school had been shit since they'd moved here and he'd been struggling until he'd mouthed off at the guidance counsellor on a rainy Friday afternoon. Mr Forbes was one of those teachers who thought he was so fucking cool and *down with the kids*. The fact that he even said 'down with the kids' showed him up for the prat that he was.

On that particular Friday afternoon Billy hadn't been feeling all that great about life. At lunchtime he'd seen his dad walking on the other side of the road with his new girlfriend. That alone had shocked him as he'd had no idea that his dad ever came into Cardiff. What had really killed him though was when he'd caught his dad's attention and watched as his father had registered his presence with surprise then pulled his girlfriend closer to him and directed her attention to a shop window further up the street. Billy had been devastated. When it had happened a year ago, he'd blamed his mum for the family split as his dad had always been cool and fun to be around. Lately however, he'd been wondering. His mum never slagged his dad off, not even when, as was now the norm, his old man didn't even bother showing up to get him on the weekends. And that Friday afternoon had pretty much cleared it up in Billy's mind: His dad was a prick. And that was why Mr Forbes had caught the sharp end of Billy's tongue in an uncharacteristic outburst.

Mr Forbes had been trying to engage with Billy about his *aspirations* for life after school. When Billy had been unresponsive, old Forbesy had walked around his desk and placed an arm around Billy's shoulder. The words were out of Billy's mouth before he knew it and even now, he could not recall them exactly. But it had been something to the effect that old Forbsey shouldn't be so open about being a member of the Jimmy Saville fan club while working as a teacher. Billy remembered the teacher's horrified expression and the way he'd removed his arm as though Billy's shoulders were on fire. Billy had stormed out of class and just gone home.

That night though, Kai Evans and a couple of his gang had appeared at Billy's door. He'd answered as his mum was still at work, and at first had shit himself that they were there to beat him up. Kai Evans was *the* kid at school that nobody messed with. But nothing had prepared him for the reason they had showed up at his door. Kai Evans had been in the class when Billy had turned on the guidance counsellor. And Kai Evans had thought it was the funniest thing he had ever heard a kid do to a teacher. And just like that, Billy was *in*. But being *in* meant you did what the gang did. Even when you didn't want to. And that's how the whole shoplifting thing had panned out. His first time ever doing something like that and he'd been caught, held by store security and the police called.

His mum had gone *apeshit*. The yelling and screaming had been bad enough but when she'd started crying and blaming herself, Billy had never felt so shit in his life. Nothing he said could convince her that it had only been a one-off, a way of staying in with the cool crowd. After that day she never allowed him any free time, every second of his waking hours accounted for and controlled. And that was why he found himself trailing his mother around the women's departments of every high street fashion retailer, wallowing in his own personal hell.

Her voice brought him back to the present and he died a little inside as she held up a…dress? Skirt? She'd explained the difference to him one day, but he was pretty sure that his boredom was pretty common to most 15-year-olds faced with the same situation. Billy sighed and nodded his head while he tried to think of a reply that would satisfy his mum without exposing his utter lack of interest in what she chose to wear. He opened his mouth as a giant bang shook the shop. His mum's eyes widened in fear and she dropped the dress or skirt on the floor. He'd felt the floor shake under his feet and looked down just as another huge boom echoed around the shopping centre. The windows behind him shattered and he screamed and threw his hands over his ears. He felt his mum's arms around him and he grabbed her around the waist, pulling her tight. He could now hear screaming and shouting from outside and a popping sound, like fireworks. His mum was yelling at him and he felt himself being pulled as she yanked at his arm and hauled him out of the store.

Looking up he saw people running in all directions, colliding with each other, tripping and falling. His mum kicked off her shoes and clamped her handbag under her arm, all the while retaining her death grip on his hand. Billy was terrified. He was trying to work out what was happening when a loud series of the popping noises came from up ahead. A new chorus of screaming followed, and a wall of people ran towards them, dropping bags as they fled whatever terror they had just witnessed. He looked up at his mum just as something slammed into him and smashed him to the floor. Winded and confused he sat up, only to be knocked down again as an Asian girl in a white dress collided with him and careened into the glass balustrade beside the escalator. He got to his feet on shaking legs and found his mum immediately. She was stood screaming his name as her head swivelled in all directions looking for him. She looked a bit mental, what with her make-up all running down her face, but at that moment he felt he'd never loved her more.

He yelled and she turned towards him, relief flooding her features and her arms open wide. He ran to her and opened his own arms to grab her when her head suddenly snapped back, and a fine red mist hung in the air where her head had been. A loud bang followed almost immediately, and Billy stood rooted to the spot. As his mother hit the marbled floor and the thick blood oozed from her head, he was unaware of the urine soaking his jeans. A hand grabbed him by the hair and pulled hard, knocking him off balance. Screaming, he grabbed at the hand and tried to pull free but didn't have the strength. Looking up he saw a man in a suit holding his hair with one hand and a rifle in another. Billy struggled as hard as he could and looked up again as he heard the clatter of the rifle dropping to the floor. The man pulled a long knife from inside his jacket and looked over Billy's head at something. Billy craned his neck in an attempt to see what the man was looking at and saw a smartly dressed woman filming him with her mobile telephone. For a brief second Billy thought that the woman was going to help, was filming it so that she could show the police, but as his legs were kicked from under him and he felt the steel of the blade against his throat, his final realisation was that she was there to film his terrible death.

KANDAHAR, AFGHANISTAN, TWO YEARS EARLIER

The guests would arrive within the hour. Mahmoud stood in the shade of the compound wall and shelled another pistachio, flicking the nut into his mouth as he discarded the husks onto the hard-baked earth. The smell of his wife's bread wafted through the open windows of their kitchen. He could hear his youngest son, Ahmad singing one of his rhymes as he played in the shade of the old tree. Ibrahim, his eldest would be in his room, fixated on the screen of his mobile phone, the online world far more interesting to a fifteen-year old to that of the real one.

A hand on his lower back broke his reverie and he smiled at his daughter as she offered him some green tea in a small, ornate glass. She was as beautiful as her mother and he could already see in the nine-year old, the woman that she would one day become. He smiled and took the drink. 'Tasha Khor, Gul.' *Thank you, flower.* She giggled and tucked her face away in embarrassed pleasure, making her way back to help her mother. Mahmoud watched her for a moment with a smile then blew on the tea to cool it slightly.

The vibrating in his pocket drew his attention and he fished the phone out and looked at the screen. His guests had reached the outskirts of the city and would be with him in around ten minutes. They had made very good progress from the crossing point at Spin Boldak, but then again, they were very important men and he should have anticipated that they would not be held up by the usual parasites of the Border Force seeking bribes for passage. He was about to warn Malia of their impending arrival but watched as his wife crossed the compound to the shaded area where he would host his guests. She laid the plate with the fresh bread on the carpet and covered it with a pristine white cloth. Returning to the kitchen she gave him one of her small smiles that he never got tired of seeing. He knew he'd been fortunate in his marriage to Malia; his family's status and position in Pashtun society a guarantee that he could have his choice of bride. And he'd chosen well. Malia was not like the women many of his friends and family had married; mere chattels recognised only for their ability to produce offspring to continue the family lineage. Malia was his love, his one and only and a wonderful mother to their children.

His phone rang as she came out a second time and he answered, directing the caller on how to reach his home. He walked as he talked, making his way to the heavy iron gates of his compound. He'd dismissed his security, as the identity of his visitors had to remain completely secret. As much as he trusted his personal bodyguards, he knew the men coming to see him would accept no such assurances.

These men knew all too well the value placed upon their heads by the Americans, and that every man had his price. As he unbolted the heavy doors in anticipation of their arrival, he thought about his visitors and what they hoped to achieve from this meeting. When three of the members of the Quetta shura, the *de facto* leadership of the Taliban, had sent the message that they needed to speak with him, Mahmoud had been curious. His involvement with the Taliban had ceased to be physical over a year before when he'd removed himself from the field of battle, recognising that the Americans were getting better and better at winning the fight on the ground.

He'd moved into the role of advisor, his background as an officer in Pakistan's Inter-Services Intelligence, or ISI, lending him both authority and experience with which to assist the insurgency. His familial links to Afghanistan had meant that he was the natural choice for the ISI's in-country liaison with the Taliban. He could move freely, was not on a High Value Target list due to his diligence in personal security. When he was just a fresh young officer, he had also worked with many of the mujahidin during the Soviet occupation, some of whom were now factional leaders of the Taliban or Haqqani networks. But then a raid by a British Special Forces' team had killed two ISI officers in a compound in Kunar. Both men had been carrying their ID and official documents. Washington had made it very clear to Islamabad: Stay out of this or we'll punish you hard. So, Mahmoud had been ordered to carry on with his role in a completely clandestine profile with no official links back to the ISI. He reported through a series of trusted intermediaries who carried coded notes that, even if intercepted, read as though they were standard missives between family members relaying relationship updates. One of these messages had come to him some weeks before, asking him to prepare for a visit from some of his favourite *cousins* who he had not seen for some years. Cousins in this case being the agreed code for commanders.

The sound of a vehicle approaching focussed his attention and he quickly checked his phone again, replied to a text, then opened the gates wide as a dust-covered Toyota saloon turned into his entrance. The vehicle slowed and he let it pass, closing and bolting the gates before turning towards the car. The engine was turned off and two men exited simultaneously, standing several feet from the car and scanning the compound with unwavering focus. The back doors opened and a further three men alighted, the taller one laying his hand on the arm of one of the first pair. No words were spoken but Mahmoud understood the message. *No need for your vigilance. This man is trusted.* The tall man locked his gaze upon Mahmoud, the deep blue eyes holding his attention. They walked towards each other and Mahmoud found himself embraced by the older man, who smelled of expensive cologne. Feeling the release of the embrace Mahmoud stepped back and smiled just as the second man approached and also embraced him. This man smelled faintly of mint and sweat, probably from the heated confines of the Toyota which would be unlikely to have air conditioning. The third man greeted Mahmoud more formally as the two did not know each other.

The tall man spoke. 'Come brothers, let us take some shade and rest a little before we speak of business.' He grinned, a flash of perfect white teeth, a rarity in a country where dentistry was practised with herbs, roots and mantras. 'Mahmoud, it has been so long my brother, I was beginning to think that the next time we met would be in paradise!'

Mahmoud laughed and showed the men to the shaded area under the trellis, pleased to see that while he had been busy Malia had laid out the food and refreshments for the guests. The men lowered themselves on to the rug and Mahmoud walked around them, pouring water and chai for the weary travellers. He was thanked and there was some silence as the men slaked their thirst. Mahmoud could not help but wonder at the reason these men had exposed themselves by coming into Afghanistan. The three were High Value Targets, or HVTs as the Americans referred to them. Generally speaking, men of this stature remained in the safe havens of the better suburbs of Quetta and Peshawar, protected by their ISI advisors.

He did not have to wait long. The tall man broke the silence. 'We do not have the luxury of time Mahmoud so forgive me for getting straight to the point. We have a huge problem that is causing us a big headache.'

Mahmoud spoke. 'Your words worry me Abdullah Jan. There must indeed be a serious problem for three of your organisation's top commanders to risk coming into the country.'

The man that Mahmoud did not know replied. 'Mahmoud. Brother. I am Jabbar Agha, the new Taliban governor of Khost province. A great deal of our problem lies in Khost province however if allowed to happen, it will expand like a disease into the neighbouring provinces and we will be powerless to stop it.'

Abdullah Jan expanded on his colleague's statement. 'The problem is Mahmoud, that we have been fighting the infidels for over fifteen years and the people are tired of it. *I* am tired of it. But in Khost the tiredness is leading to bad decisions that will affect our struggle.' He paused and took a slurp of his tea before continuing. 'The Tribal elders in Khost have been meeting with American officials and are ready to commit to cease supporting any Taliban activity in the province in return for agricultural investment.'

Mahmoud nodded. 'Okay, but we've seen this before where elders look for support from the invaders. This is nothing new.'

Abdullah Jan gave a quiet smile. 'Ah, but this time Mahmoud, we are talking about the *entire* province.'

There was silence around the rug as each man contemplated the seriousness of the situation. Mahmoud understood immediately the significance of the statement: The Taliban depended on the support of the local population for everything from recruitment to accommodation. If an entire province was to deny them this, others would follow, particularly if the benefits from their American backers was seen to be worthwhile. He cleared his throat and addressed his guests.

'Gentlemen, as you may or may not be aware, I have strong family connections in Khost and Kunar and I would be happy to represent your concerns to them and seek some clarity on this issue.'

Abdullah smiled and gestured with his hands to his colleagues. 'You see brothers, I told you that there was one man who could help us in this situation and, as always he does not disappoint. Come now, let us eat before the food gets cold and talk of business upon full stomachs.'

Mahmoud smiled at the compliment and watched as, for the first time since entering his compound, his visitors began to relax.

TASK FORCE OPERATIONS ROOM, KANDAHAR AIRFIELD, AFGHANISTAN

'They certainly look relaxed sir.' Staff Sergeant Eddie Brown kept his eyes glued to the screen on the wall above him, watching the meeting of HVTs in the compound. He turned around and smiled at the tall man in civilian attire who was typing rapidly on his mobile telephone. 'Looks like PHANTOM came through after all, eh?'

Crispin Faulks looked up from his messaging to acknowledge the Staff Sergeant's comments. He gave a small smile and nodded. 'Yes Eddie, have to say I had my doubts, but he came through in the end.' He returned to his secure telephone, updating Operations back at Vauxhall with the latest developments. He signed off and sent the missive, waiting for the confirmatory ping to confirm that it had been sent. Satisfied, he placed the device into the side pocket of his cargo pants and walked over to join the small team of soldiers watching the array of screens just above head level. Officially they were monitors that relayed the feed from the ISTAR assets, the Intelligence, Surveillance and Targeting systems deployed in the region; the UAVs or drones, covert cameras and overt systems. The drone monitor was always referred to as 'Kill TV', a legacy from the early Iraq days when the aerial assets were predominantly deployed on kinetic strikes or 'kill missions', to the layman. These days, while a significant portion of the platform's capacity remained in the lethal bracket, it was utilised for many other purposes.

Crispin looked around the operations centre and was happy with what he saw. A very small team, mostly hand-picked by himself, individuals he had worked with during his past nine months as the Secret Intelligence Service's Operations Director in Kandahar. The sharp end of the MI6 operation in Afghanistan, getting his hands dirty while others busied themselves with reports and assessments. He got on pretty well with the military, felt he had their respect, as he'd shown on many occasions that he wasn't squeamish about taking out targets. Today's targets, however, were different. Three HVTs rarely seen in Afghanistan now breaking bread together in a compound in the centre of the city without a care in the world. Crispin had no idea what could be so important that would entice these three into the country, but it must be big.

All three were in the top ten of the bad guys list and had been assigned operational code names: Abdullah Jan was Objective *Mako*, Jabbar Agha was Objective *Tiger* and Fahim Noor was Objective *Zambezi*. All named after sharks, in a nod to the fear and terror each powerful man wielded among the local population. Crispin thought it fitting that the moment the three sharks had crossed into Afghanistan they had been watched and followed by a hawk. Well, a Predator to be precise. Piloted by a young American Air Force officer back in Creech, Las Vegas and loaded for bear, as the Americans would say. Two Hellfire missiles that would lock on and destroy any target they were released upon.

The ringing of the secure phone interrupted his thoughts and Jenny, the analyst picked it up, speaking quietly into the handset. She stood up from behind her small partition and gestured to Crispin. 'Sir, it's for you. Vauxhall.' Crispin took the handset and listened for several moments before finishing the conversation with one word. 'Understood.' He turned to the Staff Sergeant and the Captain who now stood beside him.

'People, that was obviously my elders and betters on the line. We have been granted clearance for Op VIKER, I repeat, Op VIKER.' He glanced around him and noted the differing reactions. Jenny had thrown a questioning look at the Captain who had shrugged his shoulders ever so slightly but enough to indicate he was happy with Crispin's directive. Op VIKER clearance was rare; a lethal strike authorised while the assessed risk of collateral damage was very high. No recordings were retained of VIKER operations, minimising the possibility of footage being leaked to the media. He noted that Jenny was turning her attention to the other soldiers, desperately trying to gauge support for her reservations. The men however either dropped their gaze or got on with the task at hand. Crispin hoped that Jenny wasn't going to be a problem. She was relatively new and, if he remembered correctly, the only other VIKER strike she had witnessed had very little collateral and even those had been probable Taliban. He decided to nip this in the bud before it progressed into an issue.

He addressed the team again. 'As imperfect as the situation is, we have authority to strike. Ground assets are unavailable for capture option and PHANTOM has confirmed that the sharks will be mobile soon from the compound of Mahmoud Malikzada, but PHANTOM has no knowledge of destination. We now have ISTAR and HUMINT confirmation of PID.' He paused to let it sink in that the targets had been positively identified by both the drone and his source who had reported the targets' movements. Multi-platform PID was a godsend when it came to getting a strike authorised, most commanders at any level erring on the side of caution against killing the wrong person and having to account for it later. He continued. 'Weather is expected to deteriorate within the hour affecting our ability to manage the aerial coverage and follow their movements, therefore our options are very limited, and we need to act now if we are to get these bastards at all.' He looked for any reactions and saw Jenny and Eddie glance at each other quickly. Crispin couldn't have Jenny getting any support; dissention was like fear, once passed on to another individual it spread like wildfire. Of course, they knew the effect that the missile would have as they had conducted the collateral damage estimates during the planning of the mission. They were clearly uncomfortable with the presence of the woman and children but he'd hoped they would be able to put aside their consciences for the greater good. He would never get a better opportunity to take out the sharks and he didn't want the bleeding hearts of some junior-ranked squaddies to be a problem. He knew however, that they would not directly question his authority or that of his masters back at Vauxhall Cross. 'Okay ladies and gentlemen, let's do this.'

The team calmly took up their roles as they had done many times before, opening the comms link to Creech and Florida, where the US Air Force Operational Command oversaw the strike from their own Headquarters. Crispin put on a headset with a mic and sat at one of the desks below the monitors so that he could talk directly with the UK Headquarters back home. As it was an MI6 mission there was a limited audience, strictly cleared personnel only. He watched the monitor as the drone footage relayed the activity in the compound in High Definition. Crispin was impressed with the new camera systems and the clarity of detail that they provided; the men's faces clear in the monochrome display. He could hear the soft voice of the American pilot as he spoke with his own Headquarters confirming that he had the authority to prosecute the strike. The affirmative was given by a deeper, southern American accent.

Crispin's Captain acknowledged the order to execute and looked up to see that Crispin had also heard. The room was silent but for the transmissions between the pilot and the commands. The pilot marked the target area and relayed this across the comms. There was a brief pause and the final phase of the pilot's actions came through the radio system.

'Rifle, Rifle, Rifle, missile away.'

The silence was complete as all eyes watched the men in the compound sipping tea and sharing food for the final seconds of their lives. The screen suddenly changed to a mess of clouds, dust, and debris that took some time to clear and the picture to return to full clarity. Crispin spoke first. 'Let's stay on target for two and conduct BDA, over.' BDA; Battle Damage Assessment, surveying the kill zone and confirming your targets were dead. He heard the acknowledgement from the Americans and stared intently at the screen as the camera scoured the smoking ruins of the buildings and the crater where the main impact had been. Crispin saw immediately that it had been a good strike. Arms and legs were separated from torsos, clothes blown completely off their wearer's bodies, a head completely split in half. He turned his head to Jenny as he heard her swear. Looking back at the screen he saw a clear shot of the youngest girl, her body twisted at an impossible angle and almost completely severed at the hips. He turned back to Jenny and saw the tears in her eyes as she shook her head at the carnage being displayed in ultra-high definition. Crispin caught her eye and stared at her aggressively until she dropped her gaze and wiped her tears away before sitting back behind her desk and dropping out of sight. The Ops room was silent as the camera continued to sweep the area, relaying the horrific sight thousands of feet below back to the people who had ordered the carnage. Neighbours were starting to rush to the scene now, having waited until they were sure that no more missiles would be fired. Crispin nodded and spoke. 'Okay, all targets KIA. Bird can lift off. Good job people, some top work here today.' Removing the headset, he laid it on the desk and stretched, rubbing his hands through his blonde curly hair. Various commands and agencies acknowledged the results as he walked to the secure door and unlocked it before stepping into the corridor. He walked along the plywood-clad walls to the end door and opened it, recoiling in the unforgiving glare of the Afghan sun. Pulling a pair of sunglasses from his pocket, he put them on as he sat on the table of a wooden picnic bench set beneath the dappled shade of a camouflage net. Reaching into his back pocket he pulled out a packet of cigarettes and lit one up, savouring the flavour and hit of nicotine.

'Can I bum one of those?'

He looked around in surprise to see Eddie stood beside him, the Staff Sergeant's Oakley sunglasses reflecting Crispin's image back at him.

'Sure. Here you go.'

They smoked in companionable silence for a while until Eddie spoke.

'Can I ask you something sir?'

'Sure, go ahead Eddie. What's on your mind?'

The Staff Sergeant looked up at the sky as if seeking the drone that had just delivered its terrible payload. 'Well, PHANTOM provided the information that generated this Op and now he's responsible for the death of the three HVTs, which probably doesn't bother him if he's on our side. But surely, he'll be bothered by the death of Mahmoud Malikzada and his wife and kids? How much do you pay an agent so that this kind of thing either doesn't bother him or that the money makes it worth his while?'

Crispin stood and crushed his cigarette under his boot and into the gravel. The Staff Sergeant knew very well that Crispin would never talk about his agents in anything other than the information they provided. Knew that their identities, payments and what they did were for Crispin alone. He was tempted to remind Eddie of this but thought better of it. There was a fair bit of collateral on this one and he didn't want an upset Staff Sergeant causing problems for him later on down the line. So instead he smiled and patted Eddie's shoulder.

'Enough, Staff Sergeant Brown. I pay him just enough.' With that Crispin walked off towards the cookhouse, pulling his phone from his pocket and checking for messages. Eddie watched him for some time before stubbing out his own cigarette. He'd been in the Intelligence Corps for over ten years now and this was his third tour of Afghanistan so he'd experienced a fair bit in his time. But today just felt…*wrong*. That poor guy Mahmoud Malikzada and his family wiped out so that someone in Whitehall could tick another three bad guys off a list that never actually got any shorter, no matter how many of them they killed. Chances were that Malikzada was related to, or friends with the targets but their research had found no information to confirm this. *And the wife and kids? What the hell had they ever done*?

As he watched Crispin disappear from view Eddie shook his head and turned back towards the Operations Room. He had to hand it to these MI6 spooks, they were as cold blooded as any SAS soldier in their own way. Drop a missile on a bunch of men, women and children then pop over to the cookhouse for a spot of lunch. As he removed his sunglasses and stepped inside, it came to Eddie that he hoped that he never became that cold.

TALIBAN HOSPITAL, QUETTA, PAKISTAN

It took Mahmoud a few seconds to remember what had happened and the realisation that he was badly injured. Tears streamed down his face as brief memories of being pulled from the carnage of what had once been his home assailed him. He recalled drifting in and out of consciousness as his neighbours carried him on a makeshift stretcher away from the blast site. He remembered grabbing the arm of an old man who was striding along beside him, screaming his wife and children's names at the man who had cried and shook his head, confirming Mahmoud's worst fears. He screamed at the ceiling of the white room and doubled up in pain as something inside him tore. A door opened and firm hands took control of his body as he continued to scream. He felt a needle go into his arm and then sleep overtook him.

When he awoke the second time, he felt worse; in more pain and thirsty. His head throbbed and he coughed, sending a river of agony along his spine. His door opened and a doctor and another man entered, stopping at the foot of the bed and observing him for several moments. The doctor spoke first.

'Mahmoud, I am Doctor Abbas and you are in the general hospital in Quetta. You were brought here by your friends in Afghanistan as they did not think you would be safe there. Mahmoud, do you remember what happened?'

Mahmoud stared at the doctor for some time before running his tongue over his parched lips. 'Drone…was drone…'

The doctor looked at the man beside him and the man leaned forward, immaculate in a white *shalwar kameez* and well-groomed. 'Mahmoud, I am Colonel Hayatullah, Directorate S, ISI. We haven't met before but I am aware of your operation in Afghanistan on our behalf.' He watched Mahmoud for several seconds and then continued. 'When we heard of the strike and learned you had survived, I despatched a team to collect you and bring you here for your safety and recuperation. It would only have been a matter of time before the Americans learned that you were in Kandahar hospital. Here however, you are beyond their reach.'

Mahmoud wet his lips again and asked the only question he had in his mind. 'My family?'

The Colonel shook his head slowly. 'All gone Mahmoud. All gone.'

The Colonel continued to talk, going on about how they needed to figure out how the Americans had known about the meeting and other matters of security, but Mahmoud wasn't listening. He had lost everything, every single thing that he had cared for was now gone. And it was his fault. He had known the risks, that someday something like this could, no, *would* happen. But he had been so careful. Had worked so hard to keep the risk away from his family. But in the end, it hadn't mattered. They'd killed them all anyway. Killed them like dogs in the street, his beautiful wife and children blown to pieces by a machine flying silently thousands of feet above them.

He closed his eyes and felt the guilt consume him. He'd *known* from the start that this was a possibility, but he'd trusted the measures he'd taken to cover his tracks. Trusted in his own personal security. Trusted that his anti-surveillance procedures ensured that no-one had ever followed him to the meetings. His family had trusted *him*. Trusted him to never bring the fighting to their home. Trusted him to be a good husband and father. Trusted him…

Mahmoud opened his eyes and shut off his train of thought. He was agonising over history. Nothing he thought, said, or did would change the situation or bring his family back. That life was over. But *his* life was not. The past was agony, heartbreak and horror, but the future? The future was something different. The future was revenge.

The Colonel had stopped talking and was looking at him. Mahmoud ignored him and focused his attention on the doctor. 'How badly hurt am I?'

The doctor glanced at the Colonel before answering. 'You have a fractured skull, broken ribs, a broken femur and some minor burns to your face. Which sounds bad but, considering what you have just been through, is nothing short of a miracle.'

'So how long till I can walk out of here on my own two feet?'

Again, the doctor looked at the colonel who shrugged and gave his silent assent. 'Months to allow the breaks and fractures to heal and even more time to rebuild your strength.'

Mahmoud nodded and felt the pain in his head immediately, frowning as a spear lanced through his cranium somewhere unseen. In a slow but determined movement, he turned and met the eyes of the Colonel.

'Well let's get started. I don't have any time to waste.'

JOHNSHAVEN, SCOTLAND, PRESENT DAY

The last of the summer swells broke their crests against the barrier of the harbour wall, tall plumes of spray gushing high into the air. Lovat could hear the crash of the waves as he stood, sipping his coffee and watching the spectacle from his favourite spot in the house. He'd had the huge window put in when he'd redeveloped the harbourmaster's house, the mortgage and the cost of the work cleaning him out for a couple of years. But he'd known what he had wanted; a house as close to the sea as possible, a bolt hole for him to escape to and access the solitude he needed.

Looking around the room he felt the familiar sensation of calmness envelope him as it always did when he returned. The whitewashed walls and distressed flooring complimenting one another and allowing the room to feel flooded with the light from the panoramic window. An oversized, worn leather sofa and a couple of matching chairs dominating the far end of the cavernous space, taking advantage of the log-burner built into the stone wall at the end. His gaze took in the art on the walls; all large format photographs of the wild places he had visited on his travels.

The Torres del Paine of Patagonia, a temple in Angkor Wat, his favourite shot of the aurora above Kirkjufell in Iceland, the dead majesty of Namibia's Sossusvlei.

Travel was Lovat's antidote to the stress and strain of being a covert military operator. The refreshing of the soul after seeing the worst that humanity can produce. He always felt the same way on returning from operations; a yearning to go to the wild, away from people, from noise and chaos, from killing and violence. When he'd started looking in earnest for somewhere to live, he'd been drawn back to the east coast of Scotland, an area he'd come to love while serving as a Commando based in Arbroath. The empty beaches and unbroken seascapes a more attractive prospect than living his life in the Mess, getting drunk and fat with the other Warrant Officers eking their time out to retirement.

And he'd found his place. The Harbourmaster's House had come on the market at the right time for Lovat. He'd been operational for an almost solid five years, taking only the minimum time off that the Unit mandated and a little more to travel. So, when he'd seen the stunning period property with nothing but sea views on three sides, he hadn't hesitated. He had significant cash saved from never being around to spend it and knew that the conversion he had in mind would be expensive. But he also knew from the off exactly what he wanted; a sanctuary. A retreat where he could indulge his passions for reading and surfing. The powerful, cold, dark swells that pounded the coast in winter provided Lovat with the challenge of riding nature's giants over the sandstone reefs that shaped the enormous waves.

As he finished his coffee, he thought about the night to come. He didn't have any food in as he'd returned in the early hours of the morning, just grabbing some milk while he'd filled up at a petrol station. Walking towards the stairs he decided to drive up to Inverbervie, grab some food and drink. He descended the staircase and entered the kitchen, rinsing his mug out in the sink and then cleaning the cafetiere, placing the items on the dark wooden draining board. He grabbed the car keys from the drawer in the hall and opened the front door, stepping out and closing it behind him. He didn't bother locking it; nobody in the village did. It was a tiny, close-knit community with one road in and out so it wasn't particularly attractive for criminals. His Hilux was parked at the side of his house, a top tip from the neighbours who informed him that if he left it at the front there was the possibility a rogue wave could break over the harbour wall. Apparently, it had happened a few times over the years but never enough to cause considerable damage. He started the truck and manoeuvred the black beast through the narrow streets, up the hill and on to the main road towards Inverbervie.

Taking a good swig from the glass, Lovat savoured the frozen-pea tang of the Sauvignon Blanc. Although he didn't really know a whole lot about wine, he liked the sharp acidity of this South African. He could hear the sea outside in the darkness, the wind carrying the song of the incoming tide. The cackle of the log in the burner made him look up and he decided to let the fire go out as the house was warm enough for the time of year. He took another drink and turned the page of his book, an account of Shackleton's expedition to the Antarctic. Other than the occasional protest from the burning log, the house was silent as he lost himself in the narrative of the book.

He was getting a pleasant buzz from the wine and found his eyelids becoming heavier. Marking his page with the book's dustcover, he leaned back, yawning and stretching. Finishing the glass, he leaned over to the small table, retrieved the bottle and topped-up his glass. Completely relaxed, he let his brain wander as he gazed at nothing in particular. He thought about the change of seasons and how the autumn swells would start sweeping down from the north, a mere taster compared to the thick, heavy behemoths that would smash themselves on the reefs in winter. His thoughts turned to where he would be in winter: Afghanistan? Iraq? Somalia? He sighed and shook his head, determined not to think about work. Rising, he walked over to the far end of the window sill where he picked up a small iPad. Activating the device, he accessed the Spotify app as he returned to his seat. While he would never have a TV in his house, Lovat needed music. After reading, he loved nothing more than to be mellow drunk and listening to some great tunes. His fingers worked the screen and a moment later the concealed speakers filled the room with the saxophone intro of Van Morrison's 'Stranded'. Lovat closed his eyes and smiled, swaying his head gently and drinking his Sauvignon.

He'd progressed onto Steve Earle by the time he'd gotten half way through his third bottle, singing loudly and slightly off beat to 'Copperhead Road'. As the song ended, he lay back on the sofa and toasted Mr Earle for a *bloody great tune*. He keyed up Cold Chisel's 'Khe Sanh' and felt the tears come to his eyes as the piano intro gave way to Jimmy Barnes' gravel vocals. He sang aloud but his voice caught and a sob came out instead. He couldn't believe he'd allowed himself to let the emotions sneak up on him, teased from his carefully guarded self by the lyrics of a song from a long-ago war. Memories of loss and heartache were now rising to the fore. Friends, colleagues and fellow operators whose faces he would never see again. Angry, he wiped his face with his hand and picked up the iPad, but it fell from his fingers. He dismissed the object with a wave of his hand and downed the wine. Putting the glass carefully on the floor, he lay back down on the sofa and felt his eyes close almost immediately. The song came to an end and quiet returned to the house. Lovat's breathing became heavy and he snored lightly for a few minutes before changing position slightly. He let out a couple of small moans and his brow wrinkled as he frowned. Then his breathing deepened, and he retreated into a heavy slumber.

The noise woke him. He groaned as he opened his eyes and wondered where the hell he was. For several seconds he was confused, couldn't remember if he was in the tented accommodation in Libya or back at the Mess in Bracken. It was soon apparent that he was in his home. Sitting up, he rubbed the back of his neck which was stiff from his awkward sleeping position. *What the hell is that noise?* He traced the shrill ringing to the bottom end of the sofa and moved a cushion aside to reveal his mobile, ringing louder now the cushion had been removed. Reaching out he picked the phone up and turned it over to look at the screen just as the ringing stopped. Squinting at the message displayed, he sighed as he recognised the caller's ID; Oliver Dewar, Commanding Officer of the SIG; the Special Intelligence Group, and Lovat's boss.

Lovat groaned as he tossed the phone back to the end of the sofa. *Not already. Only home a day.* There was a moment's blessed silence until his phone beeped again, alerting him to the presence of a text message. He shook his head and picked the phone up, studying the screen. *Lovat, you know what this is about and if you don't then turn on the fucking news. Call me ASAP. OD.*

OD; Oliver Dewar. *Colonel* Oliver Dewar OBE, Commanding Officer of the SIG. Lovat knew it would be something big; Commanding Officers did not call Warrant Officers directly. They had an RSM to do that for them. But Lovat was a special case. He'd known OD since their early careers as covert operators in Northern Ireland and no matter how far up the ladder of promotion he climbed, OD would always call on Lovat just as he had back in the rain-drenched back streets of West Belfast. The memory brought Lovat's hand to his face and he traced the deep line of the scar that followed the curve of his cheekbone before dog-legging down to the corner of his mouth. He'd saved OD's life that night. Saved both their lives to be more accurate. He closed his eyes and was immediately back at the scene, OD unconscious and slung over his shoulders as he staggered along Beechmount Avenue. The rain bouncing off the road, his face on fire and his cheek flapping open as the hot blood ran down his neck and onto his chest. Angry cries and shouts behind him, the mob baying for blood and howling over their dead.

He opened his eyes and shook his head, denying the memory further traction. Returning to the present, Lovat looked up the latest news on his phone and was stunned by what he saw. Three major attacks in British cities with the death toll in the hundreds. He read several articles and watched some of the more credible news reports before he put his phone down and went downstairs to brew some coffee. His mind was racing as he worked. A killing spree of this magnitude was unprecedented in the UK and the attacks were definitely coordinated, meaning someone with skill, authority and intent had put them all together.

As he poured the boiling water into the cafetiere, Lovat was shocked that Box had failed to catch this one. The logistics and organisation alone would have necessitated hundreds of phone calls, dozens of meetings, training and rehearsals. MI5, or Box as it was referred to in the intelligence community, should have been all over it. *What the hell had gone wrong?*

He sighed as he sipped the warm brew and felt himself finally starting to spark. He remembered the night before and how drunk he had been but felt no remorse. He liked to drink. A lot. Lovat knew he wasn't an alcoholic, nowhere near it. You couldn't deploy for the better part of a year and remain dry for that period if you were, but he hit it hard on his return and made no apologies for it. *Work hard, play hard.* As he finished his coffee, he decided to shower, change, have some breakfast, then phone OD back to hear what his Commanding Officer required of him this time.

THAME, ENGLAND

Nadia woke and felt the pounding immediately. She moaned and brought her hands to her head in a vain attempt to dull the throbbing. Opening her eyes, she saw that she was not in her own room and a brief moment later the memory of the previous night came flooding back. As quietly as she could, she slipped out of the bed and began searching for her clothes in the dim light, the closed curtains keeping the daylight at bay. Seeing all of her clothing piled on a small chair she crept over to it and pulled on her pants and bra, glancing over her shoulder at the sleeping form in the bed. Her jeans and shirt came next and she picked up her handbag and shoes and tiptoed from the room, taking exaggerated care when she opened and closed the door, loath to wake the sleeping body.

Finding herself in a small hallway, she remembered it from the night before and put on her shoes, glad they were flats and not heels. She had a rough idea that she was in an estate in Thame, if she remembered the taxi ride from the club accurately. Passing a mirror on the wall she gave a small laugh that she shut down instantly, gazing at the bedroom door behind her. Her hair was all over the place and her make-up had run, making her look demented. Reaching into her bag, she pulled out her hair brush and began dragging it through her black locks, gratified to see some of the sheen come back. Returning the brush to the bag, she pulled out her phone as she opened the front door, stepping into the sunlight and squinting against the glare. Recognising the area, she called the taxi number she retained in her contacts. As she spoke to the dispatcher, she looked over her shoulder at the house she had just left. Shaking her head with a small grin, she strode towards the road junction ahead where she had arranged to meet with the taxi. *I really should cut back on these one-night stands, settle down for a bit.* As she waited at the junction, she reflected that if they weren't so much fun, she probably would.

'Are you Staff Sergeant Ali?'

Nadia pulled her earphones out and wiped the sweat from her forehead with the back of her hand, the cotton boxing wraps absorbing the moisture. 'Yeah, that's me. What do you want?'

The young Lance-Corporal stared at the woman in front of him. Despite the fact she was soaked in sweat and breathing heavily she was possibly the most beautiful woman he had seen. He'd watched her knocking hell out of the heavy bag with powerful punches, kicks and elbows as he'd wandered over and…

'Oi, stop fucking staring and spit it out. What do you want?'

He felt his cheeks glow with embarrassment and stuttered out his request. 'Sorry Staff, the CO of SIG, Colonel Dewar, wants you to meet with him tomorrow morning at ten o'clock in his office.'

Nadia frowned. *The SIG? What the hell do they want with me*? She wondered for a moment if she had messed up somewhere but couldn't recall anything. Even if she had, a disciplinary wouldn't be handled in this way. She also couldn't remember hearing of a CO wanting a private meeting with a Staff Sergeant, outside of signing off performance reports. She looked the younger soldier in the eye.

'Anything else?'

'Only he said just come casual, Staff.'

'Okay thanks. You can go now and let me finish my workout.'

She replaced her headphones and began warming back up, hooks, jabs and straights to the beat of The Dropkick Murphy's 'Shipping up to Boston', the loud aggressive song the perfect accompaniment to her routine.

The Lance-Corporal risked a last glance over his shoulder at the stunning Amazon in the top corner of the gym. He took in as much detail as he could, the rippling muscles on her long legs, the definition in her triceps and arms, the jet-black hair tied back and exposing her beautiful face. Sighing, he opened the door and stepped out of the gym, making his way to the cookhouse before it closed. He'd have to ask around after the Amazon. He'd never met anyone like her in his entire twenty-one years on the planet.

SPECIAL INTELLIGENCE GROUP, (SIG), BRACKEN CAMP, AYLESBURY

Colonel Oliver Dewar replaced the secure telephone back in its cradle and leaned back in the leather chair, crossing his arms in front of his chest as he mulled over the latest updates the Analyst Cell had just provided. Coordinated, complex suicide attacks in the three mainland capitals of the UK. Hundreds dead and many more injured. The Cabinet angry and demanding the heads of the Intelligence and Counter-Terrorism organisations explain how they had missed this. The public asking the same questions but with a hell of a lot more emotion. ISIS had claimed responsibility, but this was discounted by GCHQ who had picked up traffic between senior ISIS leadership personalities who were puzzled and confused as to who could have pulled off something like this.

Sighing deeply, Oliver stood and walked over to the metal cabinet that stood against the wall. Opening the door, he reached in and retrieved a crystal glass and a dark green bottle. Removing the cork from the bottle he poured a stiff measure of the amber liquid into the glass, the pungent, smoky aroma of the Lagavulin dominating his senses. Sitting back at his desk he opened his moleskine notebook and read through his notes from the meeting earlier that day. As he read, he sipped at the whisky, allowing the heavily-peated liquid to rest in his mouth for several moments before swallowing, savouring the taste. Closing the notebook, he leaned forward and wiggled his computer mouse, bringing the screen before him to life. With a few clicks he had opened up his diary and checked his appointments for the following day. He saw that after his routine morning meeting with the heads of departments he was scheduled to see Warrant Officer Reid and Staff Sergeant Ali. He nodded, satisfied that the arrangement had been made.

When the request had been made at the Counter-Terrorism Coordination meeting, Oliver hadn't even had to think about who he would entrust with the operation: Lovat. The government needed to be sure that there were no further attacks being ramped up and also to find and bring to justice those responsible. Quickly. The PM had actually stated that the gloves were off on this one, for the agencies to do whatever was necessary to achieve her directives. For his part, Oliver had been approached by Matthew Chivers, MI5's Director of Operations and asked to provide a couple of hunters; operators who weren't afraid to get their hands dirty in their pursuit of answers. Experienced counter-terrorism operators who could hit the ground running and start bringing in results.

And that was certainly Lovat. Taking another swig of the peaty liquid, Oliver reflected that even from their very first days together as covert operators in Northern Ireland, it was clear that Lovat had a gift for this work. Several of Lovat's operations were still briefed to the new operators coming through the course at The Branch, the Unit's training school. And Oliver had more reason than most to respect Lovat's abilities; it had been Lovat who had dragged him unconscious from a mob in a bar in Belfast and CASEVAC'd him to safety. He had no doubt that his life would have ended that night in a very painful manner. His memories of much of the incident were hazy due to the blow to the head that had knocked him out, but he had read the incident report and was obviously a major part of the subsequent investigation. He also knew that Lovat blamed himself for the incident, took sole responsibility for the fact that they were somewhere that they should not have been. That people had died because of it. Lovat's actions and courage that night easily merited a gallantry award but the circumstances and political sensitivities had made the granting of any decoration impossible.

Stretching his legs, Oliver's hand went reflectively to the area of his stomach just above the navel where the knotted scar tissue lay in a misshapen lump, a reminder if he had needed any, of how close he had come to death that night. Sipping his whisky, he thought about the last time he had spoken to Lovat, almost a month ago when he had flown out to Libya. Lovat had been running penetrative operations there against two major ISIS-linked groups in the country and was systematically taking them apart with a combination of drone strikes and Special Forces raids. *Effective.* That was the word he would use to describe Lovat if he was pushed to select a single adjective. *Very* effective. Lovat was that rare beast you could deploy anywhere in the world and guarantee an immediate impact.

But the man had his demons. Oliver raised an eyebrow as he remembered some of their extended drinking sessions through the years. Lovat liked a drink, no two ways about it. Occasionally this had become an issue when it was noticed by people he was working with. But again, Lovat had that rare ability to put the booze away like no one else but still perform in a completely different league from his contemporaries. Mostly though, a blind eye was turned to his drinking as it had never affected his judgement or effectiveness. Oliver knew he had a unique relationship with Lovat and when he was in the UK, both men would meet and have a few too many drinks together, a relationship that was completely against all protocols of a Commanding Officer's social responsibilities.

Lovat actually didn't like being back in the UK for any extended period. Hated being cooped up in the false atmosphere of the SIG and Bracken Camp. He'd once told Oliver that coming back to the SIG after a deployment felt more like a punishment than a relief. Oliver had pressed him, as the Commanding Officer of the SIG, to explain his comments. Lovat had downed his Jack Daniels and Coke and looked him hard in the eye. He'd explained that because the SIG's operators were constantly deployed abroad, the SIG building was populated and occupied by all the support elements; the techs, the drivers, the stores, the clerks. As a result of this, when operators returned from rotations abroad, they felt like strangers; the odd ones out in their own unit. Wandering the long corridors and offices aimlessly until ennui forced them to beg the operations cell to send them away again. Lovat had laughed and said that when you thought about it, it was actually the perfect system. Whether by accident or design, it motivated the operators to keep deploying, to continue plying their effectiveness in the world's shitholes.

Oliver had felt a little stung by the criticisms of his Unit but recognised the truths behind the statements. He'd looked at ways of improving it and had mentioned some of his ideas to Lovat who had simply held up his hand and said that he should be grateful that his operators couldn't wait to be as far away from the SIG as possible. Had asked him to imagine trying to motivate these same people to deploy over and over again if the SIG suddenly became an amazing place to spend time.

Oliver regularly felt frustrated at Lovat's apathy in gaining promotion. He could see that Lovat had the potential to be an effective officer and have a very productive career and decent pension with which to retire on. Lovat, however, saw it differently. He'd joined the unit to be operational, not chained to a desk in a building full of wankers, as well as being in charge of these same wankers, as he'd put it in his inimitable manner. It infuriated Oliver that Lovat couldn't or wouldn't see his potential but there it was. *You could lead the horse to water but you couldn't force it to drink*. He grinned as he imagined how Lovat must have felt when he sent him the text on his first day of leave; angry but intrigued and hungry to be part of it, would be Oliver's guess. Yes, he was looking forward to seeing Lovat again and catching up with a good bottle or two.

Staff Sergeant Ali was another one of Oliver's personal projects. Mason Harris, Oliver's counterpart at SRR, the Special Reconnaissance Regiment, had brought Ali to Oliver's attention. She'd passed the SRR selection, being one of the first women to complete the hills' phase; a new evolution of the selection process since the Regiment had come under Special Forces ownership. SRR had then used Ali for the majority of high-threat surveillance operations in middle eastern and African countries. She had three commendations for bravery under her belt, a testament to her courage when operating in these hostile environments. But, like Lovat, she didn't quite fit the mould completely. Tough and outspoken, Ali took no shit from anyone, including senior officers. The last straw that saw her ejected from the Regiment was the incident where she knocked out a MoD official on a visit from Whitehall. As the CO of the Regiment, Mason had covered for Ali on several occasions but physically assaulting a civil servant left him no room for latitude. Ali was RTUd; Returned To Unit, back to the

Intelligence Corps where she had served before completing SRR selection. Mason, like Oliver, knew the value of good operators, even the mavericks, and had given Oliver a courtesy call updating him with Ali's background and abilities. Oliver had directed his RSM, WO1 Hudson, to keep an eye on Ali, where she was posted, how she was performing and any trouble that looked like she was heading towards.

To her credit, she seemed to be keeping a low profile, other than a minor run-in with one of the female Warrant Officers from the Imagery Analysis Wing. As it was a social occasion, and both Ali and the Warrant Officer had been drinking, the decision had been made not to take the matter to a more formal platform. The RSM had however, made Ali aware that if she ever grabbed another one of his soldiers by the throat and choked them, it would be the last thing she ever did. Having settled the matter, the RSM had privately stated to Oliver that, having seen Ali smashing the punch bags in the gym, he wasn't sure he could actually follow up with his threat.

Oliver downed the remaining whisky in his glass and placed it back on the desk in front of him. He reflected on the forthcoming operation that he was putting Lovat and Ali into and thought that, in all his days in the field of clandestine operations, he had never seen MI5 so rattled. The main concerns were the utter lack of any warning chatter being picked up by GCHQ and the ruthless efficiency of the coordinated attacks in three of the UK's capitals. The complexity of the attacks was also new. The London attacks, where a series of bombs had effectively shepherded the panicked mob into what they thought was the safety of an underground station. Where a PCSO had guided hundreds of people below ground, packed tight against each other before he detonated a significantly large suicide vest, killing dozens and wounding many more. Or Cardiff, where British citizens of Somali origin had murdered twenty-nine people in a shopping centre and cut off the head of a young boy, posting the vile footage online for the world to see before taking their own lives and denying the security forces any opportunity for arrest and interrogation. Edinburgh: Oliver's home city. Young, intelligent, middle-class, white university students from Chechnya masquerading as backpackers killing forty-seven and seriously wounding a further ninety before again, taking their own lives.

No wonder Box was rattled. The nation was reeling from the attacks and the security and intelligence agencies still had nothing to show in terms of leads or arrests with which to allay the public's fears. Not one single, tangible lead. At the earlier meeting, SCO19, the Metropolitan Police's firearms support to counter-terrorism operations, had briefed the attendees on the raids and arrests that morning. By their own admission however, it was merely a case of 'shaking the tree', hoping for something to land in their lap. Although he'd kept his own counsel, Oliver had no faith that this approach would work. Whoever was behind these attacks was clever enough to have left no warning signs or digital footprint for the security forces to exploit, so it was highly unlikely that an ISIS sympathiser hauled from his bed in Bermondsey on a rainy morning would have any involvement with such a professional strike.

Glancing at the clock on the wall above the door, Oliver nodded and stood, picking up his beret from the desk and placing it on his head. He stood in front of the long mirror and adjusted his black stable-belt, rubbing the silver of the locket and union with his sleeve to remove the slight smudges that his fingers had made. Actaeon, the Greek god holding a spear and net, embossed on the shining metal, was the Unit's badge. Although not formally a regiment, the SIG functioned as one and their badge reflected their operational role as the 'Hunters of Men'; covert soldiers who penetrated terrorist organisations, recruiting and running agents or acting as agents themselves. Although rarely in uniform when on operations, Oliver directed that when back in the UK, his soldiers don their uniforms and wear their stable-belts while in the Unit, his attempt to establish a cohesive Unit identity amongst a conglomeration of Marines, Paras, SAS, Navy, Air Force and regular Army personnel. Not an easy task when dealing with high-achieving individuals accustomed to operating in the toughest corners of the globe and usually with full autonomy for their actions. Oliver smiled as he thought about this facet of his role as a Commanding Officer. *Wouldn't have it any other way. I'd be bored shitless if my guys were not who they were.* Adjusting the position of his beret slightly he made his way to the door and opened it, stepping out into the corridor and securing the room behind him. He decided to pop down to the Operations Cell and see how Sergeant Henry's targeting Op in Yemen was progressing after which he'd make a start on his notes for briefing Lovat and Staff Sergeant Ali. He wasn't sure how the pair would get on, but he had every faith in their abilities as individuals and was sure they'd find a way to work together. As he placed his finger-tip into the biometric security pad of the Ops Cell door he gave a small grin. *Not like they've got any choice; they're going to bloody have to get on.* The mechanism clicked, and he pushed the door open and stepped into the hive of activity that always filled him with a sense of proprietary pride: His soldiers running operations on behalf of a country that didn't even know his Unit existed. *And long may it continue…*

WATFORD, ENGLAND

Ahmad giggled as he read Michelle's WhatsApp message again. This girl *definitely* loved him. He'd been worried that his return to Uni would have put her off, the distance between them too much to hope for the relationship to carry on. His fears had been groundless. Through the various social media platforms and making the most of their free weekends, they'd kept the flame alive. Now that he'd graduated, he was taking a couple of weeks off and staying at his uncle's flat in Watford, close to Michelle, while he looked for a suitable position with a good company.

His parents had practically burst with pride at his graduation ceremony. Their son, the engineer. *With honours*, as they never failed to add to conversations with the rest of the extended family and friends. For his own sake, Ahmad had been gratified to see that his father was finally proud of his son's achievements. Ahmad's father Hamdad was a difficult man to please. An imam and community leader in Leicester, his values and expectations for his only son had always been high, almost impossibly so, particularly to a young Ahmad. Ahmad's teenage years had been a constant source of conflict between father and son, the youngster's exploration of girls, alcohol and drugs a direct affront to the old-country, Islamic values of his father and a complete disregard for his status within the community. The discipline, beatings and lectures Ahmad endured had created a gulf between the two that seemed all but impossible to bridge. As Ahmad had matured and found an interest in engineering, that gulf had narrowed and the pair had begun a cautious but definite reconciliation. His acceptance to the University of Leicester and the manner in which he had embraced his studies had further endeared him to his father, erasing the difficulties of the past and paving the way for a closer relationship. His mother could finally relax, relinquish her role as mediator and peacemaker, lose the constant frown of concern she carried through those difficult timcs.

Ahmad's phone pinged again and he saw Michelle's name appear on the notification screen. Even as he smiled, he felt a small pang of regret that he could never introduce her to his family. Michelle's free-spirited approach to life and her utter disregard for what people thought about her tattoos and counter-culture dress sense were what had attracted Ahmad to her in the first place, but it was these very attributes that would shock his parents. His grin widened as he attempted to imagine a scenario where he would land on his parent's doorstep with Michelle by his side and introduce her as his girlfriend. His father would probably drop dead with shock while his mother would tear out her hair while screaming at the shame he had brought upon the family. He sighed as he took a sip of his coffee and looked out through the windows of the café at the throngs of shoppers outside.

This was the problem for Ahmad and indeed, many young men and women whose parents had emigrated from Pakistan. Their parents retained a loyalty and kinship with a country that their children had no bond with, no commonality, no links other than the oft-recited stories and anecdotes of their elders. Among his close friends, Ahmad would laugh and joke about this shared experience, each taking turns to mimic and mock their parents' loving descriptions of shopping for pomegranates in Peshawar or the pleasures of snacking on *Chana Chaat* in Karachi. While funny, he'd always felt a twinge of guilt for mocking his parents in such a way but would also feel anger at the fact that he was meant to identify with a country that he had never even seen. A country that sounded, quite frankly, to hate and police the very freedoms that Ahmad and his friends embraced as teenagers. No alcohol or drugs to get your Friday buzz on. No consorting with girls until marriage. No sneaking into nightclubs and partying hard to a brilliant DJ's tunes. Ahmad and his friends would raise whatever bottle they had in their hands and cheer this sentiment with a collective *Fuck That!* They could think of nothing worse, as young men pushing the boundaries, than that of living their lives under such a restrictive regime. It had taken Ahmad some further years to understand his parents' attitudes and their confused identities. On the one hand, British citizens grateful for the opportunities afforded to them, while on the other, concern for the moral sanctity of their children growing up with limitless freedoms. As Ahmad grew older, he could see how difficult it was to achieve a balance of any sort in these matters.

This was what also contributed to some of the radicalisation of the young men from the British Pakistani community. Those individuals who felt torn between identities; *British and Muslim or Muslim and British*? The wars in Afghanistan and Iraq polarising elements of these communities and fuelling the young men's anger, motivating them to join the defence of the perceived war against Islam being waged by western nations. Ahmad had been fortunate in that none of his circle of friends had subscribed to this particular narrative, uninterested in the whispers from unfamiliar 'brothers' waiting outside the mosques after prayers, encouraging them to join them in secret meetings. He'd been lucky enough to have begun his degree at the age where some of these young men, unemployed and alienated, had been ripe for recruitment. So here he was with his engineering degree and a beautiful, if slightly crazy girlfriend, about to embark on his own life as a man.

He replied to Michelle's message, arranging the time and place where they would meet later that evening, feeling the familiar excitement in his stomach at the thought of being together again. It had only been a couple of weeks, but it felt more like months to him. Smiling, he put the phone back in his pocket and was just about to stand when a man slid onto the stool next to him and patted his back.

'Brother, brother, please, sit down and speak with me for a minute, yes?'

Ahmad frowned and looked the stranger up and down, trying to determine if they had met before. He was of Pakistani origin and was dressed, like Ahmad, in smart casual clothing; a pink Ralph Lauren polo shirt and dark jeans. He could also see that the man kept in shape, the shirt displaying an impressive physique within. Ahmad was sure that they had never met and opened his mouth to say as much but the man stopped him, pressing a firm hand on Ahmad's shoulder and directing him back onto his own stool.

'This is not a time for you to talk Ahmad Noor Mohammed, only for you to listen. In a moment I will pass you a mobile telephone under the table. You will take it from me carefully making sure that no-one sees it. I will leave and you will then receive a call from a very important man. After that your destiny is your own, brother.' The man leaned in until his face was close to Ahmad's and he noticed for the first time the hardness in the man's stare. 'But make no mistake; whatever you do in the next minute has direct consequences for your father, your mother, your sisters, and the whore Michelle that you seem so fond of. Put your hand under the table and take the phone now.'

Stunned and shaking, Ahmad put his hand under the table and felt the man take it and place an object in it, curling Ahmad's fingers around it to ensure it was secure. As Ahmad drew his hand back the man stood and smiled, patting Ahmad on the back once again before placing his sunglasses over his eyes and walking out the door. Ahmad trembled as he put the phone into his pocket as the man had directed. His head was spinning as question after question sprinted through his mind. *What the hell just happened? Who the fuck was that? How did he know me? How did he know about Michelle? What the fuck is going on here*? He was just about to follow the man out when the phone in his pocket began ringing. He stopped and pulled the device out, staring at a basic pay-as-you-go model, no smart functions whatsoever. The small screen was illuminated and a single word displayed in its centre: *Djinn*; Demon. As the phone continued to ring and vibrate in his hand, Ahmad became aware of the disapproving looks from the seated customers around him. He pressed the call accept button and brought the handset to his ear, speaking in a croaking, hesitant voice. 'Hello?'

As he listened to the voice on the other end of the telephone, Ahmad felt his heart race and his mind reel and realised that his life would never be the same again.

SIG, CAMP BRACKEN, AYLESBURY

Lovat held up his key card to the sensor and waited for the click and the green light before entering the security turnstile. Proceeding down the path towards the main entrance of the building, he nodded at various individuals as they passed him. He opened the door and stepped inside the main corridor that for some reason always reminded him of being in a primary school rather than a base for a secret military unit. Pausing for a moment, he checked his watch and saw that he was ten minutes early for the meeting with OD. To kill some time, he walked over to the admin board and started reading through the Daily Routine Orders that were promulgated on the dark mahogany display. He flicked through several pages, unimpressed by anything that he saw. Sports notices, Mess functions, charity fundraisers, wives' and girlfriends' social evenings, reminders about speeding in military vehicles. He couldn't suppress the small shudder that ran through him, each and every page representing an existence he had long ago left behind in favour of remaining at the sharp end of operations.

A voice behind him caught his attention. 'What the hell are you doing back here so soon? Miss us that much?'

Lovat turned and grinned at the tall Major standing before him. 'Morning Terry, good to see you too, you grumpy old bastard.' He stuck his hand out and shook the other man's with genuine affection. Terry Clark was the Unit's Operation's Officer and one of the real linchpins in the success of the SIG's effectiveness. He and Lovat had worked together in various guises over the years and enjoyed a mutual respect for the other's capabilities.

'What you doing back here Lovat? I thought you were on leave for the next few weeks. What happened? Run out of exotic destinations to travel to?'

Lovat laughed and nodded his head in the direction of the Commanding Officer's end of the corridor. 'No, got a text from the Boss to get my arse down here ASAP and here I am. I'm with him in five minutes so I guess I'll get all the details then.'

Terry nodded and lowered his voice slightly, leaning in to be better heard. 'Yes…not telling tales out of school by any means but I'm pretty sure this will be about the recent attacks. Briefing today was pretty bleak; still no leads or relevant intelligence to follow up on. Apparently, Box are getting hauled over the coals so I'm assuming they've reached out for help on this one.'

Lovat nodded, Terry's analysis of the situation making perfect sense, particularly when added to OD's initial text to Lovat. 'Yeah, that sounds about right Terry. Look, you about this evening if I'm free? Catch up over a few small ones?'

Terry Clark grinned and shook his head. 'Not a chance mate. The long-haired general has her parents staying with us at the moment so I'm house-bound with the in-laws for the next week.'

Lovat grimaced and shook his head in mock sympathy. 'Mate that's awful news. Surprised you didn't get yourself away on an assessment visit to Yemen.'

Terry laughed and looked at his watch. 'To be fair even that shithole would be preferable to another one of her Dad's '*when I was on the board of directors of ICI*' stories. Anyway, I've got a VTC in five so best shoot. If you're around for a while let's do the drink thing mate. Been far too long.'

Lovat patted the other man on the shoulder and turned towards the opposite end of the corridor. 'Definitely Terry. Will drop you a line and let you know when I'm about.' Walking towards the CO's office he saw a striking Asian woman stood leaning against the wall across from the office. Lovat didn't recognise her and wondered who she was. *New joiner maybe*? Closing the distance between them he monitored her discreetly, assessing her clothing, posture, and facial expressions to provide him with any clues as to her identity. She was dressed smartly in a salmon-coloured shirt, dark jeans and calf-length boots, her clothing showed off an athletic figure. Her casual leaning on the wall across from the CO's office implied either an affected lack of respect for the man and his establishment or she genuinely didn't care. Either way, Lovat mused, it spoke of confidence bordering on arrogance. She seemed very relaxed and was just looking in front of her, not seeking distraction from a phone or reading any of the background notices displayed on the walls. In the small space of half a dozen or so steps, Lovat knew he was looking at someone with a bit more to them than a new joiner to the Unit.

From the corner of her eye, Nadia monitored the approach of the individual, indulging her programmed habit of conducting initial assessments of people's characters based on the limited information before her. It was a skill that she'd learned on her SRR selection and had used ever since, now an automatic reaction rather than something that she thought about. The man was about her height and carried himself well, the rounded shoulders and flat of his chest against his white shirt implying someone who took care of himself. He was tanned; a deep tan that spoke of a deployment abroad rather than a quick trip to the Canaries. Like her, he was dressed in smart-casual clothing; a tailored white shirt, dark jeans and tan boots. As he drew closer, she saw the huge scar that ran down one side of his face, the tissue a dull purple rather than the angry pink that would have suggested a recent injury. His dark hair was neat without being overly short and she could make out the grey creeping in around the sides and edges. She noticed him slowing as he approached the office and raised an eyebrow as he mimicked her stance, leaning on the wall opposite her.

'How's it going? You waiting to see the Boss too?'

Nadia nodded at his statement, continuing her information collection exercise. He was Scottish, judging from the accent and obviously part of this unit, his reference to the Commanding Officer as 'Boss' telling her as much. She cleared her throat. 'Yes. Got a chat at ten. You?'

Lovat raised his eyebrows in surprise. 'Me too. Ten o'clock with the man himself. Maybe he's double booked us?'

Nadia smiled. 'Well, he's an officer, isn't he? Probably got a double from Oxford but would struggle to tell you which day of the week Sunday lunch is served.'

Lovat laughed out loud at the irreverence and the humour of the remark. It was a pretty ballsy statement; there weren't many people who would have been comfortable insulting the most senior officer in the unit to a total stranger. He was about to reply when the door beside him was snatched open and Oliver Dewar's head sprang out and stared at him.

'Ah. I see you've both met. Good. That will save some time. So, if you're quite finished with your shits and giggles out here please feel free to join me where we can talk about why you're both here.' He disappeared back into the room and Lovat caught the woman's eye and again, was equally surprised and impressed to see her roll her eyes with an accompanying grin, clearly unfazed by the CO's remarks.

Lovat grinned back, stepped away from the wall and entered the doorway, hearing the woman follow him closely behind.

Oliver Dewar sat behind his desk and watched the pair enter. 'Close the door behind you Staff Sergeant Ali and both of you take a seat.' He waited until they had settled themselves on the large leather armchairs before continuing. 'Staff Sergeant Nadia Ali, meet Warrant Officer Lovat Reid. Lovat is my Unit's most experienced operator and that is why he is here today. For your information Lovat, Nadia comes to us from SRR and was one of their most effective operators in the Middle East and Africa before she was sent back to the Intelligence Corps.'

Lovat leaned over and offered his hand to Nadia who accepted it and nodded to him. Leaning back into his seat he continued to listen as the CO spoke.

'I don't have much time to get you up to speed on this so you are going to have to hit the ground running with immediate effect. You're both here because Box has requested our assistance in finding out who is behind these recent atrocities and bringing them to justice.' He paused and took a sip of his coffee before continuing. 'So, I have hand-picked you two as the best that we can offer them, so you will work as a team seconded to Box.' Seeing Lovat frown and lean forward, Oliver raised his hand. 'Not so fast Lovat. Yes, you are seconded to Box and are under their remit but you have full autonomy in how you carry out your operations as long as you touch base with our Ops Cell and make them aware of it and any support you think you need.'

Nadia shook her head. 'Wait sir. I've *never* heard of anything like this before. A Box operation but we have full autonomy and support from here? In my experience if you're not one or the other the whole thing just ends up in a big bun-fight about who is in charge of who.'

Oliver nodded. 'Agreed Nadia. However, from the mouth of the PM herself, the gloves are off on this one. I've laid out the terms of your involvement with Box and have the signed Memorandum of Understanding, the MoU that authorises your participation.'

Lovat was impressed. With a signed MoU there would be no inter-agency squabbles or pissing contests over who had ownership of what. He could feel the familiar sensation of anticipation starting to build within him at the thought of a new operation, with all the support that they would need at the end of a telephone. He was brought back to the present as the CO continued his brief.

'The Ops Cell have a starter pack with all the relevant points of contact you'll be engaging with as well as a standard mainland kit issue to get you up and running ASAP. Box will issue you their comms and encrypted phones, tablets and lap tops so you have access to all their intelligence as well as forwarding your own reports through their systems. Lovat, I know you're familiar with this, Nadia, not too sure of your exposure of MI5's procedures but I'm sure Lovat will bring you up to speed.'

'I've done a fair bit of work with them over the years' sir and pretty happy with their working methods.'

Oliver nodded and took a sip of coffee, grimacing as the now cold liquid went down his throat. 'Excellent. We're already ahead of the curve then. I don't really have much more for you, so I suggest you get yourselves down to the Ops Cell and draw your kit and then get down to Thames House and touch base with their team.'

Lovat cleared his throat. 'Who is the point of contact at Box, Boss?'

'Good question Lovat. You'll be pleased to hear that it's Giles again. I think they know they need a safe pair of hands on this one so they're definitely throwing their best people at it. As are we.'

Lovat was pleased with the news that Giles would be heading up the MI5 operation. He'd worked with Giles several times over the previous years and had a healthy respect for the man's intellect and experience. As well as the fact that Giles wasn't afraid to make the tough decisions that most career officers shied away from. Knew that to counter terrorism in the UK meant working within the grey areas of legality and compliance in order to take the bad guys off the street. His presence on the operation further buoyed Lovat's anticipation.

Nadia glanced at Lovat before turning back to the CO. 'Erm…not to sound ungrateful or anything sir but you do know that I am not part of your Unit and I'm also not part of SRR anymore so I'm a little bit confused as to my status here.'

Oliver leaned forward. 'Okay, let me make this simple for you. Do you want to be part of this operation, yes or no?'

'Yes. Absolutely.'

Oliver smiled and leaned back, clasping his hands behind his head. 'Well, I'm glad. Because as of ten o'clock this morning you were posted into the SIG on a temporary assignment basis on an open-ended engagement. And I would have looked a right twat to the drafting office if you'd said no and I'd had to re-post you back to the Intelligence Corps half an hour later!'

Nadia laughed and shook her head. 'That was a pretty cocky shout sir. Fair play though, looks like you called it bang on.'

'Nothing cocky about it Nadia; I'm good friends with your old CO, who, by the way, thinks very highly of you and asked me to keep an eye on you for him. This wasn't guesswork on my part. I knew immediately that the only people that I *want* on this job are you two. And I also knew that, given who you are, neither of you would turn down an opportunity to operate on home soil against the deadliest killers we've come up against.' He looked at his watch before meeting their eyes once again. 'Now, I have to get going and you have to get started. I'll be kept abreast of your efforts through the Ops Cell but again, if you think I can help personally, don't be frightened to pick up the phone.' He stood and walked around the desk as the pair followed his lead and also stood up. Shaking them by the hand he nodded towards the door. 'Now get out of here and go show those snobby Oxbridge toffs what we can do.'

BUSHEY HEATH, ENGLAND

Ahmad could feel the sweat trickling down his back despite the coolness of the autumn day. Entering the park through the wrought iron gateway as he'd been directed, he walked along the bitumen path, flanked by rows of trees almost devoid of foliage. He looked around as he walked, eyes wide and breathing ragged as he struggled to remain calm. The voice on the end of the telephone had been passing him a series of directions and instructions for the past two hours and Ahmad could feel the tension inside him ready to explode. He'd begun his journey, as directed, by getting on a bus in Watford and taking it to Northwood. The second call had told him to get off the bus and go into a small supermarket and buy something. The third call saw him jump on another bus and take it to Bushey. From there he had been ordered to make his way through a large park, up the hill and into the suburb of Bushey Heath. He'd been instructed to go into the supermarket and buy a cold drink before the next call came and directed him to the park.

The voice on the other end of the line left no time for either questions or confirmation. It was calm and commanding, someone accustomed to wielding authority. Despite his fear and anxiety, in the forefront of Ahmad's mind was the threat to his family and girlfriend. Ahmad wasn't stupid; he knew that only a very serious individual would have gone to such lengths to learn about him and put him through this elongated journey. Even though he had been looking throughout each change of travel, Ahmad had not managed to identify anybody following him. *Is that the point of all this? Are they checking to see if I'm being followed?*

As he negotiated the path around a small water feature, he started as a man appeared by his side and walked alongside him.

'Keep walking Ahmad and act naturally. I'm only here to talk.'

Ahmad felt his heart racing as he complied with the command. He resisted the urge to stare at the stranger, sure that this would anger the individual and possibly lead to a reprisal that Ahmad did not want to be responsible for. As if sensing this the man spoke and Ahmad could hear the smile in his voice.

'Good. I know you really want to see who you are dealing with but you resisted the temptation to turn and stare. I knew you were smart.'

Ahmad cleared his throat, knowing that his voice would sound strange due to nerves. 'Who are you and why are you doing this to me?'

'Who I am would be of little relevance to you Ahmad so please don't concern yourself with such trivialities.'

The stranger's accent was strong, and Ahmad concluded that he had not been in the UK long, despite the perfect grasp of English. His diction was precise, and he was clearly well educated. Ahmad looked at the man as he felt his hand upon his back.

'Come Ahmad, sit with me a moment and let us talk of my requirements.'

Ahmad allowed himself to be directed towards a bench sat within an enclosure of hardy bushes and shrubs. As he changed direction towards it, his legs felt stiff and his gait awkward, and a cold fear took hold in his stomach. Sitting down, he turned to look at the stranger's face now that they were sat close together. The man looked to be in his late forties or thereabouts and was well groomed, his jet-black hair neatly combed and his moustache trimmed. He was wearing a pale-blue shirt that contrasted with his dark skin and he seemed incredibly relaxed considering the situation. Ahmad leaned forward and hissed at the stranger.

'What do you want from me and why are you threatening my family? I don't even know you!' The man looked at Ahmad with an expression akin to amusement and the young man felt anger well up inside him. 'You think this is funny? You tell me right now why I don't just go straight to the police with your fucking threats.'

The moment the words were out Ahmad saw the man's expression change, a tightening of the face and a hardening of the dark eyes.

'By all means Ahmad Noor Mohammed go to the police. Go and tell them what has happened to you. Give them my description and what I have been saying to you. I will simply disappear and you will never see or hear from me again. But…' The man paused and leaned in closer, Ahmad registering the briefest hint of an expensive after-shave. 'Then I will post a clip of your sister being gang-raped by a hand-picked group of the lowest, junkie scum I can find. I will also make sure that she is so out of her head on meth that, to the viewer, it will look like she is enjoying and encouraging the act. The shame and humiliation for your parents will almost kill them however I am hoping that this doesn't happen as I have other plans in place for your second sister.'

Ahmad began to shake his head to attempt to get the man to halt his horrific narrative but the stranger continued. 'Your second sister Ayesha will be found dead in an incident that the police will identify as an accident in a drug lab. The trail of real and digital evidence that I will leave in place will allow even your incompetent British Bobbies to draw the conclusion that Ayesha was running a meth operation that went wrong. They will also point out that it was Ayesha who got Fatima hooked on the drugs that will eventually kill her.'

Ahmad held his hands over his ears and shook his head violently from side to side. 'Please…stop, please…' He felt the stranger's cool hands grip his wrists and lower his hands from his ears as the vile speech continued.

'Again, through a clever and wholly believable chain of evidence, Michelle will be identified as assisting you in the construction of the IEDs that killed people in London, Edinburgh and Cardiff. She helped you by purchasing equipment and acting as a courier which, again, I have much evidence for the Police to follow on this line. She will definitely face a long prison sentence which I will ensure will be a living hell for her for every day of her existence.' The man paused and leaned back on the bench, smiling as a shaft of sunlight illuminated his face. 'And you? What of you? What of Ahmad Noor Mohammed? Well, you were obviously the terrorist mastermind behind all of the attacks which you funded through making your sisters operate the meth production on your behalf.'

Ahmad leaned away from the man and attempted to sound more confident than he felt. 'That's all lies and there's no way that you can do any of this without the Police catching on to the fact that it's a set up.'

The stranger chuckled and leaned forward. 'Ahmad, Ahmad, Ahmad. *This* is what I do. *This* is what I have done for nearly thirty years. I am one of the best in the world at my art. And it *is* an art, believe me. Digital cookie trails, bank transfers, mobile telephone connections with known insurgents, caches of money and weapons throughout the country…all these things are in place *now* Ahmad, ready to be provided to the authorities a little at a time to make them believe that they are finding the evidence rather than being given it.'

Ahmad dropped his head in his hands and sobbed but the man was relentless.

'But the most important thing that you haven't thought about is how much the British Police and MI5 will *want* to believe this. They still have not one suspect for the deadliest attacks on UK soil and pressure is mounting. Then suddenly they have a lead on a *stinking Paki boy* running a meth operation with his sisters to fund these attacks and corrupting an innocent white girl to do his running around? It's a gift Ahmad, like Christmas Day come early. You and your family will be front page news for weeks and there will be medals for the Police and Security personnel who uncovered this *dastardly* plot.' The man was smiling as he finished and placed a gentle hand on Ahmad's shoulder. 'Or…'

Ahmad looked up and wiped the tears from his eyes. ''Or?'

'Or you do what I tell you and none of what I have just spoken about will ever happen. And when our business is concluded it will be as though nothing has happened. No one will ever know of our relationship or activities together. On that you have my word.'

Ahmad sniffed and shook his head. 'Your *word*? You've just threatened to destroy my whole world and everyone in it and I'm supposed to accept your *word*? Whatever it is you want me to do, you're just going to use me and kill me now that I've seen your face.'

The man threw his head back and laughed, a genuine, deep guffaw. 'Oh, my dear Ahmad. You watch too many bad detective movies. I'm not going to have you killed because you have seen my face. This is the way I do business. There is nothing that you can say or do that would cause me concern for my safety and freedom. Nothing. But for you, I own everything. Your whole life and that of everyone that you love. So, the fact that you have seen my face is of no significance to me whatsoever.'

Ahmad was quiet for a moment before the plea left his mouth. 'What is it that you want me to do?'

The man nodded. It was always the same way, whether with an Agent he was recruiting, or a prisoner being interrogated. The moment they broke completely was always signalled by the same, or at least a very similar statement. The brain finally accepting the inevitability of the situation and the mouth vocalising it.

'Ahmad, you are a very gifted young engineer with no criminal record or even links to criminals. To me you are a very valuable asset that I require for a short-term operation. I will need your engineering skills to assist me in several plans I have in place and once complete, you will never hear from me or see me again. All the evidence against you and your family disappears and their lives will continue as normal. And that's it. Short-term pain for long-term gain.'

'But what? What the hell is it I'm being expected to do? Build bombs? IEDs? Make weapons? I can't do any of that!'

'You will do everything that I ask of you, no matter what it is. And you will do it within the timeframe that I set you. One failure or disappointment will set the whole operation against you and your family into action. Once *that* plan is activated it cannot be stopped or slowed. Everything I told you would happen will happen with absolute certainty. So, what are you expected to do? *Anything* I ask you because for you there is no alternative.'

Ahmad stared with glazed eyes at the stranger, conflicting emotions of fear and rage coursing through his body. A fantasy of strangling the man to death flitted quickly through his mind but Ahmad was no fighter and was sure that the man had thought of such a reaction and probably had reinforcements nearby. He was brought back to reality as the man spoke again.

'I can see that you want to kill me. That's good. That's healthy. In your shoes I would be exactly the same. But know this; If I ever see that look on your face again, you'll have your sister's gang-bang footage on your news feed within the day with the rest of the nightmare following on. You see, I want *you* to help me on this task but if you are too much of a headache, I will find someone else. But only after I am satisfied that your punishment is complete.'

Ahmad's shoulders sagged and the tears rolled down his cheeks. 'Okay. I get it. I'm completely screwed. I'll do whatever you want just please promise me that you will leave my family and Michelle alone. Please?'

The man took Ahmad's hands in his own. 'Look at me Ahmad. Right now, to you, I am the devil, and I won't pretend to be anything different. I *am* the devil and I carry out my work with no feelings or emotions for those I kill or destroy to achieve my aims. That much I am sure you have worked out.' He leaned in closer, forcing Ahmad to meet his eyes. 'But I never lie to someone I make a bargain with. I don't have to and I don't need to. I will not hurt your family or your girlfriend as long as you uphold your side of the bargain, you have my word on that.'

Ahmad shivered and took in a shaky breath. 'Okay, can we get started so I can get this over with as soon as possible? Please?'

The man smiled and sat back nodding with satisfaction. 'Good. You are obviously as smart as I thought you were. Yes, let's get started. For this you will need your engineering head with which to assist me in an idea that I have. What do you know about railway tracks?'

THAMES HOUSE, LONDON, ENGLAND

Nadia glanced around the drab walls of the reception area, noting the tired appearance of the room. As the headquarters for the British Security Service, MI5, she'd always felt that the least they could do was give it a fresh lick of magnolia to tart the place up a little. In recent years Nadia had been working more with MI6 because of the international nature of her operations and had spent quite a bit of time in their headquarters across the Thames at Vauxhall. In contrast to the MI5 building, no expense seemed to have been spared for the sibling across the river. The controversial building dividing opinion but creating an architectural statement regardless of which side of the fence you stood. Even within the building itself, there was a fresher feel to the offices and meeting rooms than one encountered here on the north bank. Nadia got along equally well with officers from both organisations, but she knew that MI5 felt themselves to be the poorer cousins of their colleagues across the river, leading to some acrimony from time to time.

In the past, she had worked alongside A4, MI5's surveillance unit, on joint operations against Islamic fundamentalist targets in the UK. She'd found their operators to be every bit as professional as her and her SRR colleagues, albeit in a slightly less intense way. In SRR, the task was everything; the rest of your life took second place to retaining control of the target. With A4 however, while very professional when on task, she'd noticed that their lives came first, the job scheduled around child-minders and trains home to Brighton and Pinner. Nadia had once mentioned this observation to her Ops Officer who had explained that MI5 was a civilian organisation staffed by civilians. Whereas SRR was composed of highly motivated operators drawn from all branches of the armed forces and put through a harrowing six-month selection process. He'd gone on to explain that soldiers were mission-focused by nature and indoctrination; nobody resting until the task was complete. Agencies like MI5 were composed of civilians accustomed to working under equality and diversity policies, being managed by Human Resources and complying with office directives and protocols. Their lives and career pathways took precedence over the task, which effectively was just another job around which they juggled their domestic existence. It didn't make them any less effective when on target, but she had felt some frustrations when the occasional job was postponed or put on hold because of the operators' pressures at home.

She pulled herself out of her reverie and glanced across at Lovat who was engrossed in the newspaper he had brought in with him. They had spoken in the car on the drive down from Bracken and learned a little about each other in the process. They knew some of the same people from within the Intelligence and Special Forces community and it had been heartening to learn that they shared very similar opinions about those individuals. She recalled the laughter in the car when the inevitable questions about how they got on with certain individuals had been addressed. To both of their surprise, they shared the same disdain for some people and respect for others. This commonality endeared Lovat to her, as well as the fact that he was quite up front about his opinions.

He'd asked why she had left SRR and she'd told him that it was too long a story for such a short car journey but that if he was still interested, she would bore him with the details over a beer or two. In return, she had asked him about the scar on his face. He had laughed and said that it too, was a longer story best told over alcohol and agreed to divulge the details at a better time. She'd learned that he lived alone in a coastal village in Scotland and that he loved surfing big waves. Like her, his life was operations, with little appetite for desk roles of any sort regardless of the promotional trade-off. She'd asked about Giles, the MI5 officer they were to be working with and Lovat had explained that Giles was one of the good guys, someone who knew how to get things done. She was just about to say something to Lovat when the door opened and a rotund, heavily-bearded man bowled into the small room, his voice booming in the confines of the reception.

'Lovat Reid, you ugly bugger. How are you? I see you haven't got any more handsome since we last met?'

Lovat grinned and stood, crossing the small room to meet the man whom he greeted with a hug before stepping back and appraising him. 'Good to see you too Giles although it might take a while to see *all* of you as you've been piling on the pounds fatty!'

Giles' laugh was loud and deep. 'Good to see you again pal and really chuffed it's you that's running point on this with us.' He turned to Nadia who had stood and was watching the exchange between the men with amusement. 'And you must be Staff Sergeant Ali?'

Nadia nodded and held out her hand which Giles grasped and shook warmly. 'Yep, but Nadia will do just fine.'

'Excellent, excellent, and I'm Giles. Not fat bastard or beach-ball belly or whatever else this turd has told you to call me.'

Nadia laughed. 'Nice to meet you Giles and to be fair, in his defence, Lovat hasn't actually told me to call you anything.

Giles laughed again and nodded. 'I can see we're going to get on great here Nadia. Now, let's get upstairs where we can have some coffee that doesn't taste like cat's piss and I'll brief you up on developments so far.'

Giles brought the presentation to an end and the screen before them turned black. He reached behind him and turned the lights back on before taking his seat again and turning to face Nadia and Lovat.

'So, in a nutshell; no advance communications or chatter to warn us of the attacks. No *credible* claimants, all discarded because we actually have intercepted communications where *they* are asking each other who the hell is responsible. No communications at all regarding the coordination of the attacks and lastly, no-one left alive that we could even question about the attacks.'

Lovat nodded and sipped at the coffee before replying. 'That's pretty grim Giles and I must say, pretty surprising. There isn't a single lead on this at all? What about HUMINT?' Despite the fact that nothing had been picked up on communications intercepts, Lovat was hopeful that at least HUMINT, Human Intelligence, would throw up a few lines of enquiry.

Giles swallowed a gulp from his own cup before speaking. 'We have nothing from our Sources at all Lovat. SO15 in Luton got a tip off about a bunch of toe-rags hanging round the mosques but it was completely unrelated.'

Nadia tapped her pen on the notebook in front of her. 'Okay then, where's our start point? From what I can see we don't have a single viable lead we can begin investigating.'

Giles grimaced. 'Nail on the head there Nadia. I don't have a single thing to give you on this I'm afraid. GCHQ are working round the clock hoovering up any conversations and messages linked to the attacks but so far they've all been after-the-fact discussions.'

Lovat scratched his head. 'So, let me get this straight; no comms *at all*, either to set up or coordinate the attacks. Nobody credible claiming the most significant attack on British soil. And nobody has any idea who did it or if and when they are going to strike again. That about sum it up?'

Giles nodded. 'Yep. That's about the size of it mate. This is completely new to us. Whoever put this together is the best we've seen, or not seen, to put it more accurately.'

Lovat leaned back in his chair. 'Okay then, a new group with a very effective leader and utter control over the whole scope of their operations. For not one of these people to fuck up and drop a text, email or chat with someone, is phenomenal control.'

Giles leaned forward. 'That's the theory we're working on too. This is someone we believe is new, possibly new to the UK but if not that, then certainly they are not using or co-opting any of the existing networks.'

Nadia spoke. 'I take it you're liaising with immigration?'

'Yes of course but we're not holding our breath. They're generally not much use to us on conventional queries so I don't hold out much hope for anything on this one.'

'What about recovered weapons, explosive trace, biometrics on the dead terrorists etc. Anything there we can use?'

Giles sighed and shook his head, meeting her eyes. '*Nada.* We've tracked all the weapons and explosives and the general provenance is through thefts from criminal gangs which is pretty ballsy when you think about it. It also shows that whoever is behind these attacks has an exceptional intelligence network to be able to identify and procure this stuff. We've also grilled the families of the dead and interrogated their phones and devices but got nothing to indicate any support or connection to the attacks.'

'And none of the Sources have reported any new power struggles, ideology clashes within the communities, new groupings emerging?'

Giles waved his hand. 'Nothing out of the ordinary Nadia, just the usual shit that we've investigated and put to bed as routine really.'

Lovat whistled. 'Bloody hell Giles, we've got our work cut out for us here mate.'

For the first time since they'd began the presentation, Giles smiled. 'Well, that's why we reached out to SIG and they sent us down Beauty and the Beast to help us out.'

Lovat wagged a finger in mock anger at Giles. 'No, no, no; I won't have that. Staff Sergeant Ali is not a beast and I will be taking this up with our equality and diversity officer on our return to Bracken, you misogynistic bastard!'

Giles laughed and stood, opening the door behind him. 'Piss off Scarface. Right, you've left me feeling really guilty that I haven't given you much in the way of a start point for your operation so as way of an apology I'll treat you both to lunch.'

Nadia held up her hand. 'Yeah, but not here if that's all the same to you? I've eaten here before and its pretty shit to be honest.'

Giles raised his eyebrow and nodded at Lovat. 'They're clearly paying you squaddies too much money when you're offered free food and you get picky over it.'

Lovat nodded. 'Agreed Giles. But she has a point; it is pretty shit food here.'

Spinning on his heel, Giles led them down the corridor muttering under his breath about the lack of gratitude and that he wasn't sure he could stretch to the Savoy and hoped they wouldn't be too disappointed with a Pret a Manger.

STEVENAGE, ENGLAND

From the small rise above the tracks, Ahmad watched as the London to Aberdeen train sped through the countryside below him, the sound reaching him a second or so after the train came into view. Looking through the binoculars, he could make out the faces of the passengers as they stared listlessly out of the windows or nodded to the beats from their headphones. Laying the binoculars on the grass beside him, he reached into his jacket pocket and retrieved a small notebook with a pen attached to the spine. He unclipped the pen, opened the notebook and added another line of figures to the existing list before returning the notebook to his pocket. Standing up, he stretched and picked up the small backpack, putting the binoculars and the small towel that he had been sitting on into the depths of the pack. He took a quick look around him to confirm that there was no one watching, then shouldered the pack and made his way back down the farm track towards his car.

Ahmad was content that everything was now ready for the plan to be put into action. As he walked down the rutted track, he considered the variables that might affect it negatively. He soon reached the conclusion that the plan's simplicity meant that there was very little, if anything, that could go wrong once the apparatus was in place. Chewing on the inside of his cheek, he thought about the call he would make to Djinn. He'd made up his mind that he would do this one thing, this one *terrible* thing for the evil man then he would ask to be released from his obligations. Djinn had almost hinted as much at their last meeting, telling Ahmad that if this operation was a success, he would be willing to renegotiate the terms of their arrangement. Ahmad snorted at the memory. *Arrangement? Like I had any fucking choice in the matter.* But he grasped on to the statement like a drowning man, desperate for rescue.

Ahmad wasn't stupid; he'd known right from the initial briefing what he was being asked to do. He knew that many people would be injured and some killed because of what he was about to do. But what choice did he have? He could not be responsible for the vile things that would happen to the people he loved. Could not bear to live to see what would become of his family and Michelle once Djinn put his plan into action. He just wanted it all to go away. He wasn't sleeping or eating properly, any food that he put into his mouth devoid of taste or texture. Michelle had met him a couple of times, but they'd argued at their last meeting when she'd asked him for the hundredth time what was wrong with him. He'd mumbled something about the stresses of job hunting but she hadn't been convinced and defaulted to the position that there was something amiss with their relationship.

He'd wanted to tell her everything, wanted to grab her and pull her close to him and pour out the whole story, praying that she could provide a way out of his situation. But he'd resisted the impulse. He loved Michelle but he knew that she would go straight to the police with the information, so he'd kept his secrets and burden to himself. She'd stormed off in a temper and they hadn't spoken for several days until she'd texted him and re-established communication. By that time, he was already working on the planning and the design of Djinn's task, knowing that the fate of his loved ones depended upon it. Today was his fourth and final observation of the target and he was content that he had all the information at hand and that his design would work. It would have to.

Returning to his car, he unlocked it with the remote, the confirmatory beep of the mechanism loud in the confines of the country lane. He stepped around a muddy puddle and opened the back door, swinging the small rucksack onto the seat before closing the door and getting behind the wheel. Starting the car up, he put it in gear and headed off down the hill and back towards Stevenage. He had to pull in to allow a tractor to pass and acknowledged the farmer's wave of gratitude with one of his own. As he drove on, Ahmad felt a flicker of resentment for the easy day that the farmer was having in comparison to his own. Not for him, the pressure of being blackmailed by a maniac to assist in terrorist operations. *Probably only worried about his fucking sheep or cows or whatnot.* He shook his head as the tears of frustration rolled down his cheeks. Sighing as he wiped his face with the sleeve of his jacket, Ahmad turned his attention back to the present and joined the minor B-road that would take him back to the dual carriageway.

It was cold in the large warehouse and Ahmad shivered. One of the men who stood by the welding equipment saw him and sneered. 'You think this is cold? Try the mountain passes of Logar Province in February. *That's* fucking cold boy.'

Ahmad looked away from the man's intense gaze and tried to think of a suitable reply. He was just about to say something when a voice reached them from the far corner of the warehouse.

'I thought my directions were very clear Faisal. No discussions of our past or private lives with each other. Was this not the case?'

Ahmad's eyes widened as he identified Djinn's voice. They had been told that Djinn would send someone to oversee the building of the apparatus and that they should wait in the warehouse for the individual to arrive and direct them. He could also see from the astonishment on the other men's faces that none of them had expected Djinn either. The man who had made the remark stammered his answer.

'I am so sorry Djinn. I did not mean to talk to the brother about my past. I don't know why I did it or said what I said.'

Ahmad watched as Djinn emerged from the shadows with a silent accomplice walking behind him. Ahmad recognised this man as the individual who had approached him in the café in Watford on the day his life had changed forever. Djinn was dressed in a smart suit and black shoes and continued towards them smiling as he spoke.

'I'll tell you why you said it Faisal; because you wanted this young man to feel inferior. Wanted him to look at you with wide eyes and worship you for your experience and commitment to *jihad*. Wanted to soften him up so you could get him into your bed tonight and fuck that small, tight arse perhaps?'

Ahmad watched as the man physically blanched and held his hands up before him, a look of panic now dominating the once confident face. 'Djinn…no, I swear…no…it was a stupid thing to say and I swear it will never happen again. Please Djinn, it was a moment of forgetfulness, nothing more. I swear by all that is sacred it will never happen again.'

Djinn had reached the man and stood before him, staring impassively into the eyes of the terrified individual. 'Oh, I know it won't happen again Faisal. And *you* know it won't happen again because if it does…'

Ahmad watched as Djinn pulled out a mobile telephone and pressed a button. Holding the device to his ear, Djinn was silent for a moment then his face broke into a smile and he spoke into the handset.

'*Salaam Alykum. Khaif Halaq*? Good, good. I am with a friend of yours who would like to speak with you, is that acceptable at the moment? Tremendous, I will put him on.' With that, Djinn handed the phone to Faisal who looked at it with a puzzled frown and put it to his own ear.

'Hello…'

Ahmad could not hear the conversation on the other end of the phone. He did not need to. The shock and terror evident on Faisal's face told him that he had just learned that Djinn was aware of someone that Faisal loved deeply and knew that Djinn's message was clear; Fuck up again and this is the person who will pay the price for your errors. As he watched, he heard Faisal mumble an end to the conversation and hand the device back to Djinn who replaced it in the inside pocket of his suit jacket. Faisal stood, shoulders slumped, tears running down his face as he gazed at the floor. Djinn laid a hand on his shoulder and waited until the other man met his eyes before speaking.

'As I said Faisal. We both know you won't make such a mistake again so let us move on from this unpleasantness, yes?' The man nodded gratefully and straightened up, wiping his face with the sleeve of his jacket. Djinn clapped his shoulder and moved across the floor towards Ahmad. 'And you, my little engineer. You say we are ready?'

Ahmad nodded and licked his dried lips, still unnerved from the exchange he had witnessed. 'Yes Djinn. I have tweaked the design a little and identified the location. We just need to update it and put it the apparatus in place at the right time and it will work.'

'You're sure of this?'

'I'm well aware of what will happen if it doesn't so yes, I am sure that this will work. It is too simple for it not to.'

Djinn stared at him with that terrifying intensity Ahmad had experienced several times before. The demeanour changed in an instant and a huge smile transformed Djinn's face as he turned towards his silent companion. 'You see Abdul Malik; didn't I tell you our little engineer was smart?'

Ahmad watched as Abdul Malik gave a small nod, his face devoid of any expression. Djinn clapped his hands twice, making everyone in the room jump. 'Okay gentlemen. Work on the apparatus starts immediately under Ahmad's direction and plans. Faisal, Hafiz and Samir will have the apparatus ready for transportation to the area by eleven o'clock this evening. Questions?'

There were none as each man understood their role and the generous time frame with which they had to complete the task. Djinn continued. 'At eleven o'clock the transport team will arrive and again, under Ahmad's direction, they will load the apparatus and deliver it to the location. They will remain there overnight and emplace the apparatus at the specified time before extracting. Ahmad, you will direct the emplacement team to the location and oversee the placing of the apparatus. The driver of the transport team has the extraction plan so you will take your direction from him once the apparatus is in place. Understood?'

Ahmad's mouth was dry and his heart was racing. *This is really happening. I'm actually fucking doing this*! He could hear the nerves in his voice as he replied. 'Yes Djinn. Understood.'

'Good. This is a one-time-deal gentlemen. For all of you. Mess this up and you will see I am a man of my word, believe me.' He paused and glanced at his watch before looking back up and nodding at each man as he addressed them. 'Right, to work then brothers. Let's get this thing done as our American friends would say. Abdul Malik will remain here with you in the unlikely event that there are any problems. He speaks for me so you will respect him as such. I'm not going to wish you luck as you are all professionals and I have every confidence in you but work hard and be successful and you will hear from me soon.' With that, Djinn leaned in towards Abdul Malik and spoke quietly for several minutes before walking back across the warehouse floor and into the shadows from where he had emerged, the click of his shoes on the concrete floor the only sound in the building. A barked command jolted Ahmad from his reverie as Abdul Malik stepped forward.

'Well? What are you waiting for? Get on with it.'

KING'S CROSS RAILWAY STATION, LONDON

John Hoynes sank back into the seat and allowed himself a small smile. The interview had gone well and he'd been offered the job on the spot. He still couldn't get over the fact that in his first job interview after 27 years in the Royal Air Force, he had smashed it; walking straight into a fantastic opportunity. He'd barely had time to allow the success of the moment to sink in as he'd sprinted between underground connections to make the train he'd reserved the seat for, but here he was. He smiled at the pretty woman typing on a lap top across from him and removed one of the cans of IPA Pale Ale from the bag on the table. He'd risked the two minutes it had taken to buy the beer from the small concession on the concourse but had been determined to toast his good fortune as soon as possible. He pulled the ring and a hiss escaped the can as the pressure inside was released. Smiling, he put the can to his lips, savouring the cool draught and malty tang of the beer.

He caught the disapproving eye of an older man at the table across the aisle and glared back in reproach, holding eye contact until the other man dropped his gaze and found something fascinating on the platform outside with which to concentrate on. *Wanker. A man can't enjoy a couple of beers on a train after 27 years' service? Who the fuck do you think you are to judge me for a couple of cans*? John was raging but calmed himself slowly as he recollected the interview and the fact that he was about to begin a whole new career as a Security Consultant for Lloyds of London. He smiled and toasted himself silently, noting the poorly disguised grin from the pretty woman across from him, clearly amused by his antics.

Paula Harris tried to suppress the smile as she watched the man across from her toast himself with a can of beer. He was very smartly dressed in a dark suit, crisp, white shirt and a red tie so she'd concluded almost immediately that he wasn't some drunken yob who was going to be a pain in the arse all the way to Edinburgh. Although the stuffed shirt at the table across from them obviously thought differently, making his disapproval quite obvious. Paula had already crossed swords with the belligerent twat who'd tutted at her as she'd struggled to get her bags in the overhead rack, invading the man's personal space as she stretched on her tip-toes to reach. She was glad smart-dressed guy across from her had put the twat back in his box with a good, hard glare.

Turning her attention back to her computer she picked up the email thread she'd been looking at before being distracted. She could feel the excitement within her as she read over the last missive in the thread, the confirmation that their opening date was a go. She closed the computer and leaned back, a wide smile of her own now apparent. It had been a huge risk to turn her back on the only employment she had ever known but today was the day she had dreamed of for the last six months; the nursery opening day was confirmed. With over thirty children already formally registered, she could finally relax, confident in the knowledge that her business venture was now up and running. She smiled and shook her head as memories of the last six months of planning, securing finance, premises, and staff came flooding back to her. She remembered the dark days when all she'd wanted to do was curl up in a ball and dismiss the whole idea as a stupid gamble that hadn't paid off, but she'd been stronger than she'd thought. And as of the first Monday of the month, Little Cherubs' Childcare of Edinburgh would be up and running. Her grin widened as the thought of all her hard work finally paying off became a reality. Looking up, she saw smart-dressed guy observing her with a smile of his own and nodding his head towards her.

'Looks like maybe someone else got some good news today.'

Paula gave a small laugh and returned his nod. 'Yes, I sure did. Best news I've had for years actually.'

John Hoynes pulled one of the beers from his bag and offered it across the table. 'Well, you're clearly a Northern lass, so if you're not driving after this why not join me in a wee toast to good news and new beginnings?'

Paula smiled and took the beer. 'Well, that sounds like a bloody good idea! I've got a taxi booked at home so why the hell not?'

She pulled the ring-top and quickly put her mouth over the aperture as foamy beer gushed out, threatening to spill onto the table. Taking a large gulp, she lifted her face back up and held out the can before her, tapping it against that of her new travelling companion. 'Okay. Here's to good news and new beginnings. Cheers kind sir!'

John laughed and repeated the toast before taking a large swig of his own. 'Alright. I'll tell you mine if you tell me yours, how does that sound? Oh, and I'm John by the way.'

Paula smiled. 'Deal, John by-the-way. You first.'

John laughed and leaned forward, happy to share the details of his good fortune with a pretty woman with a good sense of humour.

Sandy Crawford watched the interaction between the man and woman across from him out of the corner of his eye. *The suit and the silly tart.* The woman had annoyed him the moment she'd set foot in the carriage, invading his personal space as she was too weak to lift her case into the overhead rack. The arsehole in the suit had then turned up with a bag of beer and settled down for the duration. Sandy had been going to say something; just a small warning to the suit that he was in the quiet coach and should respect that. The suit had glared at him before he could speak, and Sandy had been cowered into remaining silent.

Seething as he listened to their witless conversation, Sandy leaned back in his seat and closed his eyes, reflecting on the awful day that he had just had. When he'd been called into Brian's office, he'd assumed that it was for another ten-minute session of one of Brian's corporate-speak monologues. As Managing Director of south-east England's third-largest driving agency, Brian strutted about the offices in a poor imitation of Wall Street's Gordon Gecko. He liked pulling the staff into his office on a regular basis and lording it over them as he sat behind his desk, hair slicked, sleeves rolled up and fingers crossed as he leaned back in his oversized leather armchair. Sandy hated those meetings and had to literally bite his tongue to prevent lashing out at the little prat. His coping mechanism was to imagine meeting Brian in a pub toilet and banging Brian's head off the urinal over and over again. Sandy found that this was the only way that he could get through the inane monologue without actually carrying out physical violence.

And as he'd entered bullshit Brian's office this morning, Sandy had prepared himself for the usual. When he'd been asked to close the door, Sandy realised that there was not just something different about the meeting but also with Brian. Gone was the smug self-assuredness and patronising grin. Sandy had taken the proffered seat and listened to Brian in utter silence, a sensation of dread settling like a stone in the base of his stomach. Even now, as the rhythmic clacking of the train on the tracks soothed him, Sandy could only recall the main phrases that Brian had uttered rather than the whole conversation. *Company consolidation, department re-structuring, re-allocation of personnel, market downturn.*

Opening his eyes, Sandy shook his head slightly. Irrespective of all the corporate bullshit phraseology, Sandy Crawford, aged fifty-seven would soon be unemployed and looking for work. Sandy prided himself on being a realist and recognised that the market for a business development manager pushing fifty-seven was not a large one. *Fuck*! He would get a small settlement based on his contractual agreement but it wouldn't amount to much. He'd also have to return the company car and that would mean buying one of his own, a major expense he could ill afford. Tracy was still bleeding him dry through the alimony payments even though the bitter cow had a new man with a really good job.

He eavesdropped on the suit and the silly tart's conversation and gritted his teeth as he listened to them swap stories about how fucking amazing their lives were. The suit had spent a bit of time as a squaddie or something and had just been offered a job at Lloyds of London. *Probably got it through the old boy's network; you scratch my back I'll scratch yours, kind of thing.* The tart had started some kind of kid's crèche or some shit and was waxing lyrical about her life's ambition finally being realised. Sandy rolled his eyes and turned towards the window. *Oh, give it a fucking rest love. It's not like you're Richard bloody Branson or something! I mean, anyone can…*

Sandy's head smashed against the glass of the window as the carriage flew into the air and turned on its side. He was lifted from his seat and hurled against the overhead rack, his shoulder ramming the curved edge of the compartment. Even as the agony of his broken scapula made him shout in pain, he could hear the screams of the other passengers.

John Hoynes was catapulted across the aisle and only managed to get his hands up in front of his face a moment before his head connected with the hard plastic of the seat back. He had only the briefest of moments to register the pain in the back of his hands before he was thrown back over the seat and landed upside down as a horrendous screeching of metal on metal and a huge bang drowned out the hellish din of terrified screaming.

The screams brought Paula back to consciousness and she opened her eyes and shrieked in agony as a fire of pain assailed her leg. *What's happening? What's going on? I can't move. I CAN'T MOVE!* She tried to shift position and found herself stuck fast but wasn't sure where she was or how she'd got there. A bolt of pain from her leg caught her unawares and she screamed again. She was breathing in quick gasps and panic was taking hold as she tried desperately to move. Her eyes widened as she realised that she could also smell burning and a new terror came to her;

if she couldn't move, she would be burned alive. Crying and shouting for help, she could hear, through the bedlam in the carriage, other people moving. From her position where she was wedged tight between the seats and the side of the carriage, she turned her head until she was looking across the aisle.

A man's legs poked out from under a seat, the crazy angle in which they rested telling her that they were badly broken. Next to them she saw movement and with a gasp of surprise, realised that it was John, the man she had been speaking to. As people crawled between her and John, she began yelling his name, trying to be heard above the chaos. Her eyes widened as she saw him raise his head and look in her direction. Blood was running down his face but he nodded when he saw her.

John Hoynes tried to smile at Paula to reassure her that all would be well. He could feel the blood pouring from the wound on his head but knew that the priority had to be to get out of the train. He too, could smell the burning and knew that he had to act fast. Looking at his position, he saw that when the carriage had flipped it had thrown him across the aisle and trapped him hard between the crushed shell and the seats. Pushing down with his arms he tried to lever himself up but there was absolutely no give. He paused and caught his breath then tried again, using all his strength to get his body out of the jam but he was held fast. In the dim light he couldn't see beyond the seats that were pinning him, but he could feel real pain down there and assumed that either his thighs or his pelvis was crushed between the two objects. He looked over to Paula to try and communicate with her just as someone crawled between them.

Sandy felt the hand grab him tight and yelled in surprise, turning, wide-eyed to see who had hold of him. He saw that it was the suit and that he was hurt, with blood covering his face. Sandy tried to shake the hand free and make good his escape from the hell of the carriage but the suit held firm.

John Hoynes yelled as loudly as he could at the man he was holding in his grasp. 'Help the woman. Her. Look. Help the woman.'

Sandy followed the suit's nod of direction and made out the wide eyes and tear-streaked face of the tart, pinned under a pair of seats. Looking back at the suit, Sandy nodded to show that he understood and changed his position slightly, angling his body to face the woman.

Relieved, John Hoynes let the man go, happy that Paula now had some help and a chance to get out of the carriage before it caught fire. He wiped the blood from his eyes and looked up to gauge the man's progress. Frowning, John wiped his eyes again to be sure of what he was seeing then began to yell. 'No, no. You can't leave her. Get her out of here. Help her you bastard. HELP HER!'

Sandy scuttled forward, his teeth gritted against the agony of his shoulder. He cracked his head against an unseen obstacle and emitted a yelp of pain. He had no intention of helping the woman. This place was going to go up in flames at any moment and Sandy Crawford was not going to be caught up in *that*, thank you very much. The smoke was beginning to catch at his throat as he scrambled over the crazed arrangement of seats, tables, and luggage that were strewn the length of the coach. A small twinge of guilt arose when he thought about the woman's fate, but it was hardly *his* fault. He remembered reading somewhere that people who were drowning often took their rescuers with them as they panicked and that would probably happen here. He had no intention of being killed just because some silly woman couldn't hold it together long enough to be safe. No. Not with his shoulder. Not worth the risk. *As soon as I'm out though, I'll get the emergency services to go get them. Yes, that's a better plan.*

Paula sobbed and dropped her head as the smoke began to sting her eyes. Her hope had disappeared with the arsehole when he'd abandoned her. She could hear John yelling hoarsely across the aisle but she couldn't make out the words against the cacophony of terror in the carriage as bodies struggled over each other to escape. Coughing hard, she tried once again to move position but she was completely stuck. She thought about the fact that she would never hold her nephew Harry ever again and began screaming and pounding the seat with her fists.

John Hoynes leaned his head back and coughed as the smoke agitated his throat. He knew he was going to die here and that his death would not be a good one. He smiled as he thought about the irony of surviving operational tours of Northern Ireland, Iraq and Afghanistan only to be killed in a fucking train crash. No doubt that would be brought up in a moment of black humour at his funeral. He could hear Paula screaming across the aisle but recognised that they were both beyond help and that, she too, would end this life in the smoking ruins of the 1400 London to Aberdeen. *What a shit way to go.*

Sandy Crawford hauled himself over a youth who was trying to pull his leg free from a tangle of twisted metal. The youth was blocking much of the coach door while he attempted to extract himself and was crying and screaming in panic. The smoke was now visible as its tentacles advanced through the door and into the carriage. Clambering over, then kicking the youth behind him, Sandy snaked through the door and gave a gasp of relief as he saw the light streaming from the shattered window above him. *I've made it! I fucking made it*! Pulling his legs underneath him, he pushed upwards and pulled himself towards the window, feeling the fresh air on his face and breathing deeply. He could hear himself moaning as the realisation that he was safe began hitting home. Ignoring the shards of glass digging into his palms, he grabbed the edge of the window with both hands and hauled his upper body through the open aperture. He saw that the train was lying on its side and he had found one of the side doors that was now pointed towards the grey sky. Tears of relief streaked down his face as he shuffled the rest of his body through the broken window. He grunted in pain and heard himself sobbing as his injured shoulder protested at being twisted and turned to gain exit through the aperture. Free of the window, Sandy tumbled to the ground below, screaming on impact as his shoulder took the brunt of the fall on to the gravel. Rolling on to his side he moaned in a combination of agony and relief and struggled his way up to a sitting position. Remembering the smoke in the carriage he stumbled to his feet and began staggering away from the train and up the small bank of high weeds and bushes. Looking around he could see other people in various states of disarray stumbling or crawling from the wreck. As his brogues struggled to gain purchase on the slippery slope, Sandy thought that perhaps he wouldn't have to worry about work after all. Surely there would be serious compensation for this? This was someone's *fault.* There were no such things as accidents anymore; someone was always liable. Nodding to himself as he continued his precarious climb, cradling his arm against his body, Sandy wondered just how much money he could milk this situation for. *Millions? Possibly. Hundreds of thousands? Definitely.* Reaching the crest of the small slope he saw a group of people walking along the bank in his direction. He lifted his good arm and waved it in the air.

'Over here. I'm over here. I'm injured and need help, quickly.' As the men approached him, Sandy noted that they were not dressed in a manner that suggested that they were from any of the emergency services. They were carrying equipment of some sort and he assumed that they were probably workers from the local area who were responding to the crash. He was just about to tell them to hurry up when he saw the first man raise something in front of him and point it at Sandy. Sandy Crawford never heard the sound of the bullet being fired from the Glock 17; the round had already entered and exited his skull before his ears could register the retort. His body remained upright for several moments, his mouth agape and a neat hole in his forehead oozing blood, before he tumbled backwards, rolling down the embankment and coming to rest beneath the very window he had escaped from.

SIG, CAMP BRACKEN, AYLESBURY

The conference room was silent as the analyst ran the slides of the presentation on the large screen at the front of the room. When the last slide had been shown the analyst paused and turned to face the attendees. Oliver Dewar cleared his throat.

'Thank you, Corporal Harkins, that'll be all.'

The analyst turned the lights back on before leaving the room and closed the door behind him. Oliver turned in his seat to take in the three individuals sat at the table. 'Thoughts?'

Lovat nodded towards the blank screen. 'A train derailed at one hundred and thirty miles an hour by an improvised ramp. The survivors then either set on fire or shot by an armed gang. This gang then all turn up crispy as KFC in a burnt-out people carrier near Luton. That about sum it up?'

Giles stretched in his chair and regarded his military colleague. 'That's about the size of it Lovat. We're still getting feedback trickling in regarding the forensic investigation but the truth of the matter is we're not getting much to go on.' He turned to face the Commanding Officer. 'I'm getting my balls squeezed pretty fucking hard on this one Oliver because my director is taking a kicking from Number 10. So, forgive me but I make no apologies for the fact that you won't be seeing much of your guys here until we nail these bastards for good.'

Oliver Dewar nodded. 'Well that's why you've got these two Giles. If there's anything that can be found I have the utmost confidence that this is the team that will find it. So, use and abuse them as much as you need.'

Nadia leaned forward in her chair. 'Look, I'm sure I'm not the only one that's thinking this: There's something very different about these attacks. One; they're brilliantly planned and executed. Two; there is never any evidence or anyone left alive to question. Three; this is a campaign, not a series of linked attacks. There's more to come. So, the question I think we need to be asking first is *who*? And I think we're all in agreement that this isn't one of our known or suspected scumbags so that leaves the probability that it's someone new. Someone either brought in or who has sneaked in to the UK in the last year or so.'

Giles nodded. 'Agreed. We've got every asset we have working on this and we've had a couple of leads that we followed up on but they were all either utter bollocks or unrelated.'

Lovat sighed. 'Look, these guys are very good. Best we've seen on mainland UK soil but let's not forget that they *need* four things for their campaign; weapons, communications, finance, and people. *And* they have to coordinate all of these elements each time they launch an attack so they are definitely open to penetration but we just haven't found the weak link yet.'

Giles gave a small smile and a sigh of his own. 'Unfortunately, Lovat, time is something we do not have the luxury of having. Another attack like this could happen any day and slaughter even more people. We also have the added pressure of the backlash against Muslims; only this morning we had another two mosques burned in Bradford. Let's hope that Cheltenham have managed to hoover something up to give us somewhere to start.'

Lovat was quietly hoping for the same thing. They were waiting on a conference call from the team at GCHQ in Cheltenham that had been dedicated to supporting the hunt for the terrorists. The virtual meeting should have started over an hour ago but their technical colleagues had sent a rushed message requesting a short delay. Like Giles, Lovat hoped this was an indicator of good news rather than poor timekeeping. On more occasions than he could possibly remember, Lovat had been hugely impressed by the capabilities of GCHQ. From telephone numbers, text messages, emails and encrypted chats, the agency had provided Lovat with a lot of help throughout the years.

There was a moment of silence as each individual sought to think of something that could assist in generating a start point for the investigation. A soft knock on the door interrupted their thoughts. Oliver Dewar looked up. 'Enter.'

The young analyst walked into the room and pointed at the large television screen at the other end of the room. 'Sorry sir. GCHQ on secure conference VTC. They're ready to go.'

'Thank you, Corporal Harkins. Patch them through.'

'Yes Sir.' The analyst strode to the screen and picked up a remote control from the small console table in front of it. The screen came to life and a set of options appeared which the young corporal swiftly selected. Two individuals appeared on screen and the analyst nodded back at his Commanding Officer before exiting the room. Oliver Dewar nodded at Giles who turned back to face the screen.

'Good morning Peregrine, Anthony. With me is Oliver Dewar, CO of SIG and my team, Lovat Reid and Nadia Ali. Please tell me we have something to go on.'

The two men on the screen looked at each other and Lovat thought he detected the smallest flush of excitement on Peregrine's cheeks.

'Giles, good morning to all of you and, well, yes. We believe we may have something you can use. I'll hand you over to Anthony as it was his guys that first picked up on this.' The clipped estuary English was replaced by a gentle Scottish brogue as his colleague took over.

'Good morning all. Look I know we're all under the cosh here so let me get right to it. We got a ping on a phone associated with someone we were monitoring some years ago. He dropped off the radar and it was assumed had either gone abroad or ceased with his activities. The day before the train derailment this number was called from an unknown mobile being used in an industrial estate in Stevenage.' The speaker paused and adjusted the wire-rimmed glasses on his face before continuing. 'We tracked the movements of this Stevenage mobile and, well, it appears that the owner was also in the vicinity of the train derailment mere hours before the attack.'

The sense of excitement in the room was palpable as Lovat looked across the table at Nadia who was smiling and giving him an enthusiastic nod. Lovat turned back to the screen as the speaker continued.

'This number went dark around the time of the attack and hasn't reappeared since, leading us to believe that it has been destroyed but we were able to map the network of contacts associated to it and we've sent them on secure means along with the information we have on the individual that this mobile was calling.'

Giles clapped his hands together. 'Anthony that is tremendous news. This is the first real lead that we have had in four attacks. You and your team have done bloody well mate, bloody well indeed. Anything else, gents?'

The two men on the screen exchanged a glance and shook their heads slightly before Peregrine spoke. 'No Giles, that's all we have I'm afraid. We're still following through on each associated number but will get anything of relevance to you in real time.'

'Peregrine, that's fantastic and again, big thanks to you and your guys. Tremendous job.' As Giles watched, the two men on the screen nodded and Anthony leaned forward and then the screen went black. He turned back to face his SIG contemporaries. 'Plan?'

Lovat spoke. 'We need access to all CCTV in and around the estate and look to link vehicle and people movements with the timings of the mobile telephone patterns. We can then identify the phone's owner and track them through the systems, walk the cat back and see how this person made their way to the estate, where they came from, who else were they with etc.'

Nadia nodded and addressed Giles. 'Soon as we have something to go on, I'll get around the estate and start doing the face to face stuff. I'll lead with the…*intimation* that I'm tracking down a paedo ring thought to be using some of the warehouses.' She gave a grin. 'People won't think twice about helping out a Paki if she's investigating the worst scum of the earth.'

Lovat laughed at Nadia's self-deprecating humour but recognised the truth in her statement, the backlash against Muslims as bad as it had ever been. He turned to Giles. 'You going to look into the network they've pulled from the phone history mate?'

Giles nodded. 'Yes, I'll get the guys in the cell to start putting faces to names and pull all the backgrounds up. Shall we say back here at nineteen-hundred for a debrief?' Seeing the nods of assent, he stood and straightened his tie.

'Okay. Let's not squander what little time we have. See you all tonight.'

Nadia punched in the code to her personal cage, entered, and closed the door behind her. She dropped her bag on to the table and pulled a set of keys from her pocket before unlocking a large metal locker. Opening a drawer, she reached inside and removed several folded wallets and examined each one before identifying the one she required. The photograph on the warrant card was very recent, the whole document only weeks old, made the day after she'd formally joined the team. MI5 had provided them with all the essential documentation that they could possibly need in order to operate freely. Today Nadia planned to use the Police identity to encourage people to talk to her. She'd already formed a loose cover story for the more curious members of the general public, something around the activities of an armed paedophile grooming gang operating in the area. The recent high-profile arrests of gangs of Pakistani men involved in these activities would lend credence to her story. And the warrant card would do the rest.

Looking around her she smiled. She liked having her own cage. When she had agreed to join the unit, Lovat had shown her to her allocated cage where she would store all her operational kit, weapons and communications. He had shown her his own cage and how he stored and secured everything in accordance with the Unit's security compliances. As the operators had access to the building and their cages any hour of the day or night, security was a pretty big deal. Nadia liked this. She'd always worked better when she had the freedom to come and go as she pleased. She was either blessed or cursed with one of those brains that would wake her up in the small hours of the morning with a vital fact or new idea for an operational requirement. To be able to act on those impulses as and when they happened was now a reality for her. No more waiting until morning when the armoury was open or the ops room staff had cycled in from whatever dormitory town they'd chosen to base themselves.

Ramming the warrant card into the front pocket of her suit trousers, she removed a set of car keys from a hook on the side of the locker, then secured everything before locking up and making her way out of the Ops wing of the building. As she walked along the main corridor towards the front exit, she wondered how Lovat was faring with his trawling of the CCTV systems. Pushing open the large glass doors she gave a small grin. Spending hours hunched over an array of TV monitors was definitely not her idea of a good day. No, she had undoubtedly got the better end of the deal today.

Lovat leaned back in the chair with his hands behind his head as he felt the excitement start to take hold in his stomach. The old, familiar sensation he always experienced when he knew he was on the trail of a bad guy. It had taken him the best part of the day, and he felt tired from the constant strain of sifting through days of poor-quality CCTV footage but it had paid off. He now had a name and address for the mobile telephone's owner and vehicle details of another two cars that looked to be associated with the Stevenage estate. *Faisal Wali Omar. Who are you and what is your involvement here*? Lovat closed his eyes as he mentally summarised what information he had learned as a result of his hard work.

Using GCHQ's information, Lovat had narrowed down the timings of when the mobile phone had been present in the industrial estate. From there he had analysed hours of CCTV coverage, logging the details for every car and individual coming in and out of the estate. And he'd done it: He had his man. Once Lovat had been certain that the vehicle and individual were linked to the phone, he had reversed the individual's route, scanning hours and various CCTV networks and coverage areas until he had a full picture of the individual's journey. A check of the address, listed occupants, and DVLA records showed that the individual he had first identified was one Faisal Wali Omar, British citizen of Afghan origin, unemployed and living in a middle-class housing estate on the outskirts of Stevenage.

Lovat had tracked Faisal's movements from his home to a unit on the industrial estate and then from the estate out on to the M1 motorway but then had no more coverage of him after junction five. Lovat thought that this was probably when Faisal had left the motorway and made his way to join the attack on the train in an area where there was no CCTV coverage. *Smart.* Of more concern to Lovat was the fact that GCHQ had told them that Faisal's phone had gone dark at or around the time of the attack and had not been active since. Lovat knew that there were only two conceivable reasons for this: either the phone had been destroyed after the attack to preserve security or Faisal was currently one of the charred corpses melted into the framework of a burnt-out people-carrier. Instinct told Lovat that it was likely to be the latter.

He was considering this when his own phone buzzed angrily in his jeans pocket and he retrieved it, glancing at the number as he lifted the device to his face. *Giles.* Giving his colleague a cursory hello, he then listened in silence to the latest development for several minutes before ending the call. He placed his phone down on the desk as he assimilated the information that Giles had excitedly voiced down the secure telephone: Cheltenham had come up trumps again and decrypted a message between Faisal and one of his contacts. It was a short message that Giles had read verbatim to Lovat and it was very easy to remember: *This new Emir might have been an unfriendly neighbour but his arrival is a flaming sword to the kuffirs.* Even though a short missive, Lovat's experience and knowledge of his country's enemies allowed him to interpret the cryptic content. Islamist terrorists often referred to senior commanders as

Emir; a prince or leader. *Unfriendly neighbour* probably meant a Pakistani, given that Faisal was an Afghan and the term was not uncommon for Afghan's to use when describing the nation to their south. And the reference to a *flaming sword to the kuffirs* was fairly standard jihadi-speak for delivering a just and brutal punishment to the unbelievers.

Lovat nodded slowly and leaned back in his chair, one hand self-consciously touching the scar on his face as he thought through all the information they now had at their disposal. While still not a direct lead to the group responsible, they had a solid starting point and in his experience the information would now start coming in more regularly as connections were made and further leads established. He gave a small smile, his first of the day, and stood, arching and stretching his back to ease the stiffness from his hours of sitting. *I'm on your trail now Mr Emir. Might be a while yet, but I'm on to you.*

With a renewed sense of purpose, he closed down the computer application and logged off before leaving the small enclosed booth. Entering the main area of the Operations cell he nodded to a few familiar faces before exiting the room and heading for his cage. He wanted to change and get a quick run through the woods in before the evening brief. If he hurried, he knew he could crack a decent six miles and a shower before the briefing started.

Nadia was first into the secure briefing room and retrieved her lap-top from her bag and began attaching it to the projector leads. She wanted to present her findings to the team and had some interesting footage to show them which would help with their operation. Her day around the estate had proved fruitful once she'd broken down most people's wariness and deployed her cover story. She had struck gold when speaking with the owner of a small warehouse across from the unit they had identified as that used by the terrorists. The owner of the warehouse had informed her that he might actually have some footage of the cars that entered and left the unit across from him. Nadia mentioned that she couldn't see any cameras pointing that way and the short, tubby man had laughed before looking around him in a mock secretive manner. He'd explained that as a small delivery company, he sometimes took on agency workers to support his operation during busy times and that a lot of these temporary workers were not shy about squirrelling away the odd parcel or two for themselves. To gain evidence of this, he'd emplaced two cameras facing the driver's loading bays but had ensured that they could not be seen with a casual glance. With a mixture of pride and excitement he'd taken Nadia to his cramped, untidy office and accessed a surprisingly modern CCTV system. She'd asked him to bring up the footage from the discreet cameras and then scroll to the day of the attack. It had taken some time and they were sometimes unable to see the building opposite due to the company vans being in shot, but then

then she'd seen it; a group of cars and individuals arriving over a short time frame. She could see also that the men were Asian in appearance and she knew then, that she was looking at the group who had attacked the train.

Grabbing the remote for the projector, she powered the device on and adjusted the focus of her first slide. After she'd copied the footage from the company's hard disk, she'd gone to work throughout the afternoon, cropping images and footage and isolating faces and vehicle details. She'd finished with a collection of fair-quality imagery of three men and three vehicles which she'd expanded and sharpened to bring out the maximum details. Satisfied that her presentation was good to go, she looked up just as the door opened and Giles walked in accompanied by a tall, athletic individual with a shock of blonde hair and a thick beard. Nadia grimaced as she recognised Giles' companion. Before she could say anything, Giles placed his hand on the man's shoulder and nodded towards her.

'Nadia, this is Luke. He's the SFE from Hereford and will be working with us on the exploitation elements of the operation.'

Nadia groaned inwardly as she took on board the information. The Special Forces Element or SFE, was an SAS or SBS officer attached to MI5 for specific operations and worked closely with the team, managing the high-threat physical elements of the operation. Luke had actually been one of the instructors on Nadia's SRR selection and had gone out of his way to make what was already a living hell far worse for her. Catching his eye, she saw Luke nod discreetly towards her, a mocking look in his Nordic-blue eyes. *Yeah, he fucking remembers.* She gave a nod to Giles. 'Yeah Giles, Luke and I know each other from old. Luke was actually the first Olympic-standard wanker that I'd ever met. In fact, come to think of it, he's *still* the finest Olympic-standard wanker that I've met!' She almost burst out laughing at Giles' stunned expression but caught the flash of rage that flitted over Luke's face, hardening his eyes, and she caught her impulse. The moment was fleeting and the SAS man recovered quickly and addressed her in his upper-class London accent.

'Different times Staff Sergeant Ali and clearly stood you in good stead based on what Giles has been telling me. Now, I don't know about you but I'm here to get the fuckers that are ripping my country apart and put them in a box where they belong so what say we put the past behind us and get on with the task at hand, eh?'

Nadia nodded. 'Suits me, *Sir*.' When he'd addressed her by her rank, Nadia knew that Luke was making a point about his seniority in the military chain of command and she wasn't about to roll over on it. Luke had been a young Captain when he'd been on the selection staff so he would probably be a Major by now. *Well, a major prick at any rate.* Giles cleared his throat and regarded the pair with some unease.

'Erm…we're not going to have any difficulties here are we people?'

Nadia sighed and shook her head. 'No Giles, absolutely not. Luke's right; the past is the past and we're both professionals so whatever personal differences, they won't have any bearing on us working together. Right Luke?'

There was the briefest hesitation before the SAS officer broke into a beaming smile. 'Couldn't have said it better myself Nadia. Looking forward to working with you.'

Giles nodded, happy with their affirmations, and began pulling out his own computer. Nadia turned away and busied herself with her notebook, checking she had all the points listed that she wanted to cover. From the corner of her eye she watched Luke take a seat and check his phone, ostensibly ignoring her. She thought about his remark regarding putting the past behind them and wondered if he'd been as completely full of shit as she had. Her thoughts were interrupted when Lovat walked in, face shiny and ruddy from whatever physical activity he had just been carrying out. Introductions to Luke were made and Lovat took a seat beside the Special Forces officer. As Giles was seated also, Nadia cleared her throat and caught their attention.

'Gents, some good news from today: Decent footage of faces and vehicles associated to the activity within the unit in Stevenage. Haven't had time to put the info into the system yet as I came straight from the job. To summarise though, we have potential identification for four individuals involved in this attack.'

Giles clapped his hands together hard. 'Yes! This is what we're after people. Bloody good work Nadia. Now, why don't you continue with what you have, then Lovat can show us what he's dug up.'

Nadia was about to reply when the door opened and a stranger walked in, dressed smartly in a tailored suit, nodding confidently at the puzzled faces before closing the door behind him. Tall and tanned, he regarded them for a moment before smiling and placing a placatory hand on his chest.

'Lady and gentlemen, please forgive this intrusion but, as I'm sure I have no need to point out to your good selves, time is somewhat of the essence here. As of now, I will be assisting this operation as a representative from my department at Vauxhall, having, as I do, a not insignificant amount of experience in the Afghan/Pakistan CT sphere.' The man paused and widened his smile, the perfect white teeth in contrast to the tanned skin. 'I'm Crispin. Crispin Faulks.'

WATFORD

Ahmad rubbed his eyes, wincing at the gritty sensation. He was exhausted, having had little to no sleep for the past few days. Since the train derailment and the non-stop news coverage of the event, he'd been consumed by guilt at his role in the attack. His design and management of the construction of the ramp that had derailed the train was all that he could think about. The dead and the dying. The horrific images of the surviving passengers being gunned down or set alight. The Prime Minister's public assertion that every effort was focused upon catching those responsible.

For the first two days after the attack, Ahmad had not slept at all, convinced that any one of the noises he could hear outside signalled the arrival of armed police sent to bring him to justice. He'd been sick; rushing several times to his small bathroom to vomit into the toilet. He'd also been tempted to go to the police, tell them everything and get them to get his family safe before Djinn could get to them. But he couldn't risk it. Djinn had hinted on more than one occasion that he had access to police officers on his payroll and Ahmad was almost certain that the moment he set foot into a police station Djinn would know.

He groaned and rolled on to his side, looking at the red digital display on the alarm clock next to his bed before closing his eyes again in the forlorn hope that he would get some sleep. He needed it; Djinn had messaged him last night and told him he needed to meet with him today. Ahmad had no idea what this meeting would be about but was sure it would involve the planning for another attack. Djinn had complemented Ahmad on his work with the train-ramp but in the same breath warned him that he still had work to do. When Ahmad had seen the news reports about the burnt bodies found in the wreckage of a vehicle, he'd known instantly that it was Faisal and the other men he had been working with. It had been a further demonstration, not that any was really needed, of Djinn's utter ruthlessness.

Opening his eyes, Ahmad decided just to get up. There would be no sleep today. He threw his legs out of the side of the bed and picked up a pair of tracksuit pants from the floor, pulling them on before making his way to the chair in the corner and grabbing the hoodie draped upon it. He was walking out the room when the buzz from his mobile startled him. Lifting the device, he looked at the screen and saw Michelle's name and a brief message all in upper case to highlight her obvious displeasure. He stared at it for a further moment before putting the phone into his pocket and leaving the room, making his way to the kitchen. There was no point replying to her, not when he had no real answer that would satisfy her question; *WTF is going on????*

'You look tired my little engineer. Are you not sleeping well?'

Ahmad looked up from his coffee and stared at the man who had destroyed his entire existence. He took in the dark, intelligent eyes, the sardonic smile and the scar tissue just visible under the hairline. 'No Djinn, I'm not sleeping.'

'But you must sleep Ahmad. I need you firing on all cylinders as the English say. Need you to be fighting fit, as they also say. What worries you so much that it keeps you awake at nights?'

Ahmad gave a small snort of derision. 'Well Djinn, I'm not sure really. It could be my terrible diet or how worried I am that my favourite is going to get voted off from *I'm a celebrity* or, oh wait, I remember, it's the fact that I helped murder and maim dozens of innocent people!' He hadn't meant to be so sarcastic and held his breath as he waited for Djinn's response. The other man merely raised an eyebrow and lifted his coffee to his lips, all the while maintaining eye contact with him.

'Very amusing but please don't talk to me like that again. I don't much care for it. I am, however, well aware of the fact that you will be experiencing a lot of guilt and shock regarding your participation in the attack but there's nothing I can say or do that can alleviate that. I feel no guilt or remorse because I know that we are fully justified in our actions and consequently I sleep like a baby every night.'

Ahmad opened his mouth to reply but was cut short by Djinn's raised hand.

'And frankly, your guilt and shock are of no concern to me except for how they affect your work with me. And if it does affect your work, then you already know the consequences that your family will suffer. To that end, I am content that you will be able to put your feelings and emotions to one side and ensure your performance remains professional.'

Swallowing hard, Ahmad nodded. 'Djinn please, I am tired but I won't let you down, I promise.'

Djinn reached out and placed his hand on the younger man's shoulder. 'I know, my little engineer. I know. You are stronger than even you know. But enough of this going over old ground. Let us move on to our next operation. I think that you will find this one a little easier to stomach as we will be hitting our enemies directly; no normal citizens this time.'

Rubbing his eyes once again, Ahmad nodded in resignation. 'Okay, what are we doing this time?'

Djinn smiled, his white teeth gleaming in contrast with his dark skin. 'We're taking the battle directly to the very people who are killing our brothers and sisters across the globe: We are going to war with MI6.'

Ahmad shook his head. 'How? They must have some of the best security in the world. Is this even possible?'

Leaning back, Djinn regarded the stunned expression on the younger man's face. 'It's *more* than possible. I have already planned the attack and conducted the reconnaissance and know exactly how this is going to work. Think about it Ahmad; attacking the assassins as they go about their work! This will be *our* best work yet.'

'And what is it you want me to do as part of this operation.'

Djinn nodded, pleased that they were getting down to business. 'I will need your knowledge of ballistics, physics and some other things for this one. I have the plan ready to go and will tell you exactly what I require of you but believe me, it will be nothing too difficult. Oh, and Ahmad?'

'Yes?'

'If you work well and this is a successful operation, you will never hear from me again. It will be over for you and it will be as if I had never existed.'

Ahmad's eyes widened as he dared to hope. 'Seriously? This works and it's over for me? You won't ever come near me or my family again?'

The older man smiled and patted Ahmad gently on the knee. 'I told you some time ago my little engineer that I wouldn't lie to you and that hasn't changed. Work well for me on this operation and your ordeal is over.'

Ahmad could now feel the moisture in his eyes as the relief began to sink in that it was possible, *just* possible, that he would make it out of this. But he had a feeling that if Djinn was willing to hold true to his word, this next attack would be much deadlier than the previous one.

MI6 HEADQUARTERS, VAUXHALL

Crispin Faulks regarded the military officer sat across from him for a moment before continuing with his brief. 'So, you see Luke, that is where we are and that is why we can't allow our colleagues across the river or SIG to be privy to this intelligence.'

There was silence in the large office for several seconds, the soundproofing cocooning the men from any external noise.

'I completely understand Crispin. Very much a need to know basis as far as I can see. This information is pretty sensitive so we can't risk it going public.'

Crispin nodded. 'Absolutely. If it was common knowledge, this would set us back about twenty years with the Pakistanis. As it stands, our Director of Operations is engaging them in discreet, closed door discussions.'

Leaning forward, Luke Taylor reached for his coffee, took a sip and replaced the cup on the table. 'Okay, but in the meantime, if we get the opportunity to take this guy down, we don't have to request any formal clearance?'

'No. We're running with the narrative that he's rogue ISI, as much of an embarrassment to the Pakistanis as he is a threat to us. Islamabad don't really have any option but to follow us on this as any other course of action from them suggests they knew about his intentions.'

'Do you think there's a chance that they do?'

Sighing, Crispin laid his hands flat upon the table in front of him. 'My gut instinct says no; they wouldn't be this stupid. I can't, however, discount the possibility that they may have learned about him and allowed him to run, just to give us a bloody nose while maintaining plausible deniability.'

'Motivation?'

'Some years back we killed several ISI officers in a strike in Kunar Province. We didn't know it at the time but when you guys did the follow-up on the ground, the ISI were carrying their official ID papers. As best we can understand they just got lazy; didn't bother cleaning themselves down before crossing the border into Afghanistan. Their presence was leaked to the media and Islamabad was hugely embarrassed at being caught red-handed. Washington came down hard on them and heads were rolled so to speak. After that they have always held a grudge, however well-hidden.'

Luke nodded. 'Yeah, I remember this. I was running the Close Protection teams for the Embassy in Kabul when this happened and it was a really big deal. And you think that's what this has all been about? Revenge?'

'One way or the other, yes, I truly do. But even if we're wrong, we've got to stop it and that's why you've been brought into the loop: We need someone we know we can trust with this information to bring this madness to a halt.'

'Okay, let's speak clearly here Crispin. You and I have worked together quite a few times over the years and, as far as I can tell at least, we've always done a pretty good job.' Luke waited for a nod of agreement before continuing. 'So, you give me whatever you can to help me and my guys get this murdering bastard and I will make sure there is always an alternative explanation for how we got the Intel. We've been here before so it's not exactly new territory for either of us.'

Crispin knew that Luke was referring to an operation that they had worked together in Beirut some years back that had involved the Special Forces' officer orchestrating the kidnap of a particularly nasty Hezbollah commander. The fallout of the operation would have been quite considerable however it had been conducted to appear typical of an Israeli snatch and grab, leaving no trail of breadcrumbs with which to associate any involvement from Crispin or MI6. Luke had received a Queen's Gallantry Medal in the New Year's Honour's List for his role in the operation although the heavily redacted citation referred only in general terms to courageous service to the British Embassy programs in the Middle East. Then, as now, Luke had been given privileged information to enable him to carry out the operation without attracting any negative attention to the Service. Crispin was confident that the SAS Major could repeat his earlier successes and it was for this very reason that Crispin had ensured that it was Luke who had been assigned as the SFE to the operation. Of course, fat Giles and the squaddies from the SIG didn't know this. As far as they were concerned, Luke was assigned to the operation from Directorate of Special Forces, Luke's masters. But Crispin could not leave anything to chance on this one and wanted control of all the pieces.

When his Director of Operations, the DO, had requested an emergency meeting, Crispin had been curious. Very little happened in the top corridors of the Vauxhall building that necessitated such urgency. Ten minutes into the meeting however and Crispin's head was back in the dusty thoroughfares of Kandahar and Lashkar Gah. More importantly, it was remembering and reliving his actions and activities during his deployment to the region. The meeting had lasted no more than twenty minutes at the end of which the quiet-spoken Director had fixed his subordinate with a cold glare and uttered only two words: *Fix this.* And Crispin was determined to do just that.

Looking at the SAS major across the table, Crispin sighed and leaned forward, engaging the other man's attention. 'So, full disclosure: I wasn't selected at random for this task as you'll probably have guessed. The ISI officer we're chasing is not unknown to me and is actually someone I thought I'd taken off the board a couple of years ago.

Seems that the reports of his death were, as the cliché goes, somewhat exaggerated.'

'Personal element to the revenge then?'

'Possibly, given that his family were killed in the strike.'

Luke Taylor considered this for a moment. 'What are you doing at this end to develop the intelligence picture on him?'

'Again, no further dissemination on this please, but I have reached out to one of our agents we have within the ISI and we are starting to get some interesting information, particularly regarding his access to funding and logistics.'

'Good; the money trail is always a great start point. He's got to get his cash from somewhere and that means a physical appearance at a real location, whether that's to receive money or allocate it.'

'Agreed and it looks like this will bear fruit very soon. What about your team? Are they prepped and ready to go?'

The Special Forces officer nodded. 'Absolutely. They're on immediate notice to move. I'm leaving them based at camp until we get a location then I'll forward mount them as and when.'

Crispin leaned back and nodded, satisfied with Luke's preparations. The SAS team would be responsible for the physical operation to kill or detain the target. Home Office approval had been given with none of the usual hand-wringing or demands for ridiculous justification clauses. This was one of the few occasions where Crispin could remember witnessing a completely concerted effort to bring a terrorist to heel without everyone trying to cover their backsides from any legal or political fallout. *Works for me.* He was brought back to the room as Luke spoke again.

'The team's a good one. Got lucky to snag a Team Leader from B Squadron who's just rotated back from a spell in Libya where he's been doing a lot of snatch and grabs of some top tier bad guys. The rest of the guys are all experienced operators and have done this kind of thing before.'

'Good. I was quite sure I could leave this in your capable hands and I can see you're all over it. So, think all that's left is to give you a full briefing on the target then introduce you to my team here who are collating all the actionable intelligence.' With that, the MI6 officer picked up a remote control and pointed the slender black device at a large flat-screen display mounted on the wall. The familiar white crest of the Service dominated the black screen before the next screen flashed a red warning that the contents of the presentation were classified as Secret with no further dissemination permitted. Crispin operated the remote and clicked on to the next image, that of a well-groomed man dressed in traditional Pakistani clothing. 'Luke Taylor, meet Objective SCIMITAR, formerly of Pakistan's Inter-Services Intelligence or ISI for short.'

Luke stared hard at the high-definition photograph of the target, committing every aspect of the man's features to memory. 'How recent is the image?'

'We believe that's around seven years old so here's one that our analysts have done their wizardry upon to reflect the effect of age etc.' The next image showed the same photograph but the man's face was slightly heavier with some wrinkles in the skin and a greying of the hair at the temples. Crispin allowed the SAS officer a few moments to observe the new image before continuing. 'It is also possible that he has some scarring on his face and body but we have no current confirmation of that, just a good possibility seeing that he was flattened in a drone strike just over two years ago.'

Luke grunted. 'Still surprises me how hard it is to kill some of these bastards.'

'Agreed: The strike that hit his compound killed another nine people all within yards of SCIMITAR and yet here he is, alive and well and tearing our country to shreds.'

'Well, not for much longer. I take it we've got the face into OMNI?'

Crispin nodded. 'Yes. As we couldn't give what we had over to Five and the SIG we've had SCIMITAR's mug programmed into OMNI but no hits so far.'

Luke made a small note in his moleskine diary. He had no doubt that if anything was going to get a physical sighting of SCIMITAR it would be OMNI, MI6's covert facial recognition program that was embedded into practically all of the UK's major CCTV systems. SCIMITAR's image would have been uploaded into the program and the moment that any camera in the UK caught and matched the image, SIS would be alerted through OMNI's notification system. OMNI also tracked the movement of the target from camera to camera and all without the knowledge of the camera operators or owners. Although he struggled to understand how OMNI worked, Luke knew that the program had provided the initial leads on several major operations that had resulted in the arrest of some serious individuals. It was also one of the Service's best-kept secrets, as much for protecting the capabilities of the program as it was keeping the human-rights lawyers and activists from shrieking in horror at the perceived privacy abuses. He looked up as Crispin advanced the presentation and found himself looking at a biography of the target as the SIS officer read through it.

'Okay, as you can see, SCIMITAR is a very experienced intelligence officer and no stranger to getting his hands dirty. Strong pedigree from his days working with the Muj against the Russians, then effectively running with the development and structuring of the organisation we now refer to as the Taliban. His family connections are also significant, giving him access to most of the power brokers in the entire Afghan/Pakistan sphere.' He paused as he heard Luke chuckle and looked at him as his military colleague pointed his pen at the screen.

'I don't believe it! He trained at Sandhurst as a military cadet, then had CIA and MI6 training when he was fighting the Russians. Well, that has certainly come back and bitten us on the arse, hasn't it?'

Crispin felt a surge of annoyance at Luke's comments but kept his expression neutral. He had to remember that the military was a far simpler creature and had little or no understanding of the vagaries and dynamics of international intervention and nation-building. To them the world was binary; you were a good guy or a bad guy, with us or against us. What soldiers like Luke couldn't see was that the world wasn't as simple as black and white; it was grey. And navigating that grey world was the preserve of people like Crispin and his Service. People who *understood* it. He turned his attention back to the screen and advanced the next slide.

'Right, while we don't have any corroborated reporting on how he entered the country, our agent in Islamabad provided a few of the ISI's tried and tested methods…'

WATFORD

The old woman struggled to keep her small trolley upright as she dragged it behind her, the small tartan receptacle bouncing off-balance on the cracks in the narrow pavement. She paused and took a drag on her cigarette before sighing and carrying on with her journey. She looked up to gauge how much further it was until she reached the new pavement outside the community centre. Her expression changed as she saw she was going to have to move over to allow the approaching person to pass her. Lip curling in distaste, she hauled on her trolley and pulled it closer to her side as the person brushed past her. The old woman shook her head and followed the departing, black-clad form as it made its way along the road. *Shouldn't bloody well be allowed. Go back to your own country if you want to dress in that shit.* Taking an angry draw on the cigarette, she tugged on the handle of the trolley and, head bent, toiled towards the newer paving where, for a short stretch at least, her journey would be easier.

Beneath the black niqab, Nadia spoke quietly as she pressed on the small transmit button. 'Zero, Echo, fifty from HOTEL, over.' The acknowledgement from the operations room was immediate in her covert earpiece and she turned her attention completely to the area around her through the slit aperture of the restrictive veil covering her face. Other than cars, the old woman that she had just passed had been one of the few people Nadia had seen on the street. She was now only fifty metres from the target's home address, a fact that she had just informed the operator back at the safe house. She heard Lovat's voice in her earpiece just as a car drove past her.

'Echo, Delta, have you visual and going static in fifty, over.'

'Roger Delta, you are going static.' Nadia watched as Lovat drove his vehicle further along the road then parked it outside a small row of shops, almost directly across from the target's home, designated as code-word HOTEL. Lovat would be the close cover for Nadia as she conducted her foot-based approach to the area of the target's house, ready to support her instantly if something went wrong.

Maintaining her vigilance for anything unusual or out of place, Nadia again had to hand it to Lovat for this lead. After his scrutiny of all the CCTV footage, he had visited the site of the attack and then identified all the areas where someone could have monitored the location. He'd done the hard graft of the door to door but had, by his own admission and humility, gotten lucky with a farmer. The farmer had remembered a car with an Asian driver that he'd seen on one of the lanes beside his property. The farmer had remembered not just the encounter but also the first three numbers of the vehicle's registration, as he'd been concerned that it may have belonged to thieves caching his property. It had taken no time at all to identify the registered owner as one Ahmad Noor Mohammed. They had also linked his vehicle to the industrial unit in Stevenage and both the case and the team's excitement had built rapidly. Although there were no subversive or criminal traces associated to him, there was absolutely no doubt that, at whatever level, Ahmad Noor Mohammed was involved in the attack on the train. Lovat's working theory was that the target, or ANM as they were calling him for sake of brevity, was a clean skin, someone deliberately recruited due to their lack of criminal or terrorist links.

The analysts had quickly put together the Target briefing pack for the team with all the family background, names, addresses, vehicles, friends and associates and telephone numbers. All these numbers as well as email and social media accounts were being interrogated and monitored even as the operation unfolded to identify any useful information or evidence of involvement. The decision to mount a surveillance operation was made in order to allow the intelligence picture to be developed further. With no positive identification for the terrorist mastermind they were hunting, they couldn't be sure whether ANM was that individual or a mere pawn in a supporting role. With the accepted wisdom that the latter theory was the more probable, the team needed to see where ANM would lead them. As he was now a sanctioned and cleared Target, Ahmad Noor Mohammed was officially designated as Objective DAGGER.

From the imagery that the analysts had provided for the address and neighbouring area, Nadia and the surveillance team had produced a plan that would allow her to conduct a walk past of the property and emplace a covert camera that would cover the front door. The high-definition imagery from the camera would be monitored and controlled from a safe house several streets away where the team had forward-mounted the operation the previous day. Motion-activated to preserve battery life, the camera would give them valuable assistance in covering the property as well as providing hard evidence for any legal prosecutions.

Nadia could see that she was close to the stairwell that would lead to the block of flats where DAGGER lived. Turning into the stair's entry she gave another transmission. 'Zero, Echo, twenty to HOTEL, over.' Once again, the acknowledgement was instant, as she would have expected on a high-threat surveillance operation. The Special Forces guys had demanded they conduct the operation but Lovat had vetoed this immediately. He'd pointed out that this was what he and Nadia did for a living and were far better at it than someone who had done it occasionally as an additional skill. It had gotten the SF guys' backs up but Giles had backed the call, well aware that the Special Forces had a reputation for not following directives and being a bit too quick off the mark with the trigger finger. But Lovat was right; if DAGGER was killed by an over-eager SF operator, the team's lead would be as dead as the target.

As she climbed the stairs, she pulled the crumpled coke can from a small pouch in her handbag and let her arm fall to her side in a casual manner. She discreetly sent another transmission as she walked. 'Zero, Echo, Oculus now, over,'

'Roger Echo, that's Oculus now, standby…Echo, Zero, that's Oculus go, I say again, Oculus go, over.'

The acknowledgement told her that the camera, codenamed Oculus, had been activated remotely by the operator at the safe house and that it was functioning and ready to be placed. Turning on to the floor where DAGGER's flat was located, Nadia slowed her pace a little as she ambled past the row of doors leading to the homes within. From the analysts' imagery she had identified several locations where the camera could be placed to gain optimum coverage but knew that until you were on target, you could never know for sure. Making her way along the covered thoroughfare she saw however that the potential spot she had identified was as good as she'd thought. It was a corner of fencing and drainpipes where litter seemed to naturally collect and there were already several soft-drink cans showing through the pile. She gave a final transmission as she approached DAGGER's door.

'Zero, Echo, HOTEL now.' She received the acknowledgement at the same time she reached the target's door, paying it no attention whatsoever as she walked several paces beyond it.

Turning her body as though she intended heading into the next stairwell, Nadia allowed her handbag to slip from her shoulder and fall on to the concrete walkway. Muttering a small groan, she knelt and began retrieving the spilled contents and putting them back into the bag. With a discreet glance around her, she used her other hand to ram the coke-can camera into a space between the drainage pipe and the pebble-dashed wall, ensuring the logo was facing towards her. Satisfied that the can was lodged tight and that some of it was covered by the other litter, she went back to picking up the contents of her bag. Her earpiece came to life as she continued with her activity.

'Echo, Zero, Oculus complete, I say again, Oculus complete, over.'

Having received the confirmation that the camera was functioning and that the operator had a clear view of the target's house, Nadia stood and dusted herself off before walking into the stairwell and making her way down to the ground floor at the opposite end of the block of flats from where she had entered them. The emplacement of the camera had taken mere seconds and nobody had been in the area to notice her presence let alone be suspicious of it. Even if they had, she reasoned, all they would have witnessed was a Muslim woman dropping her handbag then picking all the crap back up before going on her way. The area also had a sizeable population of Muslims, so Nadia was not concerned that her dress or appearance was in any way out of the ordinary.

Back on the street, she crossed the road, noting that Lovat was sat on the wall outside of a shop reading a newspaper and munching on a sandwich, to all intents and purposes just a guy on a break from work. She gave a brief transmission to the team back at the safe house. 'Zero, Echo, that's Echo task complete, clear, and extracting.' The team acknowledged her update that she was finished and heading out of the operational area. By letting them know that she was clear, they understood that she had nobody following her. Continuing along the street she noted the hostile glances from various individuals as she passed them. One older man wearing a filthy luminous work-jacket snarled as she passed him.

'Why don't you go back to your own fucking country if you want to dress like that?'

Nadia paid him no heed and continued on as though she hadn't heard him but the irony of the situation wasn't lost on her. Here she was, dressed as someone that the man had decided he hated, in order to save the lives of people just like him. A small smile came to her as she crossed the road leading to the car park where she'd left her vehicle. *If only you knew chum. If only you knew.*

Lovat tilted his glass towards Nadia and smiled. 'Well, here's to a good job today and the hope that we get something useful soon.'

Nadia returned the smile and raised her own glass. 'Cheers. We've got a trigger on him or anyone else that moves from that location now so we should start getting results.'

Taking a drink of his Jack Daniels and Coke, Lovat looked around the pub, taking in the details of the clientele and looking for any indication of interest in him and Nadia. When they'd concluded the camera emplacement and set up the reaction teams, Lovat had been the one to suggest they grab some food and a few well-earned drinks. Nadia had been quick to accept and they'd met up in the car park of the pub, just on the outskirts of town. Lovat could see that Nadia was attracting some discreet interest from the men in the bar but knew that it was because of her good looks rather than anything more sinister. Turning his attention back to his colleague he tipped his glass towards her. 'Okay, spill: What did you do that got you kicked out of SRR?'

'Oh, we're doing *that* tonight are we?' She returned his grin and took a swig of her straight vodka before continuing. 'Okay, I'll tell you mine and you tell me yours. Deal?'

'Deal.'

Nadia leaned back in the large leather armchair and nodded. 'Alright. It probably won't shock you that, from the moment I applied to attempt selection, I got a pretty fucking hard time. I was a woman and a Paki trying out for one of the most alpha-male units in the world. But I wasn't stupid; I knew exactly what I was letting myself in for. I knew I could make it but that I would have to be so much better than everyone else just to be taken seriously.' She paused and swirled the ice in her glass before taking another drink. 'So, I was eating shit from day one, week one. Luke, our current SFE, was one of the Directing Staff on my selection and he in particular, went out of his way to make me quit. I'm not gonna sit here and fucking cry about it Lovat, but it was absolute hell. Despite all that, I made it. Passed and badged and sent to Northern Ireland for continuation training. The guys out there kept giving me all the shit jobs; manning the desk, Heli-overwatch, QRF LO. Anything literally to keep me from direct involvement in operations. Eventually, a request came from MI5 for some help with a surveillance task involving a mosque in Bradford. We were given the brief by the Boss with the Box guy in our Det. As usual, the guys started suggesting how they could black-up, darken their beards and chuck on their *man-jams* and stroll around the area. I suggested that we maybe put the 'Team America' plan to one side and insert an *actual* Asian who could speak the language and was comfortable with all the protocols and cultural shit. Needless to say, it didn't go down too well with the muscle heads, but Box were very keen and that's how my start in operating against Islamic Fundamentalist targets came about.'

Lovat nodded. 'Yeah, I'd figured you wouldn't have had the fairest crack of the whip.'

'No. But like I said before, I'm not here to cry about it. I done a good job with Box and they gave my CO a nice letter singing my praises. From there, that was me set; Libya, Somalia, Kenya, Morocco, Afghanistan. Nadia the Paki touring the fundamentalist shitholes of the world and bringing down the bad men who thought themselves safe. It was after my last job in Libya that the incident happened. We were back at Crediton Hill and had just had a formal wash-up on the Libya job where MI6, MI5, GCHQ and a few of the Intelligence and Security Committee were all in attendance. We kicked off a pretty large social after it and a lot of booze was being put away. There was the usual hilarity with fire extinguishers being set off and the odd flash-bang thrown about but all good, clean fun. I'd been cornered by this fucking creep from Whitehall who wasn't taking the hint and was a bit too touchy-feely for my liking. When I eventually decided enough was enough, I grabbed his wandering hand and stuck my face in his and told him if he touched me one more time with his horrible, liver-spotted hands, I'd fucking break them.'

Lovat grinned as he waited for Nadia to finish her drink and conclude the story.

'Well, he obviously didn't take me seriously as his next move was to step in close to me, grab my crotch and inform me that no squaddie slut was ever going to talk to him in such a manner. So, I broke his hand at the wrist and knocked him out with an elbow to the face. Which obviously, didn't go down well with any of the adults who were there.'

Lovat laughed. 'So, what happened next?'

Nadia sighed and tossed her hair back. 'After all the initial chaos had died down, I was told to go and take a few days leave. When I returned, the Boss had me in for a one to one. He's a good bloke and I have a lot of time for him so I knew that whatever was going to happen to me, he would have done his best to look out for my interests. Upshot was, *Mr Wandering Hands* had pushed for a full-on assault and battery charge against me, demanding jail time for an attack against a servant of the Crown. The Boss had countered with the fact that I had approached a solicitor regarding a counter-charge of sexual assault. A compromise was agreed where I wouldn't pursue this and the creep would drop his end but I was to be RTUd. And that's what happened.'

Lovat shook his head. 'That's outrageous. The problem with these mandarins is that they've never been accountable for anything and think they have the power to do what the hell they want.'

'Well, as shit as it is, I have to say, the satisfaction of smashing my elbow into his chin and watching him collapse in a heap was almost worth the whole affair!'

Lovat laughed and raised his glass. 'Here's to well-aimed elbow strikes.'

Nadia laughed aloud and touched her glass against Lovat's before nodding towards him. 'And now your turn; the story of the scar if you please.'

Downing the contents of his drink, Lovat motioned towards her for her glass. 'Okay. A deal's a deal but let me get some refills first.'

Nadia passed him her glass and waited until he'd returned from the bar and placed a drink in front of her. She lifted her head and met his gaze with a raised eyebrow. 'Doubles?'

'Yeah. Never really got on with these tiny pub measures.'

Taking a sip of her vodka, she sat back in her chair and gave him a nod of encouragement as he started to speak.

'Like you, I started my operational career in Northern Ireland. Belfast to be precise. Cutting around the back streets of the Lower Falls, running recruitment Ops in Twinbrook and Poleglass, following agents through counter-surveillance routes. All good stuff. And I loved it. Absolutely threw myself into my work. And I found I had a bit of a knack for it. Notched up some really good results and was soon running my own Ops; unheard of for a first-tour operator. Problem was, I was beginning to believe my own hype.' He paused and took a drink, savouring the sweetness of the cola mixer. 'I'd been in theatre for two years when OD showed up fresh from the course, looking to take up a company commander's slot at East Det. As I was the golden bollocks at the time, I was given the task of taking OD through his orientation package, getting him familiar with the ground and our operations.'

Nadia nodded. 'Yeah, that's how we do it at SRR as well.'

Lovat continued. 'OD is a smart guy and a very quick learner. He was smashing his orientation and had learned the ground really quick. We got on very well on a personal level too and that's where the problem started. He'd heard that I wasn't averse to going into the pubs and clubs where the bad guys socialised and wanted to experience it for himself. Now, as you well know, these pubs and clubs are completely out of bounds to us for good reason. But I've always had this…I don't even know what to call it. *Disdain*…*Arrogance*…Whatever, there's always been something in me that wants to see how far I can push things, take them to the limit. So, me going into republican haunts and holding my own was bad enough, but taking another Brit in with me? Madness.' He took a longer drink and shook his head. 'But that arrogance I mentioned, it *wanted* me to do it. It *dared* me to do it. I could see that, although OD should have been appalled by the fact that I was going off the reservation, there was a part of him really wanted to experience it for himself. And that's how it happened.'

Nadia interrupted. 'Lovat, that is mental. You were taking your new commander drinking in republican bars in an operational area?'

He gave a sad smile. 'I told you Nadia; I know exactly how bad it sounds and I offer no rational explanation for it other than it's something that's always been inside me.'

'Okay. Go on. What happened?'

Lovat's eye's glazed over as the memory of the night returned to him. 'We'd already had a few in the Det bar when OD suggested we head out and grab a couple in the *Badlands.* I tried to talk him out of it but not all that hard in all honesty. I had that flutter of excitement in my stomach, the anticipation of crossing the boundary of what was safe. I got into my Ops car and drove us into the Beechmounts area, parking the car a few streets away from Boyle's Bar. I picked that one because even though it is a staunch IRA haunt, they do get the odd visitor in now and again. We were armed with our Sig Sauers, tucked into our waistbands and covered by our shirts and jackets. The pub was busy, some kind of function on upstairs with a band playing on the bottom floor as well. We got a few looks as we walked in but we smiled and manoeuvred our way to the bar just like any man with a right to be there would. We'd decided on a loose cover story based around looking for real estate opportunities in the city and that we were taking a wee break tonight and that Boyles had been recommended to us as a great bar.'

Nadia could see the change in Lovat's face and had registered that his voice had also altered as the story progressed, his tone softer and quieter.

'I'd ordered the first round and although the barman raised an eyebrow at my accent, he didn't seem that bothered. A man sat on a stool asked me where I was from and we got into a conversation about Belfast now being an up and coming city in its own right. I saw that OD was being chatted to by a couple of women who seemed to be enjoying his company. So far, so normal and I was completely relaxed.' Lovat sighed and took another drink, gauging Nadia's reaction to his story. He could see that he had her undivided attention and continued.

'It's always what you don't know that fucks you up and that is exactly what happened that night. While we were downstairs in the bar, congratulating ourselves about how fucking cool we were to be able to just waltz into enemy territory and be accepted, upstairs a serious meeting of senior IRA men was taking place under the cover of attending the function. The IRA Army Council was using the function to mask their coming together for a meeting. No-one had any idea that this was happening or if they did, nobody had informed us. Because of this, the IRA had deployed a shit-load of security while the meeting was happening. At some point, word must have got to the security that there were a couple of Brits in the bar and the balloon went up from there, I guess. We were blissfully unaware of any of this and were just enjoying the craic and banter with the locals. Behind the scenes however, an IRA operation to kidnap, torture and interrogate us was already well under way. The first hint I had that something was wrong was when I noticed that a couple of guys had joined the little group I was chatting with. These men seemed pleasant enough, but I had caught the odd glance they'd been passing each other and although I couldn't really say what it was, my antennae were up. I looked over to OD and saw that there were a few more people in his close company as well and that they didn't seem to be quite as relaxed as the others. Another drink was pushed into my hand and my back slapped with a hearty cheer and just as I was knocking it back, I caught sight of two or three people slipping out of the bar's side entrance, looking scared. They made eye contact with one of the bigger guys in my company and I saw him give the slightest of nods to acknowledge them. But that was enough: I knew we were being set up.'

Nadia watched as Lovat took another large drink and ran his fingers through his hair before meeting her eyes.

'I was sober in an instant. I continued to laugh and joke but my mind was racing, looking at all the angles. They'd done a fantastic job of separating me and OD without us even noticing. I could hardly see him now and there were far more men of an athletic build around us than had been when we entered. Unknown to me at the time obviously, but the Army Council had all left from an upstairs fire exit and the focus of the security men was to get me and OD in a van and out of the city within the hour. A team had been stood up in South Armagh to get us over the border and into the Republic where our torture and interrogation would take place. All I knew at that moment was that we were in deep fucking shit.' He took another drink and sighed. 'They went for OD first.'

Nadia shook her head slowly as she imagined the appalling position that the two men had placed themselves in and watched Lovat's face as he returned to the night in question.

'I saw a bit of a commotion start around OD and heard someone yelling. Glasses were breaking on the floor and women were screaming. It was happening. I rammed my whisky glass into the face of the man nearest me, booted the balls of the guy standing in front of me and elbowed the head of a big bastard standing at my side. As they all dropped and fell, I'd created enough space around me to draw my pistol and managed to get it out but the mob was still rushing me and grabbing at my hands. I couldn't get the weapon up as my arms were trapped against my body and I was taking some serious punches to my face and head. I couldn't even see where the fucking gun was pointed but knew if I didn't do something soon, we were fucked. So, I pulled the trigger. The noise and the shock made everyone jump back and a man in front of me dropped to the floor pissing blood from his stomach. I looked over at OD and saw that he had a bit of space around him but just as I was moving towards him someone grabbed his hands as another guy stabbed him repeatedly in the stomach.'

Lovat paused and ran his fingers over the scar on his cheek. 'And while my concentration was on OD's predicament, one of the scumbags behind me tried to stab me in the neck. I caught a glimpse of the blade just before it struck and managed to duck my chin down and protect the arteries. This mess that you see here is a result of a fucking big blade slashing right through my cheek and mouth. And believe me; adrenaline running and all, it still really fucking hurt. But it also snapped something inside me and I lost all sense of panic or concern and a weird calmness came over me. I shot my knifeman at point-blank range through his right eye, turned and advanced on OD's attackers, dropping three of them even as he was collapsing on to the floor. One of the crowd went for OD's gun that had fallen from his hand and I shot her too, somewhere on her shoulder. Must have hurt like a bastard as she started screaming and rolling about on the floor. I made it to OD and saw he was in a bad way. He'd been beaten till he was almost unconscious and he was clasping his hands around his stomach, which was pissing blood. I fired another couple of shots into the floor in front of the mob and used their retreat to grab OD's gun and get him on my back in a fireman's carry position. I remember yelling at the mob that I was heading straight out the door and that any fucker that got between me and that exit would be dead before they knew it. I fired again to show them I meant business and marched straight out into the street. A few of them followed me, screaming and yelling the usual shit and I saw a couple of guys step out of a van further along the street. It was obvious who they were so I fired a couple of rounds at them and managed to hit one. The others grabbed him, chucked him in the van and took off sharpish. Behind me, all I could hear was screaming and shouting but all I kept thinking was that I needed to get to the car and get OD to hospital. And that's what happened. I made it and got OD to Musgrave Park Hospital where they operated on him and saved his life. I called the Det from the car and they sent a team to the hospital to guard us while we were being treated.'

'Holy shit Lovat, that is some serious crap. What was the official fallout from it all?'

Lovat shook his head. 'A lot. Three dead republicans and around a dozen injured or wounded. Two undercover soldiers wounded and scarred for life. The Unit was brilliant to be fair. Made sure that OD and I had a decent story from which to explain our presence in the bar. OD couldn't give a statement for weeks, so he was basically slipped a copy of mine to work with. Sinn Fein went mental of course, the republican PR machine straight into hyper-drive. You can imagine it Nadia; *British spies massacre local residents, shoot to kill in our very homes, Assassins of the Crown kill well-loved father of two* etc., etc. I went through the mill with interview after interview with both the Military Police and the PSNI. Initially I was happy to come clean but as the Boss said to me, it wasn't just my life I'd be fucking up it was OD's as well, and he was just starting his military career. The Boss also pointed out that those bastards could easily have just kicked the shit out of us and thrown us out of the bar, but they'd chosen to try and kidnap and kill us instead. So, I went with it, stuck to my story of carrying out the final bit of OD's orientation and being unaware that Boyles was out of bounds. I don't think anybody really believed that but the PSNI weren't shedding any tears for the dead and wounded republicans, so weren't really trying *too* hard if you get my drift. There was significant political pressure from Sinn Fein for the British Government to give us up to be tried for murder but fortunately for us, the IRA had just fucked up massively. They'd lifted a woman from East Tyrone they thought was an informer and had killed her during questioning but had been caught as they'd bomb-burst from the farmhouse in a panic. Not only that but one of them had just made a call to Alex McIernan, the Sinn Fein councillor for Dungannon, implicating Sinn Fein in an IRA operation. So, from what I was told, there was an unspoken agreement between Sinn Fein and Her Majesty's Government that both sides wouldn't dig any deeper into the other's complaint in order to keep the peace talks on track.'

'Lovat, you have to be the luckiest bastard on the planet. First, to have managed to escape being sat on the cooker, and second not to have been hung out to dry by HMG.'

'*Sat on the cooker*. I haven't heard that expression in a good few years.' Lovat downed the last of his drink and smiled at Nadia's reference to the IRA's infamous method of interrogating suspected informers, or *touts* as they were more commonly referred to. The suspected tout would be kidnapped and taken to an isolated farm complex either near or across the border, bound, hooded and stripped naked. They would then be led into a kitchen where a four-ring cooker would be ready with each spiral ring glowing an angry red. The victim would be shown the rings and asked once if they were an informer and that if they told the truth they had nothing to fear, but if it was felt that they were lying their naked arse would be sat upon the red-hot rings. Usually the threat was enough but over the years the bodies of several RUC or PSNI informers had been found naked and hooded in the ditches of South Armagh and Fermanagh with the tell-tale spiral scarring on the buttocks and backs of the legs. Lovat looked up as Nadia shook her empty glass in his direction.

'Another double?'

'Yeah, sounds great.'

Lovat watched as Nadia walked to the counter and noted the appreciative glances of some of the men sitting around the bar. He grinned as the thought hit him that only five or six hours previously, she had been shuffling along the streets of Watford in a niqab, her impressive figure hidden from the world in a cloak of black. He looked up as she returned to the table placing the drink in front of him.

'What are you grinning at?'

'Just watching all the guys in here ogle you as you went to the bar and wonder how many of them would have felt the same way seeing you sauntering around town in a niqab.'

Nadia laughed. 'You never know, some of them might find it quite kinky!'

It was Lovat's turn to laugh and he sputtered slightly as his drink caught in his throat. 'Ha ha, maybe you're right. We should start up a dating website; *Burqa Babes*. We could be millionaires!'

'*Burqa Babes*! You've got too much time on your hands Warrant Officer Reid.'

There was a companionable silence for several moments before Nadia leaned forward across the table. 'So, what's your take on DAGGER's role in all of this?'

Lovat thought for a moment before replying. 'I think he's a clean skin. Everything points to him being a good kid making his way through Uni and into a decent job. Somewhere along the line he's become radicalised and is now helping out in some capacity we haven't yet identified. That's why I wouldn't let the SF guys take this; we need to let DAGGER run so we can see who he's working with. They would have either killed or arrested him and been back at Hereford in time for tea and medals. And the real terrorists would still be out there, plotting and planning the next atrocity.'

'I agree. We need to let the situation develop until we get some concrete leads on the rest of this outfit. The kid's probably just small fry at the moment.'

Lovat took a drink and leaned in towards his colleague. 'Here's a question for you that's been bugging me from the start: What the hell is Vauxhall's role in this?'

Nadia cocked her head to one side. 'How do you mean?'

'Well, think about it; Crispin shows up claiming some kind of expertise on the type of guy we're after but then gives us absolutely nothing. Not a thing. No short list of potentials, no de-classified reports to help us build a better picture, no offer of extra manpower to help with the surveillance. Nothing.'

'Yeah, I see what you mean. Have you asked Giles?'

Lovat nodded. 'Yeah, but obviously there's no love lost between their organisations and Giles just puts it down to typical Vauxhall being up their own arses. As Giles put it, *they do not work or play well with others.*'

'You think there's something else going on here?'

'I don't know, I really don't. But something just feels off, not quite right.'

Nadia took a drink and considered Lovat's statement. He was right; the MI6 officer had brought nothing to the party so far but maybe that was because he was as much in the dark as the rest of them. It did strike her as slightly odd that Crispin had declared himself to be something of an authority but had then given them nothing with which to support his claim. She looked up and met Lovat's eyes as he continued.

'Look, it might be nothing but I think we should keep our eyes and ears open around that guy. I'm sure he's got a lot more to offer than he's giving us but he's obviously got his own reasons for not doing so.'

'Okay, I'm with you. Let's keep a discreet eye on him and see if we can identify what he's really up to then. You think he's maybe just playing his cards close to his.chest so he can hog all the glory at the end?'

'Maybe. Either way, let's just watch each other's backs on this one.'

Nadia raised her glass. 'As our American cousins say; *I've got your six*.'

Lovat clinked his glass against hers. 'And I yours. Cheers.'

'Cheers.'

They drank in silence until Nadia noticed Lovat's attention was diverted. Following his gaze, she saw an attractive blonde woman at the bar looking in their direction. She prodded Lovat's elbow and caught his attention.

'See something you like Warrant Officer Reid?'

Lovat returned the grin. 'Yes, as a matter of fact Sergeant Ali. I see a very attractive lady giving me the once over and very happy with what she sees.'

Nadia turned and took a longer look at the woman who was now sat with a brunette. 'Yeah, she's pretty. Blonde's your thing then?'

Lovat shook his head. 'I don't have a *thing*. Blonde, brunette, redhead. As long as they're not a complete munter and have a bit of a personality, I'm easily pleased.'

Nadia threw her head back and laughed. 'See yourself as a bit of a ladies' man, do you?'

'Hey, I'm forty-three years old and still single. Does that sound like a ladies' man to you?'

'Do you mind if I ask why you're still single? I mean, have you ever been married?'

Lovat took a drink before replying. 'Never been married Nadia. Came pretty close when I was younger but spent too much time away on Ops. Truth is, I find it easier to be single. I love the job and the job is being operational, far from home, for months at a time. I figured out early on that it's unfair to ask someone to put their whole life on hold just to fit in with mine.'

'Yeah, I completely get that and I'm in pretty much the same boat. The couple of serious relationships I was in tanked because of how much time I was being deployed away for. But like you, I wouldn't want it any other way.'

Lovat laughed. 'Listen to us; at this rate we're going to end our lives as bitter, twisted singletons, feeding our cats and smelling of piss.'

It was Nadia's turn to laugh and she raised her glass again. 'To singledom, cats and smelling of piss!'

Lovat met the toast and downed his drink. As he rose to make his way to the bar, he saw that the blonde woman was once again looking over at him and he gave her a smile. She dropped her head and laughed, turning to her companion and saying something that caused the brunette to smile. He smiled again and gave a small wave which both women returned. He looked down as he heard Nadia's theatrical groan.

'You are such a tart Lovat Reid!'

He feigned surprise, a wide-eyed expression of innocence on his face. 'What? I'm just returning a friendly smile that's all.'

'Just get the drinks in and stop batting your eyelids like a love-sick puppy.'

Lovat laughed and made his way to the bar. Nadia was very good company and he felt completely at ease around her. As he was reaching in his pocket for some change, he was struck by the thought that her teasing and banter about the women may have been more than just funny quips. *Surely not?* His brow furrowed as he tried to remember any instance where Nadia had hinted or implied that she was attracted to him. He couldn't recall any but then again, he'd never been particularly adept at picking up on the subtle signals that women tended to deploy. For his part, as attractive as she was, Lovat had made the conscious decision to resist any attraction and maintain a professional relationship. He really liked working with her and knew for a fact that, should their relationship spill into a personal dynamic, the working partnership would suffer. And until now he'd been convinced that Nadia felt pretty much the same way.

He turned his attention back to the bar as his drinks arrived then, on a whim, ordered some tequila shots. The barman loaded the drinks on to a tray and Lovat paid for the round then made his way back to the table, noting Nadia's eyebrows raise in surprise.

'Erm, on a bit of a mission are we Lovat?'

'Hey, we've got a late start in the morning and I think we've earned a bit of a session, don't you?'

She answered him by picking up one of the tequilas and downing it in one swallow. Banging the empty glass back on the table she smiled at him. 'Couldn't agree more!'

They finished the drinks and Nadia took her turn at the bar, returning as Lovat had done, with another round and several shots. She was enjoying Lovat's company. He was that rare breed of guy that didn't feel he constantly had to impress you with stories of how hard or amazing he was. The stories he was telling were all funny or self-deprecating and had her in stitches. She had told a few stories herself which he had found very funny, particularly when he'd known the individuals concerned. She could feel the flush and the heat from the alcohol and was having real fun for the first time in a long time. Lovat was in the middle of a story about one of his friends who'd been arrested for defecating in the back of a police car when the barman gave the call for last orders. She watched as Lovat stood up and quickly made his way to the bar. He returned with another tray of alcohol and they set about knocking the fiery shots back.

He was laughing at a story she'd told him about getting stuck in a drainage pipe in Libya while on a surveillance operation when she saw his gaze drift towards the two women from earlier in the evening. Following his gaze, she saw the two women stand and begin putting on their coats, the blonde woman looking over at them with a small smile.

She watched Lovat down his drink and continue looking over at the women. She saw the blonde one smile and indicate with her head towards the door, the non-verbal communication quite clear; *Joining us*?

Lovat returned the smile and nodded, standing up and giving Nadia an apologetic grin. 'Hey, sorry to bail on you like this but I think my presence is requested elsewhere. You good to get a taxi back?'

Nadia returned the smile and stood, putting on her own jacket. She stepped around the table and put her hands on Lovat's shoulders, moving closer until her nose was almost touching his. 'You're really not great at picking up on the obvious signals are you Lovat?'

Lovat's smile dropped as he considered her words and he was about to reply when she hushed him by placing a finger on his lips and leaned in and whispered in his ear.

'It's not you she wants to take home with her you moron. It's me.'

With that she gave him a huge grin and picked her handbag up from the back of the chair. 'Sorry to bail on you like this Lovat but you'll be okay getting a taxi back on your own, won't you?'

He watched open-mouthed as she made her way to the attractive blonde and put her arm around her shoulders before they left the pub together. He shook his head and laughed aloud as he imagined Nadia watching his ridiculous attempts to flirt with the blonde woman all night. *Brilliant.* Someone cleared their throat beside him and he turned to see the blonde woman's brunette companion smiling at him.

'Looks like we've both been ditched. I'm Julie and I'm not a lesbian.'

Lovat grinned and held out his hand. 'I'm Lovat and I'm not a lesbian either.'

They laughed and made their way out of the pub. As they entered the car park Lovat grinned again as the thought came to him that he should stop being surprised by how much life surprised him.

WATFORD

Ahmad ended the call on his mobile and stared at the wall of the living room. Djinn's instructions had been brief, merely a location and a time to be there but to prepare to stay overnight. With no other information to go on, Ahmad could not even speculate as to what it was that Djinn had in store for him. What he *did* know was that this was it; after this it would all be over for him and he and his family would be safe. Rubbing his tired eyes, he uttered a silent prayer that Djinn would be true to his word and cut him loose once he'd finished whatever terrible task had been allocated to him. Snapping out of his reverie, Ahmad looked at the screen on his mobile and realised he needed to get moving if he was to get to the location on time.

A shower, clean clothes and some coffee and he felt far more positive about the day ahead. The last day of his involvement with Djinn and his murderous schemes. Putting on a jacket, Ahmad grabbed his car keys from the table and made his way out of the flat, locking the door behind him.

'Standby, standby. That's DAGGER mobile from HOTEL and towards southern exit of building.'

Lovat acknowledged the message and pulled out from the small lay-by he had been parked in. As he drove along the road, he spotted a parking space near the shops that would give him a clear view of the entrance to DAGGER's flats. In his earpiece he could hear the other operators sending their movements and intended locations. Pulling into the space, Lovat pressed a small, concealed button on the steering column.

'Zero this is Delta, I have eyes on HOTEL, over.'

The acknowledgement that Lovat had visual oversight of the flats came through instantly, as he would have expected. This was the most crucial aspect of a surveillance operation; the Trigger and the Follow. Triggering the target from their location and taking them in a controlled follow. Losing DAGGER at this stage would mean he would be running free with Lovat and the team completely clueless as to where he was going or what he was doing. They hadn't been able to fit a beacon or 'lump' as it was referred to, on DAGGER's car as it was parked outside a busy area of the flats and directly under a streetlight so they were under even more pressure not to lose him. Lovat felt the excitement rise in him as he watched a figure leave the flats' entrance and walk along the pavement towards the street.

'All callsigns this is Delta. That's DAGGER from HOTEL towards CHARIOT, over.' With the team now aware that the target was heading towards his car or CHARIOT as it was codenamed, Lovat listened as his colleagues adjusted their positions to be better prepared to follow DAGGER's movements. As the last member of the team gave his position, Lovat nodded. They were set. There was no direction that DAGGER could take that was not covered by one of the team. Once the target's direction of travel was established, the operator who committed him would follow directly behind him as the rest of the team then scrambled to form up at a discreet distance behind the first operator and continue with the follow.

DAGGER was almost out of sight from Lovat and he was just about to update the team on this when he heard Nadia's voice in his earpiece.

'All callsigns, this is Echo. I have DAGGER and he is entering CHARIOT, over.'

Lovat and the rest of the team acknowledged and he could almost imagine the baited breaths as they waited for the committal. His earpiece buzzed again as Nadia spoke.

'I have DAGGER mobile and that's a left, left, left at junction.'

Lovat's earpiece was now constantly busy as the team updated their progress in getting on the route that Nadia was following the target on. Lovat was running with a five-car team that allowed him good flexibility and reaction to any changes of direction the target might throw in.

Nadia's voice cut through the general commentary from the other operators.

'All callsigns, Echo; DAGGER is straight, straight, straight onto dual carriageway.' Lovat heard his team acknowledge the call, in alphabetical order of their callsigns. Another voice interrupted the team.

'Delta, this is Zero. We have details from comms intercept and possible locstat for DAGGER's destination. Roger so far? Over.'

Lovat responded. 'Roger.'

'Capture of message content indicates Sphere Industrial Estate south of St Albans. HADES alerted and forward mounting to area.'

Lovat cursed as he negotiated a roundabout, his mind still visualising the locations of his team following DAGGER while he dealt with the unwelcome news that the Special Forces team, callsign HADES, had been dispatched to the area. He would have preferred to have housed DAGGER in a location and used technical and mobile surveillance to identify why he was there and what he was doing. As it was, the SF guys would more than likely go for the quick result and take down DAGGER. *Shit*!

He heard Nadia request someone take control of DAGGER from her as she had been behind the target for several miles now. Lovat nodded as callsign Kilo acknowledged and closed the gap between them, allowing Nadia to leave the pack at the next junction. His mind was still turning over possibilities when he heard Kilo send the message that he was now behind DAGGER.

A thought struck Lovat and he punched in a number on his hands-free set. The ringing of a phone came loud through his vehicle's speaker system and he turned the volume down using the control on the steering column. A brief moment later he heard Giles' voice.

'Lovat, what's up?'

'Giles, HADES team are forward mounting to Sphere Industrial Estate in St Albans. Mate, any chance you can get up there with them and provide a level head?'

'Shit! Yes, absolutely. I'll get on to it now. See you there.'

As the call was terminated, Lovat felt a moment of relief. Having Giles on the ground underlined the fact that this was an MI5 operation and that, ultimately, he was the man who gave the go or don't go to the SF. With that issue dealt with at least for the time being, Lovat concentrated on the task at hand, monitoring his team's progress and positions. They were doing well, had full control of the target without any sign that DAGGER was aware. Their drills were good too; nobody being greedy or getting fixated on the follow but instead orchestrating smooth changeovers and handovers when they felt it necessary.

They were heading north on the M1 when Zero interrupted their running commentary once again.

'Delta, Zero. We have lockdown on the phone that contacted DAGGER, over.'

'Delta, roger.'

'Yeah, Delta, that mobile is static in a cluster of buildings in the industrial estate, over.'

Lovat thought for a second. 'Zero, roger that. Do we have positive ID on the locstat?'

'Delta, negative. A group of three buildings but narrowing down options now, over.'

'Delta.' Chewing on the inside of his mouth as he pondered this information, Lovat could feel a ripple of excitement in his stomach. If the tech spooks had locked down the location of the phone that had contacted DAGGER earlier, this would have to be a key player in the terrorist grouping. Perhaps even the ringleader himself. Maybe having the SF on hand wasn't such a bad idea after all. He was roused from his thoughts by the voice in his earpiece informing him that DAGGER was indicating to leave the motorway at the next junction which would be the exit for South St Albans. Lovat listened as his team co-ordinated their positions to ensure they retained control. Looking at his watch, Lovat shook his head in frustration. There was no way Giles was going to make it there before the SF. He speed-dialled the number again and was answered almost immediately.

'Yes, yes, I'm doing my best here but I'm about twenty minutes away. Don't worry though, I've spoken with HADES command and there will be no move until I am at location.' The call was terminated and Lovat smiled to himself at the thought of Giles bombing along the motorway to get to the industrial estate before the SF team went noisy. *Good man.* The pack had slowed now that they were entering the ring road and accosted by a series of roundabouts. This was a problem area as the target could easily be lost if the backing callsign got blocked at one of the junctions for any period of time. Lovat decided to err on the side of caution.

'Oscar, Kilo, this is Delta. Can you both get ahead of DAGGER? Over.'

Their acknowledgement was immediate and although he was too far back to see them, his team's running commentary in his earpiece updated Lovat of their progress. Getting a couple of cars out in front of the target was a smart tactic when traffic was involved. It meant that even if a backing callsign lost the target, the team in front could pick him up again.

As it was, he need not have worried as it became clearly obvious that DAGGER was heading towards the industrial estate. When he turned into the entrance for the estate, Kilo and Oscar were already there, meaning that no-one had to follow DAGGER in and arouse any suspicion. Lovat heard Kilo's voice come through his earpiece.

'All callsigns, Kilo. I have DAGGER and he is a stop, stop, stop at the warehouse next to Euro Car Parts.'

The team acknowledged and parked up in various locations that once again, covered every possible option that DAGGER could take if he drove back out again.

'All callsigns Kilo. That is DAGGER on foot and walking to door of building. Wait…that's DAGGER into the building and door closed. Zero acknowledge.'

'Zero roger. For information, this location tallies with general location of the other telephone, over.'

Pulling his car into a large lay-by behind a burger van, Lovat gave a small smile. He could almost taste it; that moment when you were so close to the target and they had nowhere to go that wasn't covered by the team. Glancing around to make sure no-one was stood beside his vehicle he spoke.

'Zero, Delta. Any info on the ID of phone owner? Over.'

'Delta, Zero, that's a negative so far but looks like a burner, over.'

Lovat hadn't really expected much more. The use of pay-as-you-go phones was prevalent among criminals and terrorists alike, well aware of the tracking abilities of the security and intelligence agencies. Still, it was a good start; the phone associated with an as-yet unidentified player, and their main lead, Objective DAGGER, coming together in the same location. Lovat monitored the locations of his team as they positioned themselves around the various entrances and exits to the industrial estate. Content that there was nowhere anyone could enter or leave without being triggered by his team, Lovat gave the command.

'All callsigns this is Delta. PANDORA, I say again, PANDORA.' The acknowledgements from everyone involved came swiftly to confirm his statement that the targets were now completely boxed in by his team. Lovat sighed as he looked out of his window at the drab, industrial buildings around him. All they could now was wait.

And he hated waiting.

ST ALBANS, ENGLAND

Crispin knocked on the door of the unit and winced at the pain in his knuckles as they struck the corrugated metal. The door was snatched open and a bearded individual glared at the MI6 officer for a moment before smiling and nodding.

'Alright Boss, come on in.'

'Thanks Nick. Where are we at?'

The bearded SAS soldier waited for the door to close behind him before speaking.

'Pretty good actually. We have DAGGER complete in the building and confirmation that the mobile associated to the UKM is still in the area.'

Crispin nodded. 'Good. Let's just hope that our UKM isn't a UKM for much longer and that we've got this one in the bag.'

The soldier smiled his agreement. A UKM, or Unknown Male, was of little use to an intelligence-led operation where exploitation was concerned. A UKM could hold up Home Office clearance for such operations, the civil servants reluctant to place any faith in probabilities, regardless of circumstantial proof. He pointed into the depths of the building.

'Luke's down at the bottom end running through the breach options with the team.'

Crispin nodded his thanks and made his way to the back of the unit where he could see a cluster of SAS soldiers in civilian clothes huddled around a table. He smiled as the thought came to him that sometimes, the absence of uniform was a uniform itself. The men were very much identical in Fjall Raven or other expensive outdoor branded jackets and jeans or cargo trousers. As he approached, he cleared his throat and met Luke's eyes as the SFE looked up.

'Luke. Gents. How are we progressing?'

Luke pointed to a diagram drawn on a whiteboard, a representation of the layout of the warehouse where DAGGER was currently occupied, Crispin presumed.

'We're good Crispin. Breach and entry teams good to go and we've got confirmation that we have DAGGER and one other Zulu inside.'

'Confirmation from who?' Crispin was curious as to how the SAS team had determined the fact that there were two suspects within the warehouse.

'We deployed LADYBIRD into the unit and got good quality visual of two individuals present.'

Crispin was impressed. LADYBIRD was the code name for a state-of-the-art miniature camera system that was deployed on a robot framework no bigger than that of a small beetle, hence the name. It would usually go completely unnoticed even in the smallest of locations. 'Any possible ID for the Zulu?' Glancing around to make sure he couldn't be overheard, Crispin leaned in. 'Any chance it is SCIMITAR?'

'Not sure. We can't get clear imagery of his face due to ground limitations for LADYBIRD.'

Crispin placed his hand on the SAS team leader's shoulder and looked him in the eye.

'Okay, time to talk turkey, as our colonial cousins say. We cannot wait any longer for this situation to develop into anything worse and I have VIKER authority for immediate action.'

Luke smiled and looked back at his team, giving them the thumbs-up sign. The VIKER clearance was a welcome development. *Gloves off.* He turned his attention back to Crispin as the MI6 officer continued.

'To that end you now have Tactical Command of this operation and I would think you should prefer to do it sooner rather than later.'

Luke slapped the bench in front of him.

'Okay Team Leaders, you know what to do. Let's get this thing done.'

There was a flurry of activity as the group broke up into smaller teams and began assembling weapons and equipment. Earpieces were fitted and radios tested to ensure clear communications. The harsh sound of pistols and carbines being loaded and made ready echoed through the cavernous space of the unit. Crispin watched the flurry of activity with a feeling of apprehension. This needed to go well, without any fuck-ups that could be laid at his door. His DO had made that quite clear in their last meeting. He turned to Luke.

'Okay, what's the plan?'

The SAS man walked over to the whiteboard and used his finger to run Crispin through the operation.

'Simultaneous breach at front and rear with entry teams straight in. Looking to capture Zulus for exploitation rather than kill but this will be determined by Targets' reactions. LADYBIRD footage seems to indicate Zulu is armed as we can just about make out the butt of a rifle cradled in his lap.'

'Good. Just remember though, as much as we'd like them alive, these individuals have shown their utter disregard for human life and the last thing I want to see is one of your guys being carried out of there on a stretcher.'

Luke frowned and thought a moment before speaking. This was highly unusual. In all of his dealings with MI6, he had never heard them express concern for anything other than themselves or any associated negative publicity. It was refreshing to hear it, but the SAS officer couldn't help but feel there was something he was missing here. Shaking his head to clear his paranoia, he met the intelligence officer's eyes.

'Thanks Crispin, we appreciate that and don't worry; it won't be any of my men getting carried out of there.'

'Good to hear Luke. Good to hear. I'll leave you guys to it then, shall I?'

With that, Crispin walked over to a small plastic chair and lowered himself into it, pulling out his telephone and typing away at a message before sending the missive. Content, he put his phone away and watched the Special Forces Team prepare their assault. A knocking at the door disturbed them and each man looked toward the intrusion. Nick, the bearded Trooper who remained stationed at the entrance, opened a small hatch and just as quickly closed it before opening the door fully and admitting two people inside. Crispin frowned then cursed silently as he saw who the new arrivals were. *Fatty Giles and that Asian squaddie. What the hell are they doing here*? He rose from his chair and walked across the concrete floor to meet them. Giles saw him and raised his eyebrows in surprise, clearly not expecting his presence.

'Crispin? I wasn't even aware that you were here. What's going on?'

'Giles, hi. Yes, apologies for the lack of communication but we really needed to get on top of this one and fast, so the usual niceties were put on the back burner I'm afraid.' He watched as the MI5 officer visibly coloured and pointed a shaking finger at him.

'Niceties my arse Crispin. This is *my* operation and you do not just charge in here and start chucking your weight around.'

'Sorry old boy but as of fifteen minutes ago this is now designated a VIKER cleared operation and, as I'm sure you are aware, that pretty much means that I *am* going to be chucking my weight around.' He almost smiled as he watched Giles' mouth open in surprise, but he was interrupted by Luke who had walked over to join them.

'Crispin, imagery from LADYBIRD is good and we have security teams covering the building's external ready for the assault. My teams are ready. Are we go?'

Never dropping his gaze from that of his MI5 colleague, Crispin spoke quietly but confidently.

'We are go. I say again, we are go.'

With that, Luke walked back to the teams and they began moving out through the rear entrance of the unit, armed and carrying various pieces of equipment to enable them to gain access to the target location. One of the team who was staying behind monitoring the operation handed Crispin a small radio which he took and checked that it was turned on.

Nadia watched the SAS teams leaving the building and shook her head, well aware that the MI6 officer was playing power games, clearly looking to get all the glory for the success of the operation. *Lovat needs to hear* this. She turned away and pulled out her mobile, stabbing at the screen before bringing the device up to her ear.

'Hi, it's me. Look, HADES are going in now. No…no, our friend from Vauxhall seems to be running the show now. Fuck knows…yeah, yeah, I'll keep you posted.' She returned the device to her pocket and looked at Giles. 'Well?'

Giles sighed and rubbed his hand over his tired face. 'Well what? We're too late, the operation's underway, we can only wait and see what happens.'

She could feel his anger and disappointment at being usurped, and the helplessness to influence the outcome. But Giles was right: All they could do was wait. Making her way over to the team of operators monitoring the footage from the LADYBIRD camera and the communications from the SAS, Nadia watched as they formed up at their entry points. She looked at the large-scale diagram on the wall, annotated with Red spots that indicated the positions the teams would take on the ground. Standing beside Crispin, she returned his nod of recognition before he resumed his focus back towards the screens in front of him. Once again, Nadia found herself recalling Lovat's words that there was more to the MI6 officer than met the eye and certainly his takeover of the operation seemed to confer an unusual authority for the country's external intelligence agency. But then again, these were unusual times.

A clear, confident voice came through the speaker system grabbing her attention.

'This is Alpha. I am complete Red One.'

There was a brief pause before another voice was heard.

'This is Zulu. Complete Red Two.'

The operator on the desk replied.

'Zero, Roger. Both teams complete. Charlie?'

A third voice came over the speaker who Nadia assumed would be the Security Team Leader, the guys who would go in after the initial entry teams to secure the location and the subjects.

'Charlie complete Red Three.'

There was another pause for a brief moment.

'All callsigns, Alpha. Standby, standby.'

A second later two deep booms sounded and the corrugated metal walls of their building shook. As Nadia watched the LADYBIRD imagery, she saw one of the individuals in the target building fall off the vehicle he was sat upon in shock. Two pairs of boots then moved past the small camera and two balaclava-clad SAS soldiers took control of the shocked individual.

'Zero, Alpha, location secure and BINGO. I say again BINGO.'

BINGO: The code-word for the successful detention of the suspects. And all done in under thirty seconds. Nadia was impressed. Even though she had been witness to this type of operation before, these guys were slick. But then she supposed that the constant exposure to these operations had honed the Special Forces' soldiers to a very fine edge. She started as she felt a hand on her shoulder and turned to see Giles looking at her.

'Right, now that the action men have done their bit, fancy having a chat with our bad boys?'

Nadia nodded. 'Absolutely. Let's get them before the shock of capture wears off. I'll just let Lovat know what we're doing.' With that she called Lovat and brought him up to speed with the latest developments and to let him know that the surveillance could stand down now that the suspects were detained. Duty done, she terminated the call and rushed towards the building's rear entrance where she caught up with Giles just before he exited the door.

Lovat leaned back in his seat. He'd informed the rest of the surveillance team that the operation was concluded and directed them to return to the Forward Mounting Base for a debrief on his return. He didn't follow them immediately, something nagging at the back of his mind that he couldn't quite put his finger on. The interference from Crispin still rankled and he struggled to believe that it was a simple matter of a power play, the MI6 officer far too slick for Lovat's liking to stoop to such a base-level play. *But what the hell is he doing?*

Fuck it! Lovat opened his door and exited the vehicle, making sure his shirt hadn't ridden up to expose his pistol. He had intended heading back to conduct the debrief of the surveillance team but decided to join Giles and Nadia and see if there was anything of value coming out of the Tactical Questioning, or TQ as it was usually shortened to. He made his way towards the Operations' unit first to check in with the team there and let them know he would be entering the target location to assist Giles. The door was open and he stepped inside the building, nodding to some of the SAS soldiers who were unloading their weapons and stowing them in the carry bags. As he walked towards the individuals seated at the monitors, he saw Crispin talking into his telephone, an intense expression on his face. Lovat touched one of the analysts on the shoulder and indicated with his thumb.

'Hey mate, I'm heading into target location to assist Giles with the TQ, okay?'

The analyst nodded and annotated the record on his computer screen as Lovat walked towards the rear exit. Just before he reached the door, he turned, intending to catch Crispin's attention and see if the MI6 officer was going to accompany him. Lovat frowned as he took in Crispin's expression. The MI6 man had terminated his call and was staring at the floor at his feet. Lovat stopped and was about to call to Crispin when a huge explosion sounded and battered the thin metal walls of the building, shaking the fluorescent lights in the ceiling.

The unit was filled with loud curses and shouts as the SAS teams ripped their weapons from the bags and reloaded, sprinting out of the door. Lovat followed them, drawing his own weapon and running towards the billowing grey cloud that was now rising above the target location. His only thoughts were of Giles and Nadia and the hope that they hadn't made it into the building before the explosion. As he reached the target building, he coughed as the acrid, powdered dust caught the back of his throat. Muffled shouts and screams of pain filtered through the thick screen of smoke and as he walked through rubble and twisted sheets of tortured metal, he paused at each casualty that the soldiers were attending to. The fourth casualty was Nadia and Lovat dropped to his knees beside the SAS Trooper administering medical aid. Nadia's face was a mask of pale-grey powder and blood streaks but he could see that she was breathing. The SAS soldier gave Lovat a brief glance as he continued with his work, skill born of practice making his movements quick and confident. Lovat spoke, voice hoarse from smoke inhalation and emotion.

'How bad? She's one of mine.'

The trooper didn't even look up. 'Unconscious, blunt-force trauma to head, broken ribs and possible punctured lung. She'll live mate but no idea if there's any brain damage yet. CASEVAC in five.'

Lovat felt his eyes water as he took in the information. The fact that Nadia was breathing was welcome but the brain injury was a blow. He stood and continued further into the building, leaving Nadia in the capable hands of the Special Forces' medic. He had to find Giles. Just beyond Nadia he saw a cluster of soldiers get to their feet and pick their weapons up, moving further into the gloom and leaving a body lying on the floor. It only took Lovat a couple of steps to confirm his fears. Giles' body was lying on its back, the torso naked and pale against the blood-darkened floor beneath him. Lovat knelt by his friend's body, reached out a hand and as gently as he could, closed the eyes. A huge gash was visible in Giles' head, deep and a visceral red with a shock of white showing where the skull had been cleaved. Wiping his eyes, Lovat then patted Giles' shoulder. 'Goodbye old mate.' His voice was cracked and he cleared his throat as he stood. The SAS medic who had been treating Nadia approached him and nodded back towards the door.

'Your girl is on her way to the Heli now mate, we've done all we can here.' Lovat nodded his thanks as the soldier turned his attention towards Giles' body. 'Another one of yours?'

Lovat shook his head. 'No, he was Box, but one of the good ones and a friend as well.'

The medic removed his helmet and shook his head. 'I don't suppose it's any consolation mate but your friend died instantly. He wouldn't have felt a thing.'

Turning to face the soldier, Lovat nodded. 'You're right; it's no consolation but I appreciate the effort.'

The medic clapped his shoulder then made his own way out of the building. Another soldier appeared from the gloom and Lovat stopped him as he made to pass.

'We got any idea what the fuck happened here?'

The SAS man locked eyes with him and Lovat saw the rage and grief apparent.

'Massive IED concealed in the car. No idea as to the initiation method yet but they got us fucking good; I've got four dead mates in here as well as Luke.' The soldier leaned in and stared hard at Lovat. 'Was this your intel?'

Lovat shook his head. 'No mate. I've lost people too. This was Vauxhall's shout.'

The soldier dropped his gaze and ran his hand through his hair. 'What a fucking cluster. Some bastard's going to pay for this.' With that he turned and strode out of the building, booting a plastic container across the floor as he went.

Lovat took a deep, shaky breath and wiped his eyes on his sleeve. More medics arrived with one of them carrying body bags, making their way into the building. Deciding he didn't really want to see his friend being placed into one of these receptacles, Lovat made his way out of the rear of the building and back towards the operations unit. A rage was building inside of him as he stepped into the unit, eyes searching for the one person he was sure could give him the answers that he needed; Crispin. Sirens were sounding in the distance, the police and emergency services no doubt rushing to the scene. Lovat could hear one of the SAS Team Leaders talking on the phone to an SO 15 officer to alert them to the incident and requesting a Liaison Officer to deal with the regular police.

Lovat stood still as he swept the interior of the unit for his target but couldn't see him anywhere. Frustrated, he approached one of the analysts and tapped him on the shoulder.

'Hey mucker, you seen the Vauxhall bod anywhere?'

'No mate.' The analyst turned around and pointed towards the main entrance. 'Last time I saw him was about ten minutes ago over there.'

Lovat cursed and jogged towards the front door, hoping to catch the MI6 officer before he left the area. He shouldered the door open, almost falling over the threshold in his haste to get outside. Scanning the area for any sight of Crispin, he saw one of the SAS Team Leaders loading equipment into the back of a black Range Rover.

'Hey mate, you haven't seen the Vauxhall rep, have you?'

The soldier slammed the tailgate shut and looked over at Lovat.

'You mean the fucking weasel who orchestrated this clusterfuck?'

'Yeah, that'd be him.'

'He left about ten minutes ago. But when you see him give him a message from me and the guys will you?'

Lovat knew what was coming. 'No problem. What is it?'

'Tell him we won't forget this and we'll make sure he won't either.'

'Be my pleasure. Got a couple of scores of my own to settle with him.'

The Team Leader nodded. 'Yeah, I heard. Well, if you get to him first try and leave something for us, will you?'

Lovat's smile held no trace of humour. 'I'll try but I can't make any promises.'

The Team Leader raised a hand in farewell and got into the driving seat of the vehicle and took off out of the parking area. Lovat watched the vehicle until it was out of sight then began walking towards his own. He stopped to allow two police cars to pass him and enter the unit's parking space. Two pairs of policemen exited the vehicles and were met by the Team Leader who had been talking to SO 15. Lovat looked on as the SAS man handed the police officers a mobile telephone which they began speaking into. Continuing back to his car he decided to make his way to the hospital to check on Nadia's condition before making himself available to the inevitable investigation that would be ramping up.

Turning the ignition key, he recalled the look on the MI6 officer's face when he'd observed him in the Operations' unit. *That fucker knew something. No two ways about it.* With five SAS soldiers and an MI5 officer dead, there was no way Crispin could hide from his responsibility.

And there was no way on earth that Lovat was going to let him.

EDGWARE ROAD, LONDON

The man called Djinn took a sip of the hot tea and sat back on the chair, enjoying the afternoon sunshine on his face. Picking up his cigarette from the ash tray, he took a long draw before exhaling the thin smoke cloud. He watched the people walking past the café, hurrying along to whatever business they felt needed their immediate attention. Taking another sip of tea, he reflected on his situation and what he needed to do next.

The operation in St Albans had worked even better than he had dared to hope. From his vantage point some distance away, he had watched both the explosion and the follow-up from the security services. The body bags that were carried from the scene surprised him at first; he had expected two to three but when he'd counted nine being taken from the ruins of the building, he'd been very happy. This morning's newspaper headlines had made him even happier: Five of the dead were SAS soldiers, labelled as heroes by the press. There was also the rumour that a senior

MI5 officer was among the slain but this had not been confirmed.

No MI6 officer, which was very disappointing but Djinn had already known that. Had watched as Crispin had entered the other industrial unit but had not joined his colleagues who had gone to their target. Although frustrated, Djinn had enjoyed calling the MI6 officer on his phone and after the silence that followed the initial shock of Djinn's introduction, relaying his intentions to Crispin. A clear statement, short and to the point. '*You will live to fight another day my friend but for your colleagues, you have just witnessed their final breaths in this world.*' He'd terminated the call and taken the phone apart, scattering the pieces down the grate of a drain he stood beside. He'd then used another phone to ring the handset that was connected to a three hundred-pound improvised bomb in the shell of the car he'd placed in the unit. The blast had been, as always, satisfactory, a confirmation to him that his skills remained as good as they ever were. He'd made his way out of the area and back into the city to the safe house he'd set up several months before. He turned his attention back to the newspaper reports of the bombing.

Although not mentioned, was the fact that two individuals associated to Djinn had also been killed. No doubt this was the result of a directive from MI5, keeping certain details out of the public domain until they had determined if they were of any sensitive intelligence value. Djinn allowed himself a rare smile. No doubt the British spies thought that the bomb had been an accident or perhaps detonated as an act of martyrdom by his two colleagues.

But it had been no accident. Djinn had set the bomb and detonation mechanisms himself. He had coordinated getting the little engineer and Abdul Malik together in the full knowledge that the security services had identified the little engineer's involvement. As this had always been the plan from the start, Djinn was more than satisfied with the result. He was leaving no loose ends to chance and as both Abdul Malik and the little engineer were the only individuals who could provide any real information about him, they were always going to be sacrificial pawns in Djinn's game. And Djinn *had* kept his word to his little engineer; his ordeal was over, and he would never see or hear from Djinn again.

Closing his eyes behind his Ray Ban sunglasses, Djinn reflected that the next phase of his plan would ensure that the attention was drawn back to where he needed it to be; the Great British public. The death of the legendary SAS soldiers and an MI5 officer would remain headline news for a few days at most, but innocent victims on England's high streets guaranteed domination of the entire media.

MI6 HEADQUARTERS, VAUXHALL

Crispin confronted his image in the mirror before him and stared, transfixed as the rivulets of water ran down his face. Shaking himself out of his reverie, he grabbed a couple of paper towels from the dispenser and dried his face before dropping the damp tissues into the bin. Looking at his image once more he felt a stab of anger replace the anxiety that had been gnawing at him. *Come on Faulks. Get it together man. You're a survivor. Start acting like one.*

When the operation had gone wrong, he'd wasted no time in jumping in his car and heading straight back to Vauxhall. He knew there was going to be hell to pay from SF, MI5 and SIG and he intended being in a safe space when they all came calling for his head on a platter. So, he'd come back to the one place he knew where none of these people could touch him: Vauxhall. Anyone requiring access to Crispin would have to do so through official channels and would be denied access to the building unless express permission was given. So, he was safe. For the time being.

Checking his phone, he saw he had three missed calls from Director of Operations and two from Legal but the message on his voicemail brokered no such possibility of postponement. *My office directly on your return.* Straight from the Deputy Chief of SIS himself, Clarence Temple-Marsh, OBE. Crispin felt a wave of desperation overwhelm him as the prospect of standing in front of the second most powerful man in the Service and being held to account became a reality. And he could think of no way out of this. He'd called the VIKER clearance off his own back, convinced the operation would be a run-of-the-mill shooting of terrorists and of the man holding both Crispin and the country to ransom. The phone call he'd received mere seconds before the blast had been his only warning that this wasn't going to be the case. The phone call that had seen him frozen and stunned by its significance. *And how the hell did he get that number?* But nobody could possibly be aware of that. All that was known at the moment was that the SF had walked into either a trap or a suicide bomber killing himself rather than facing capture. There wasn't any *actual* evidence to link Crispin to the operation's appalling failure. And Luke was dead, so there would be no testimony from the SFE that Crispin had called the VIKER authority. Yes, some of the SAS soldiers may have heard him but Crispin was sure he could bluff it, claim he had said he was *waiting* for VIKER clearance.

But he'd need a scapegoat. Someone to carry the can for the disaster and satisfy the need for a head to roll. And preferably someone who could no longer speak for themselves or raise a credible defence. His reflected image looked back at him, smiling for the first time since the disaster. *Yes, someone who can't speak for themselves.* Crispin had just the person for that. With a renewed confidence he ran a damp hand through his hair, taming some of the wildness out of it. He didn't want to rock up to the Deputy Chief's office looking anything other than the consummate professional that he was. *Impression Management.* One of the earliest skills he'd learned as a fledgling Case Officer with MI6. Portraying the image and role that you wanted the person to believe in. And he *needed* his elders and betters to completely believe him if he was to have any hope of side-stepping the mess he was currently in and retaining his untarnished career record. Taking a deep breath, he straightened his shirt collar and took a final look at himself in the mirror. Satisfied with the reflection of a confident, assured officer, he nodded, turned and walked out of the bathroom.

WATFORD GENERAL HOSPITAL

Lovat grimaced at the bitter taste of the vending machine coffee. Looking down into the contents of the beige, plastic cup, he decided not to put himself through the inevitable heartburn that would plague him if he drank it all. He stood and walked over to a bin and dumped the cup and its contents into it. A figure moving along the corridor caught his eye and he nodded in recognition. *OD.* His Commanding Officer had called Lovat earlier and told him that he was making his way to the hospital to get the official word on Nadia's condition.

As he approached, OD held out his hand and Lovat shook it, looking into the officer's eyes and seeing the anger and sorrow apparent.

'Lovat, what the hell happened out there?'

Taking his seat, Lovat leaned forward and sighed. 'I'm still not sure Boss. If I was to guess, I would say we either walked into a trap that was set for us or one of the Zulus martyred themselves. Whichever it was, it got us good.

Giles and five Blades killed immediately and three others injured, including Nadia.'

'Fuck's sake. Any heads-up on Nadia's prognosis yet?'

'No, they literally rushed her straight into surgery and I haven't seen anyone since.'

OD reached out and patted Lovat on the back. 'She's bloody tougher than most men I know. She'll pull through, you'll see.'

Lovat nodded but felt none of his CO's confidence, remembering the sight of Nadia as she'd lain on the floor of the target building covered in dust and blood. 'Any word from Box yet, Boss?'

'Going to a meeting at Thames House right after this so hopefully get a bit of a feel for what actually happened. Poor bloody Giles. I still can't believe it. One of the really good guys.'

'Yeah, he was Boss. A real star. Can't imagine what his missus is going through just now.'

They sat in silence for several minutes until the double doors beside them swung open and a doctor in a white coat made his way towards them.

'Hi, I take it you're the Army chaps? I'm Iain McLeod, the surgeon who operated on your colleague.'

Both men stood and shook the proffered hand. OD nodded. 'Yes, I'm Colonel Oliver Dewar and this is Warrant Officer Lovat Reid. How's Nadia?'

The Doctor smiled. 'She's actually doing really good. There's no brain damage even though she took a hell of a whack on the head and we've taken care of the ribs. The lung wasn't punctured so we were spared that complication.' He paused and gave a small chuckle. 'She regained consciousness for a few moments just as we were prepping her for surgery. Took a few of us to hold her down despite the agony she must have been in.'

Lovat smiled in a combination of relief and recognition of Nadia's fighting spirit. He watched as OD shook the doctor's hand again.

'When can we see her?'

The Doctor shook his head. 'Not just yet, she'll still be under for a few hours. I would say come back tomorrow afternoon when she should be a bit more *compos mentis.*'

'Good enough. We'll do just that. Thanks again Iain, really appreciate this.'

The surgeon smiled. 'She's a fighter alright and no mistaking it. Is her family here as I'm happy to update them while I'm out here?'

OD shook his head. 'Actually, Staff Sergeant Ali has no nominated Next of Kin or family that she wishes to be notified. Very unusual to say the least, but there it is.'

The surgeon nodded and made his way back through the doors leaving Lovat and OD alone in the corridor. Lovat made eye contact with his CO. 'Well, since I can't see Nadia until tomorrow, any chance I can join you at this meeting? I'm very fucking keen to know exactly how this shit-fest happened and if anyone knew anything beforehand.'

'You and me both. Yes, will be good to have you there, get the view from the man on the ground so to speak.'

They made their way out to the car park, talking in low voices about the incident. Now that his fears over Nadia's injuries had been allayed, Lovat found himself thinking more and more about Giles. His eyes watered as memories came to him; Giles' crap jokes that only he found hilarious, his razor-sharp intellect, his utter devotion to his family. All gone. As he climbed into the CO's Audi, he could feel the sorrow being replaced by a far healthier emotion, at least as far as he was concerned: Rage. A cold, dark anger and a determination to find whoever was responsible for this and make them pay. As OD drove them out of the car park, Lovat began talking him through the events of the day to bring him completely up to speed before their meeting. For his part, OD did not interrupt, allowing Lovat to finish his update before asking any questions.

'So, you think Crispin received some kind of warning? That's a pretty heavy accusation Lovat.'

'I know that Boss, but his whole demeanour when he finished that call and then the bomb going off straight away. Too much to be a coincidence.'

'I know you've got great instincts Lovat but that's not going to cut the mustard. If he did receive some kind of tip off it would have had to have come through one of two means; an official warning from Vauxhall or information from an Agent he is running. If it's the former they'll have to come clean on it at some point or at least admit some level of knowledge. If it's the latter, then that's going to be impossible to prove. And they're not going to give us any details regarding his telephone activities.'

Lovat sighed. 'I know, I know. But I'm right Boss; that call he received was about the bomb and the fact that he took off right away is massively suspect as well. I've always thought his involvement in this Op was strange from the start and now I'm convinced of it.'

They drove on in silence, each man lost in their own thoughts.

The soundproofed, glass door closed softly as the support staff left the room and the tall man at the head of the table cleared his throat and spoke.

'Gentlemen, Lady. I think we've all met before but just in case we haven't, I'm Matthew Chivers, Director of Operations for the Security Service. As this is the first time that many of us have met collectively, could I ask you to introduce yourself and your current role as we work our way around the table please?'

Lovat had met many of the delegates before however some were unknown to him. Unsurprisingly, they represented every agency or department relating to counter-terrorism or national security. CTU, SO15, MI5, DSF, Home Office, GCHQ and of course, the inevitable presence of Crispin Faulks flying the flag for MI6. Lovat couldn't wait to hear what was going to come out of *his* mouth. When the introductions had been completed, the MI5 officer spoke again.

'I'd just like to say that, as much as we have already been invested in this operation from its inception, it has now become very personal for us with the loss of a well-respected officer and beloved family man. And I'd really like some answers on this please. Mr Reid, I'm informed that you were present when the device exploded?'

Slightly surprised that he was being asked to speak so soon, Lovat cleared his throat and nodded. 'Yes sir, that's correct. I'd led the surveillance team who took Objective DAGGER from Watford to the unit in St Albans. During the follow, I received the message that HADES was also *en route* to the target location. At that point I called Giles to make sure he was in the loop and he informed me he was making his way to the target location in order to retain control of the exploitation.' He paused to allow for any questions. When there were none, he continued. 'My team housed DAGGER in the warehouse and Giles and my colleague Staff Sergeant Ali entered the Operations' unit but were informed that HADES were preparing to assault the target location.'

Matthew looked over his glasses directly at Lovat. 'On whose authority?'

'I have no idea sir. I only received the information from Staff Sergeant Ali to keep me in the loop. Perhaps our colleague from Vauxhall might shed some light upon it as he was present before Giles arrived and was also there when the explosion went off.' Lovat struggled to keep the anger he was feeling from surfacing, but managed it, well aware that to the people sat around this table it would be viewed as unprofessional and immature. And he needed to be accepted as a credible contributor here if anything was to be done about Crispin's actions. There was a brief silence before the MI6 officer spoke.

'Thank you, Warrant Officer Reid. Yes, as my military colleague already stated, I was on location with the HADES team before Giles arrived. As the team was already prepping their assault, I assumed the authority had been given by Giles. Certainly, the momentum was already underway prior to my arrival.'

Crispin was interrupted by the imposing man sat across from him, clear blue eyes and chiselled features engaging the MI6 officer with an undisguised anger.

'According to the debrief I had with our HADES team the authority came from you. *You* gave the authority under Op VIKER and the teams went in under that very instruction.' Having finished his statement, Director Special Forces awaited the MI6 officer's response.

'Well..., I'm sorry Brigadier but that is absolutely not the case at all. I recall discussing the situation on my arrival with Luke, our SFE and he informed me that the Security Service had authorised their deployment and that he was just waiting for Giles to arrive for the Go.' Crispin paused and took a sip of water from the glass in front of him. 'Luke was anxious that the Objectives in the target location might move at any moment and I said, if he liked, I could *request* VIKER authorisation. Then when Giles arrived the authority to assault was given.'

Matthew Chivers held up his hand. 'Just to confirm Crispin; you're saying that Giles *personally* authorised the Special Forces' assault on the target location?

'Absolutely Matthew. I mean, it was a very busy environment what with weapons being loaded and camera footage being relayed to the analysts, and analysts updating team leaders but yes, Giles gave the order.'

DSF snorted. 'Bullshit. My guys distinctly heard you give the Go.'

Crispin shook his head. 'Sorry Brigadier but that is not what happened. I was stood right beside Giles when he said it. I *repeated* it to Luke so maybe that is where the confusion lies.'

'*Confusion*? I've got five dead soldiers, including a decorated Major. This isn't about confusion; this is about accountability and responsibility: As in who?'

Matthew Chivers interrupted the pair. 'At no time, did Giles contact us and either inform of, or request, any such authorisation.'

Crispin shook his head. 'As I've said Matthew, it was a very dynamic situation with a lot of moving pieces but I can't be any clearer; the authorisation came directly from Giles himself.'

Lovat found himself staring hard at the MI6 officer. He'd expected him to weasel out of any responsibility or accountability for his actions but to turn the blame on to a good man only recently dead, was beyond even what Lovat had thought Crispin capable of. He found himself being addressed by DSF. 'Warrant Officer Reid, I believe your colleague Staff Sergeant Ali was present with Giles during this incident and that she has survived the blast, correct?'

'Yes sir. She's also expected to make a full recovery sooner rather than later.' For a brief moment, Lovat thought he saw a fleeting shadow of concern sweep across Crispin's face, but it was gone instantly, if indeed it had been there in the first place and not just a result of his wishful thinking. He turned to face DSF as the senior officer continued.

'That is excellent news on a day when we desperately need it. To more pressing matters however; when will Staff Sergeant Ali be well enough to deliver her account of the events?'

OD placed a hand on Lovat's arm and spoke for the first time. 'She's still under at the moment sir but expected to come around tomorrow. Possibly best to give her tomorrow night to rest up and then we can assess things the following day. She's a tough soldier and I know she'll be keen to provide us with whatever help she can, but we must ensure we put her health first and foremost.'

'Agreed Colonel, and our best wishes to your soldier for a speedy recovery. You can contact me directly when you ascertain that she is recovered adequately to be interviewed. Okay, so where are we now?'

As the discussion turned towards the ongoing follow-up to the bombing and the preliminary forensic reports, Crispin maintained an external façade of interest while internally he was fighting down the panic welling up from his stomach. He hadn't expected that the girl would recover, recalling that one of the SAS medics had said she had brain damage. His plan was reliant on the fact that the only two people who could provide any credible evidence that he had initiated the VIKER authority could never do so. *Shit*! He'd even convinced his Deputy Chief that he was untouchable on this one, that MI5 had to take the blame squarely on their shoulders. He'd known that the SF guys would raise a bit of a din but had also been confident he could deal with that. He knew DSF was suspicious, could see it in the man's apparent sneer whenever he addressed Crispin, but he could deal with suspicions. Suspicions weren't *proof*. Matthew Chivers was also not swallowing the whole story but again, Crispin knew that Chivers, being a career Civil Servant, dealt in certainties and could not be certain that his man on the ground had not called the authority for the operation. He glanced out of the corner of his eye at the SIG soldiers. Crispin had underestimated the Warrant Officer. For a squaddie he was actually quite sharp, and he wasn't accepting Crispin's version of events. *No matter*. Mere soldiers were small beer to Crispin and his organisation and it would take a hell of a lot more than the suspicions of a squaddie to rattle him. The girl however was another problem. A *big* problem.

Bringing his full attention back into the room, he listened as the initial assessment of the bomb's components was delivered by a technical forensics officer. According to the expert it had been a standard device activated by mobile telephone. While this in itself was not unusual, the implication was that whoever had detonated the bomb had been watching the proceedings as they unfolded, within sight of the target location. Crispin felt a sudden jolt of fear. Had SCIMITAR been watching the whole time? Waiting for Crispin to enter the target location? He felt his heart race as he remembered the telephone call he had received, moments before the bomb was detonated. The realisation hit him that SCIMITAR *had* been watching the whole time and had detonated the bomb when it was clear that Crispin was not leaving the Operations' unit. *Too close. Way too bloody close.*

Matthew Chivers called an end to the meeting and thanked everyone for their attendance. He recommended further, daily meetings where this was possible in order to keep on top of every development. As chairs were pushed back and the delegates made their way out of the room, Lovat continued watching Crispin. The MI6 officer appeared untroubled as he closed his briefcase and pushed his chair under the table, but Lovat was sure he had been panicked upon hearing about Nadia's recovery. He followed Crispin out of the door and once in the corridor, opened his pace until he'd caught up with him. Lovat tapped him on the shoulder and when he turned to face him, punched Crispin in the centre of his face. He felt a satisfying crunch beneath his knuckles and watched with undisguised pleasure as the MI6 officer crumpled to the ground moaning loudly and cradling his face in his hands. Lovat loomed over the felled man.

'Just so we're clear you piece of shit, no-one in that room bought your story for one fucking second. But they can't prove it because, of the two people who *can* tell us exactly what you did, one is dead and the other recovering from surgery.' As Crispin attempted to get to his feet, Lovat booted his backside and sent him sprawling along the corridor again, a cry of fear and pain following his collapse. 'But you'll get yours mate. You'll get yours.' Lovat shrugged off the restraining hands and held his own up in appeasement to those attempting to control him.

OD grabbed him by the shoulders. 'Get yourself together Warrant Officer Reid. I want you out of this building right now!'

Lovat nodded and began walking along the corridor towards the elevators. He was aware of the wide-eyed stares he was receiving from the delegates who had attended the meetings and those who had rushed from nearby offices, alerted by the commotion. He looked back and saw several individuals attending to Crispin who was now propped against a wall. Lovat caught the eye of the SF Brigadier as he passed and nodded to him. The Brigadier nodded back and inclined his head towards the injured MI6 officer with a wry smile.

'I'd say that's at least a start on what the skinny turd deserves.'

'If I have my way sir, a start is all that was. He's going to pay for the deaths of my friend, your men, and the near death of my colleague. And he's going to pay dearly.' Lovat continued towards the elevators but seeing some of the delegates staring at him as he approached, he opted to take the stairs instead as it was only a couple of floors. Halfway down, he heard his name being called by a female behind him. He stopped and looked up to see a blonde woman in jeans and a sweatshirt coming down the stairs towards him. She looked familiar and then it came to him; Jenny Hughes, an analyst he'd known before she'd left the Army and joined MI5 in their Counter-Espionage department. He smiled at her as she reached him on the landing.

'Jenny Hughes, long-time no-see. What's up? They demanding that you escort me out in case I drop another officious little wanker?'

Jenny returned his smile and embraced him in a warm hug. 'Lovat Reid. Good to see you.' She stepped back and held him at arm's length. 'I have something to ask you and it might seem a bit odd and none of my business but please, bear with me?'

Intrigued, Lovat nodded. 'Sure, go ahead.'

'Why did you hit Crispin Faulks just now?'

Sighing heavily, Lovat leaned against the wall as he regarded his former colleague. 'Alright, I'm making no secret of the fact that I think that he's responsible for Giles' and the SAS soldiers' deaths. I also think he's much more involved in this whole thing than he's letting on. He's toxic Jenny.' He watched as Jenny pursed her lips and furrowed her brow, clearly deep in thought. He allowed her the silence and she eventually looked up, nodding to herself as though reaching an important decision.

'Okay Lovat. Meet me in an hour in The Duke just off Trafalgar Square. You know it?'

'Yeah, know it well, good little boozer. Mind if I ask why?'

She glanced back up the empty stairwell before replying. 'Not here, I'll tell you everything in an hour and believe me, you're going to want to hear it. Okay, I've got to get back upstairs and finish something off but I'll see you there.'

Lovat watched as she jogged back up the stairs and out of sight. Turning to continue his descent, he was curious as to what it could be that Jenny wanted to talk to him about so badly. It was clearly something to do with Crispin, that much was obvious. *But what?* As he reached the security exit, he stepped out of the revolving doors onto the busy pavement. Pulling his phone from his pocket, he sent a text to OD informing him that he wouldn't require a lift and that he would see him in the morning. Making his way through the crowds towards Trafalgar Square Lovat decided to go straight to the pub and have a few drinks before Jenny arrived. He felt as though he needed a couple just to take the edge of his mood which was darkening now that the adrenaline he'd felt when punching Crispin had worn off. Yes, a couple of rum and cokes just to settle him down a bit.

'So, Jenny; why all the mystery?'

He watched as she took a long drink of her gin and tonic and set her glass back down on the table. Leaning back on her chair, her expression became more serious as she met his eyes. She gave a quick glance around her to ensure that they couldn't be overheard before she spoke.

'Look, you remember before I left the mob, you tried to persuade me to stay, pulling all that old flannel about me being great at my job and a bright future ahead etc.?'

'Wasn't flannel Jenny. You were one of our brightest, no two ways about it and I hate to lose good people.'

She gave a small smile and her cheeks reddened with a small flush. 'Well, be that as it may, I couldn't stay in the job any more. Nothing to do with the Int Corps but more because of something I'd been a part of and hadn't gotten over.'

Lovat leaned forward and took a drink of his Kraken and Coke, remaining silent and allowing Jenny to talk in her own time.

'Back on my tour of Afghanistan I had been doing really well in the Targeting Cell when I was approached by Eddie

Brown, the Intelligence Staff Sergeant for the Special Projects' team. You remember Eddie?'

'Yeah, I know Eddie. Not a bad bloke and commissioned as a Captain recently.'

'Yeah that's him. Well, anyway, I was flattered by his offer so took him up on it and went into the Special Projects' team. Most of it was the standard High Value Target pursuit stuff but we were doing some cheeky cross-border targeting as well.' She paused and took another drink. 'I didn't have a problem with any of that. It was war, after all. No, my problem came with the Op VIKER strikes. You're aware of these I take it?'

Lovat nodded. 'Yes. High-level clearance for strikes or assaults when there is recognised collateral. Usually justified when it is a one-time chance of getting the target.'

'Exactly. I don't actually have a problem with VIKER in general, but with one operation in particular. I've never managed to put this one behind me no matter how hard I try. Oh, don't look at me like that, it's not PTSD or anything just…I don't know. It was really wrong Lovat. *Really* wrong. The collateral was horrendous.'

'Okay, but surely that is not an uncommon occurrence with a VIKER strike. Hell, I've worked on a few where we've accepted the deaths of a couple of innocents on the target site.'

'As have I. But these were children Lovat. Children and their mother deliberately sacrificed for the sake of three HVTs. And to watch the BDA and see the body parts littered around the crater was utterly horrific. And it's something I live with every day. I *knew* it was wrong but just wasn't strong enough to stand up to the Operation Control and stop it.'

Lovat shook his head and reached across the table, covering her hand with his as he saw how upset she was becoming. 'Jenny, there would have been nothing that you could have done. VIKER was authorised and initiated and once that's done you can't put the genie back in the bottle again.'

Jenny leaned forward and looked directly into his eyes. 'That's just it, Lovat; I don't think VIKER was authorised at all. You see, on a night duty one evening, I waited until I was alone and then checked out the digital call logs for the secure lines. Something had seemed really wrong to me from the start of that job and although I didn't know what it was, I began to look for something that would support my suspicion. And I struck gold with the call logs.'

'What do you mean?'

'Well, on the day of the strike, I took the call from Vauxhall to the Operational Controller, the OpCon, and passed it to him. The OpCon spoke on the phone for about thirty seconds then told us that VIKER was authorised. Only when I checked the call logs later, the call I'd taken for the OpCon came from Vauxhall.'

Lovat frowned and tried to see where Jenny was going with this. 'Yes, I know. You said before that the call came from Vauxhall.'

She let out a sigh of exasperation. 'That's just it: VIKER is only ever authorised from Permanent Joint Headquarters at Northwood. The authorisation *has* to come from PJHQ once Vauxhall request it. The order can *never* come direct from Vauxhall because of the strict protocols under which VIKER can be called.'

Lovat stared at her as the realisation hit him that Jenny was absolutely correct. In all his time hunting and killing terrorists around the globe, a VIKER strike was always sanctioned through communications with PJHQ. He listened as Jenny continued.

'So, it got me thinking; if the OpCon had pulled this trick on that operation, he had probably done it before. So, although it took me a couple of hours, I found three other occasions where a VIKER strike had been authorised but again, without any direct communication with PJHQ.'

An excitement took hold in Lovat's stomach and he felt a flush of warmth reach his face as he asked the one question that he already knew the answer to.

'Jenny, who was OpCon for all these unsanctioned strikes?'

She took a last sip of her drink before giving Lovat a small grin.

'He's an MI6 officer currently nursing a broken nose and a boot-print on his arse.

It was Crispin Faulks, Lovat.'

SURREY QUAYS, LONDON

Gently removing the ice-pack from the bridge of his nose, Crispin grimaced as the cold compress pulled on the skin beneath, bringing pain back to the sensitive area. He moaned aloud, more in self-pity than actual suffering. Resting his head back against the sofa, he closed his eyes as he assessed his current situation. He hadn't anticipated Lovat's attack. Although he'd known that there would have been some raw emotions flying around the table from various corners, the thought had never occurred to him that he could possibly be *assaulted* in a corridor in Thames House in full view of the country's leaders in intelligence and security. What stung more than that was how little support he had been give after the incident. Even Matthew Chivers had suggested that Crispin forego any formal action against the SIG soldier, claiming that no-one could really blame Lovat for his current emotional state. For his part, Crispin played the benevolence card, acquiescing to the request. Truth was, it was in Crispin's personal interest not to make a song and dance about the affair that would reach the ears of his superiors at Vauxhall Cross. That was the last thing he needed. *No*. First he had to deal with SCIMITAR and then he would take care of the SIG soldier who felt he could attack an agent of the crown with utter impunity.

Sitting forward, he gazed out at the rain teeming down the windows, blurring his view of the city beyond. He was running out of time and options. His Deputy Chief had been brutally clear with him; sort out this mess quickly and quietly or say goodbye to your career with MI6. There could be no blowback on the Service or even a hint that they'd had any involvement with SCIMITAR. No, he was on his own with this. He'd lost the trust of MI5, DSF and the SIG but that didn't particularly bother him. He'd always regarded the SIG operators as bottom feeders anyway. Yes, they might be relatively capable when the bombs and bullets were flying but they were hardly strategic intelligence officer material. Still, with all that hatred flying around, Crispin knew that he'd have to watch his back, Lovat's assault on him an indication, if indeed any was needed, that people felt there were scores to be settled.

He stood and made his way to the kitchen, desperate for coffee. The layout was unfamiliar to him as he had never been in this flat before. It was one of several high-end safe houses his Service retained throughout London for debriefing their Agents. After his call from SCIMITAR in St Albans, Crispin had decided not to use his own home, unwilling to take the risk that SCIMITAR may have identified the location. He'd called the support team and provided a cock and bull story about having to be seen by a potential target as living in the Rotherhithe area and they'd provided him with the details of the safe house there that he could use. His problem was where to go from here. He had no leads on SCIMITAR's whereabouts to follow up on but there was one last vestige of hope: His Deputy Chief had discarded the soft approach to the Pakistanis and had given them a direct ultimatum to find SCIMITAR and deliver the information to MI6 or there would be a leak to the media that SCIMITAR was an ISI officer running free in the UK. By all accounts, the threat had been received with the typical Pakistani denials and bluster but Crispin could see that it left ISI with no room for manoeuvre. The SCIMITAR Ops team at Vauxhall had been briefed to update Crispin directly and react to any developments only on his authority. It was a clever move by the Deputy Chief, allowing the Service plausible deniability of anything that Crispin sanctioned. Leaving the door open to laying the blame for any negative fallout at the feet of an over-enthusiastic Case Officer gone rogue. The upside as far as Crispin was concerned was that it allowed him to dig himself out of the hole he was rapidly falling deeper into, without attracting any further official attention.

He let out a deep breath and focused on his options. He was limited in what he could do as he needed to leave a minimal footprint of his activities. That ruled out approaching other agencies for help in CCTV tracking, mobile phone patterns or haranguing forensic teams for any biometric traces on the VBIED. He jumped as his mobile buzzed on the table beside him. Flipping the device over to look at the screen he noted the four-digit code that signified the call was coming from the Ops cell. Sitting forward he took the call and listened intently to the information being relayed to him. When the call was terminated, he accessed his notes application and typed a list of various points that he would need to refer to. A smile crossed his face and he felt his heart rate pick up. He was back in the game.

ISI had requested an informal meeting with the Head of Station in Islamabad, the senior MI6 representative in country. In what appeared to have been a frank and unusually honest discussion, the ISI officer from Directorate S had provided a list of contacts and safe houses that they believed SCIMITAR would potentially access while in the UK. According to the Ops team in Vauxhall, what was especially surprising about this information was the fact that not one person or location on it was known to MI6.

Crispin felt his pulse racing as the possibility that he was finally going to be able to deal with SCIMITAR once and for all became a reality. Letting out a long sigh, he reached for his lap top, opening the lid and waiting for the blue screen to appear before stabbing at the keyboard and accessing the secure portal. He skimmed through several screens before he found the one that he wanted. Leaning forward he gave this screen his undivided attention, occasionally nodding as a specific piece of information resonated with him. Half-way down the page of one of the online documents he stopped and re-read the content, wanting to be sure he understood it properly. He slapped his thigh and gave a grunt of pleasure. *This is it. I've got you now.*

The Ops team at Vauxhall had worked especially hard on this one and had, probably without even knowing, provided Crispin with a start point with which to start hunting down his nemesis. One of the safe houses that had been identified on the Edgware Road was familiar to Crispin, a fragment from a conversation long ago in a different land. His eyes closed as he concentrated on remembering the exact words that PHANTOM had used. They'd met at a safe house that MI6 was using in Kandahar city. PHANTOM and Crispin drinking hot, sweet tea as they pored over maps identifying the locations of targets that PHANTOM was providing. Burly SAS men in civilian attire monitored the outside of the building from windows and doorways, carbines and automatic rifles never more than an arm's length away. Crispin recalled a comment he'd made about one of the streets in the market district reminding him of a section of Edgware Road in London to which PHANTOM had chuckled.

'Ah, the Edgware Road. I have very fond memories of that area my friend. There is a Lebanese café near the International Community School, you know this place?'

Crispin had nodded and said he was vaguely familiar with the area.

'I lived close by for a time when I was operating in London from our embassy, as an…undeclared I think you call us?'

Crispin had laughed at the Agent's knowledge of MI6 terminology for foreign intelligence officers operating under official cover.

'It was my favourite place to be in the whole of London. The best food, the best tea, the best coffee and an easy place for a man such as myself to blend in.'

Crispin had caught the wistful tone of PHANTOM's statement and made a comment to the effect that it sounded as though the Agent missed the place.

'Absolutely I do and believe me, if I was to return to London tomorrow, it would be the first place that I would return to.'

Crispin's eyes snapped open at the recollection and the significance of it. He leaned back and let his gaze wander over the unblemished ceiling as he marshalled his thoughts. The remainder of that conversation in a warm room in Afghanistan's second city had centred around PHANTOM's potential resettlement in the UK. Crispin's agent was a very smart man and from his initial recruitment, had stated that his end-game was for a life in the UK for him and his family and the funds with which to maintain this. In return, MI6 would be running the ISI Directorate S Officer responsible for Pakistan's covert assistance to the Taliban in Afghanistan.

Crispin had, of course, intimated that this would be an arrangement to which Her Majesty's Government would be happy to oblige; providing the information PHANTOM delivered was deemed of proportionate value. And that value would be determined by Crispin alone in the standard manner of a professional intelligence officer. Never letting the Agent become aware of the *real* value of their information, always downplaying it, hinting that you knew most of it already or that it might be worth looking into. The delicate balance of stick and carrot, taking care to ensure the Agent worked hard to gain better information but without allowing them to become despondent or worse, suspecting that their information was deliberately being portrayed as low-value. The relationship between an Agent and his Case Officer was always a difficult dynamic; a balance of trust and suspicion on both parts with each believing they were the ones in control of the twisted marriage.

Crispin smiled as he recalled with fondness, the congratulations he had received from the top floor of Vauxhall Cross on his recruitment of PHANTOM and the first operation they had conducted based upon his information. He had returned to the UK for a two-week break shortly after that operation and had received a call from the Director of Operations telling him to attend a meeting the following morning and to dress appropriately for senior management. A glow of pride warmed his chest as he remembered the closed-door drinks with the Deputy Chief and senior Operations staff in the DC's office where they had toasted Crispin's success and hinted at a very rapid career path ahead. The memory evaporated as he remembered now how close he was to messing the whole thing up. All those years of taking the postings that the Service deemed High Threat Environments, making a name for himself as someone who could get things done, all now going down the pan because of an ex-Agent with an axe to grind? *No. No fucking way.*

He knew what he needed: A surveillance team to pin SCIMITAR down and an executive team to carry out the physical operation. It would have to look like an arrest and detention operation but Crispin had no intention of letting SCIMITAR live. He couldn't; the former Agent knew too much to be left alive and interviewed by some bloody *Guardian* correspondent eager to air the Service's dirty laundry. Having SCIMITAR killed on target was the least of his worries, that would be very easy to achieve. His main concern was where the hell he was going to get the surveillance and strike teams from, now that he had burned his bridges with MI5 and DSF. He cradled his head in his hands as frustration bit at him. He was so close but without the assets he needed, all he had was information.

He looked up as the thought struck him that there *were* other entities he could engage with. A smile broke his grim countenance as a surge of hope assailed him. He knew what he had to do now, but, more importantly also, how to do it: *Contractors.* MI6 retained the services of former Special Forces and covert Intelligence Operatives that they used from time to time on sensitive tasks where the Service's involvement had to remain secret. Vetted and retained for sole use by MI6, these individuals were used only when absolutely necessary and usually in the grey areas of legality and justifiability. Grabbing his phone from the table, Crispin scrolled through his contact list until he found the name he was looking for. *Nick Brechin.* Crispin had only worked with Nick on two previous occasions but had found him professional and discreet. The last time they'd met had been in Beirut along with the recently-deceased Luke Taylor. Nick and his team had been brought in to conduct the surveillance on the target as the Service needed plausible deniability if anything went wrong and the scope to make it appear as a botched Israeli operation. Nick was a quietly confident ex-SRR operator who retained his professional pride while working in the private sector. His team were all hand-picked by him and consequently very faithful to their superior. Crispin nodded as he congratulated himself on securing a surveillance team that he knew he could trust to be discreet.

The next contact he stopped at gave him pause for thought. Colin Hamer ran a team of former Special Forces soldiers all in their mid to late forties. The Service employed these men on snatch and grab operations where the use of conventional UKSF troops would contravene international laws or treaties. Crispin had met Colin twice; once in Turkey and another time in Cyprus and on both occasions had been impressed by the actions of Colin's teams. He'd witnessed their effectiveness when carrying out the abductions and renditions of High Value Targets in friendly countries without raising any suspicion of UK involvement.

Crispin's problem was that he was aware of the close links Colin maintained with his Regiment at Hereford. No doubt Colin would have been made aware that SAS soldiers had died during an MI6 operation and Crispin's name would have been mentioned. He was certain however, that he could get around that, convince Colin that Fatty Giles and MI5 had dropped the ball, that MI6 had no domestic jurisdiction that gave them the power to authorise such an operation. Maybe even concoct a couple of documents that he could show Colin, *offline* of course, that laid the blame at the hands of MI5 and, even better, SIG.

He knew he was wasting time. Taking a breath, he hit the contact details for Nick and was rewarded after several rings with the familiar cockney drawl.

'Hi Nick, Crispin here. Look, just needed to sound you out about a house I'm thinking of renting.' There was a brief pause as the phrase was interpreted at the other end and Crispin received his answer. Smiling he nodded as he spoke. 'Perfect, that's perfect. Shall we say 7pm tonight, the bar in the Park Plaza Waterloo? Yes, the Westminster one. Excellent, see you there.'

He repeated the same call to Colin Hamer but noted from this man's tone that his call was not quite as welcome. Obviously, Colin had been talking with his SAS colleagues but no matter, he knew he was obliged to meet with Crispin as part of the conditions of his contract and agreed to do so. Crispin stood and stretched, arching his back and putting his plan into action in his head. His confidence returned and he clapped his hands together, turning on his heel and making his way to the bathroom, whistling as he walked. He had to make himself look as confident as he felt. The bruising wouldn't help but he could explain that away as a legacy from the blast. Colin might have heard about Lovat thumping him but again, Crispin would demote this to a bit of push and shove while tempers were high. Play the benevolence card again. As he turned on the shower and watched the steam rise behind the glass partition, he was already adding another element into his plan. An element that made sure that Warrant officer Lovat Reid of the SIG got exactly what was coming to him.

With a wide grin, Crispin stripped off and entered the shower enclosure, washing both the dirt, and the day's tainted memories, away.

WATFORD GENERAL HOSPITAL

'You reek of drink Warrant Officer Reid!'

Lovat grinned at his colleague, both in pleasure at her jibe and the fact that she was clearly on the mend. Nadia still looked a little pale, propped up against a mound of pillows and a large dressing on her head but he could see her eyes retained their usual intensity.

'I may have had one or two small ones last night but that doesn't make me a bad person, does it?'

It was Nadia's turn to grin. 'Not at all. Just wish I could have joined you.' She grew serious and looked Lovat in the eye. 'The Boss was in first thing and told me about Giles. I'm so sorry Lovat, he was a great guy.'

'Yeah, he was and I'm still raging about his death and your near death because of some slimy shit from Vauxhall with his own agenda.' Lovat spent the next few minutes bringing Nadia up to speed with the events after the bomb and the subsequent meeting at Thames House. She laughed as he described punching and booting the MI6 officer along the Millbank corridor.

'Shit Lovat, I'm surprised he didn't have you arrested.'

'To be honest, I think there was more support for what I did than he expected. Look at it this way; MI5 and DSF have openly stated they think his explanation stinks. Along with us they know he's responsible but, as the old saying goes, intelligence is not evidence so we can't prove anything…yet.'

Nadia touched the dressing on her head, wincing slightly at the touch. 'I told the Boss today what I remembered about Crispin authorising the VIKER operation and giving the go to the SF. OD says he'll get that straight to Matthew Chivers at Thames House and I'll be required to make a formal statement for the inquest and investigation.'

Lovat shook his head, the anger flushing through his face. 'I *knew* he'd given the Go. Told him as much, but he's laying the blame at Giles and MI5. Bastard!'

Nadia reached out and put her hand over his. 'What are we going to do about this?'

He looked up and covered her hand with his own. 'First, you concentrate on getting better and let me figure out how we call this prick to account for what he's done. Then, when the time's right, we'll make sure he pays for it.' He felt her grip tighten on his hand to the point of pain and looked up to meet her eyes.

'I'm already getting better Lovat. It'll take more than a bump on the head and some bruised ribs to keep me down. So, if you even *think* about taking him down without me, I will literally kick the living shit out of you. *I'm* the one he *nearly* killed, so I'm warning you; whatever you have in mind, it waits until I'm part of it, agreed?'

Lovat laughed. 'I've seen you on the bag and don't want to be on the receiving end of any of that.' He leaned forward and laid his hand on her shoulder. 'I give you my word, I won't move against him until you're ready. It's only dumb luck and the fact that you're tough as old boots that you're not dead. So again, I promise I'll wait till you're good to go.'

Satisfied, Nadia lay back on the pillow and nodded. 'Good, because I want to see his face when he realises he's screwed.'

'Well, you out of all of us have earned it the most. Look, that's not all of it either. I had a meeting with an old colleague of mine who now works for Box. She told me a very interesting story about Mr Crispin Faulks regarding other VIKER operations.' He went on to relay Jenny's conversation and watched as Nadia shook her head in disbelief.

'So, this guy has been pulling this shit for years and nobody's caught him at it? That can't be right Lovat.'

'Think about it though; if he pulls an unauthorised VIKER and it's successful, who's going to ask anything? If he takes a couple of HVTs off the battlefield, it's champagne and cigars all round isn't it? If nobody *officially* complains about the collateral, well, you know as well as me that it never happened.'

'So, this friend of yours…'

'Jenny.'

'Yes, Jenny. Why didn't she say something at the time? Or even more so, after she'd found out he'd done this before?'

'Put yourself in her position Nadia: She's a junior in the Intelligence Corps, selected to work in a prestigious team that would be regarded as well beyond her reach, and directed by an MI6 officer. She had neither the authority nor the confidence to challenge this. Bearing in mind she was the lowest rank there among a couple of Sergeants, a Warrant Officer and a Captain. In her defence, it weighed that heavily on her mind that she left the Int Corps and went and joined Box, maintaining a professional career but without having to operate at a level where she would ever be exposed to VIKER operations again.'

'Will she give a statement to this inquest and investigation?'

Lovat shook his head. 'No, she won't and to be honest, I don't blame her. She thinks Crispin will slither his way out of this as he's always done and that he'll make life a living hell for anyone who went against him.'

Nadia exhaled in exasperation. 'Come on, surely with her testimony there would have to be an investigation into those old VIKER strikes that would support the evidence for Crispin having authorised this one?'

'An investigation by who? MI6? Really? You think they're going to want to open Pandora's Box and have their dirty laundry aired for all to see? And they will *never* give full access to any investigating body assigned to such a case.

They would simply use the Intelligence Services Act to cover their refusal to cooperate.'

'So, what now? We just keep hoping something else turns up while he walks around scot-free, without a care in the world?'

Hearing the frustration and anger in her voice, Lovat again placed his hand over hers. 'No. I told you that Jenny wouldn't give any assistance to an investigation. I didn't say she wouldn't give any assistance to *us*.'

Nadia raised an eyebrow and nodded at her colleague. 'Go on.'

Lovat leaned back and folded his arms with a look of feigned smugness that made Nadia smile.

'Turns out that Jenny really wants to help in her own way so she's going to get me the dates and locations of the other VIKER strikes that she knows about. And…'

'And what, you smug shit?'

'…and she has a very good contact at Vauxhall who has no love for Mr Crispin Faulks and owes Jenny a favour or two.'

'So, what's your plan, oh wise one?'

Lovat smiled and leaned forward, clasping his hands and resting his arms on his thighs. 'Right now, Mr Crispin Faulks of MI6 will be chasing his tail and trying to cover his involvement in this clusterfuck. He will be erasing any evidence that exists and looking to provide other evidence that will, at the very least, hint that the operation was sanctioned by MI5. But listen Nadia, you still haven't asked the most important question that we need to answer and that I think Jenny's contact can help us with.'

Nadia frowned as she tried to determine what the obvious question could be. 'Okay, I'll bite. What is the most important question we should be asking?'

'Why. Why is Crispin so personally involved in this? Why, even now, can he not let go of this operation? Even at the After-Action Meeting at Thames House yesterday he is still maintaining his involvement. And there's no need; he should be handing it over to Box like a fucking hot potato. And yet he doesn't.'

'You're right. In his shoes you would take the first opportunity to bail out and distance yourself from it as far as possible.'

Lovat pointed at her, his eyes aflame with intensity. '*Exactly*! And he is taking the opposite tack. No, he's remaining involved because there is something personal here, we're just not seeing. Crispin Faulks *has* to see this out to the end. Once we figure out *why* that is, we'll have him.'

Nadia was silent for several moments as she pondered Lovat's theory. Her gut instinct told her that Lovat was right. Crispin should have been kicking down the exit doors to distance himself from the fallout of the operation but was, in fact, doing the opposite. Lovat had hit the nail on the head; the *why* was everything. Once they had this, she was sure it would explain everything. 'Okay, you're right; this bastard has a really important reason for staying involved. How do we find out what it is?'

'Jenny and her contact are going to help us out on that front as long as their involvement is never disclosed.'

'That's a given but can they cover their tracks within their own organisations? You know as well as I do that every query and document accessed within their databases leaves a trace.'

'Jenny's all over that. Says that her and her contact are more than capable of accessing the information we'll need without leaving a trail of breadcrumbs to their doors.'

Nadia nodded. 'I'm impressed. Your friend Jenny is really going out on a limb with this. What's her motivation?'

'Remorse. Pure and simple. She still suffers from the fact that she did nothing all those years ago and that because of her inaction, an MI5 officer and five SAS soldiers might otherwise be alive today.'

'Shit Lovat, she can't take that on her shoulders. Even if she'd spoken up all those years back, there's no evidence to suggest that anything would have been done other than ruining her own career.'

'I know, I told her as much and I think it got through. She's good people and she's got a conscience, which is what's driving her to help us. We just have to make sure that her and her contact remain completely under the radar on this one.'

'Done. So where do we go from here?'

Lovat moved his chair closer to the bed so that they could talk further without the risk of being overheard. 'Glad you asked. While you were sleeping, I gave Jenny and her contact a few tasks…'

HAMLEYS TOY STORE, REGENT STREET, LONDON

Cassandra watched her daughter's expression of joy with a feeling of relief. Amy had not been herself for the past week; sullen, morose and withdrawn, very unusual for the normally bubbly little blonde. It had taken Cassandra some time to get to the bottom of the problem and it had come as very little surprise that online bullying over social media had been the cause of her daughter's unhappiness.

Unknown to Amy, Cassandra retained the ability to access her daughter's social media accounts, her husband Tim insisting that no nine-year old should be let loose online without an element of supervision. Cassandra hadn't been convinced; she'd felt that as parents, they would be betraying Amy's trust in them and jeopardising their relationship with their daughter. As always though, Tim had reasoned with her, pointed out that it wouldn't be Amy that was the problem, but the people and groups she would be engaging with. And he'd been right. Amy had become the victim of a vicious, yet all-too typical bullying campaign by girls in her class at school. Cassandra had initially been stunned as she remembered very clearly how close the girls all were the year before. But then she recalled her own school days, pre-internet, where the bullying was physical and again, usually conducted by girls that had once been the closest of friends.

She'd wanted to go straight to the police, the feral, maternal rage almost immediate. Tim again, had been the voice of reason, pointing out that they were nine-year olds and that dialogue rather than official involvement would probably yield better results for all concerned. She loved that about him. How with his warm, lazy smile, and laughing brown eyes, he could disarm her and bring her back to earth. They'd contacted the parents of the bullies, copied the messages from Amy's accounts and had a meeting without the children's knowledge on how to proceed. To her relief, the three sets of parents had been horrified when confronted with the evidence of their daughters' activities and a very quick resolution was arrived at. Karen Vickery, the mother of the main culprit Katie, had taken control of the situation, informing the other parents that Katie was always leaving her iPad unattended and her social media accounts open as she knew her parents never looked at them. Karen had gone home, taken the first opportunity to grab Katie's iPad and then 'discovered' the nasty messages.

All three girls had been dragged by their mothers to apologise in person to Amy, who for her part seemed torn between relief that it was out in the open, and fear of further reprisals. It was only in the last two days that she had begun to brighten up a bit and with a trip to Regent Street with Mum on the cards, she'd seemed her old self again.

Cassandra smiled as she watched Amy become a little girl again, dancing between rows of glossy-boxed toys, smiling in wonder at the product display staff. She felt a warm glow in her stomach, a welcome feeling after a week of being on edge. She would take Amy for a big ice-cream after this. Finish the day properly. Her grin widened as Amy turned to her with a huge smile of her own, big, blue eyes wide with happiness as she pointed to the dancing robot in the centre of the floor. Cassandra raised her hand to wave when a loud bang outside of the building made her jump.

Before she could interpret what it was she had heard, the sound of muted screams and shouting came from the street outside. Fear began clawing at her insides as she rushed to Amy, screaming her name just as a second, louder explosion sounded, this time shaking the floor and breaking windows. She grabbed her daughter's hand as the crowds in the store panicked. Pulling Amy close against her she wedged them both into the corner of a display and sat down holding her daughter tight against her chest. Around her, people screamed and fell over one another in their panic to find an exit. Amy was shaking and crying and Casandra looked down into her eyes.

'Mummy, I'm scared. What's happening?'

'Shhh baby girl, it's an accident outside. Probably a gas leak so we'll have to stay here until it's safe.'

'But Mummy, everybody else is leaving...'

Cassandra rubbed Amy's hair then lowered her head and kissed her forehead. 'Yes, they are darling but we'll wait here until it's clear, okay?'

She could feel Amy shaking against her then she screamed as the loudest explosion yet shook the building and plaster and dust fell from the ceiling. With the windows of the store broken, the cacophony of awful screams and shrieks outside were no longer muted, but as loud as those inside. Cassandra covered Amy's ears and hunched over the top of her daughter, hoping to protect her from any further falling debris. Screwing her eyes shut in anticipation of this, she flinched as an explosion made the building tremble again, and then another, slightly further away.

Cassandra knew this was no gas leak, knew for certain that they were experiencing an attack and that above all, if they wanted to live, she could not panic. For Amy's sake, no matter how scared she was, she had to hold it together for her little girl. She could feel herself breathing in large, fast gulps and tried to slow her respirations down and concentrate on what to do. She noted that, while the screams and wailing continued, there had been no explosions for some time. Looking up, she saw the department they were in through a screen of dust and plaster that filled the air. In the dim light she could also see several bodies over towards the window and thanked God that her and Amy had been as far away from the windows as it was possible to be.

Cassandra continued to monitor the area around her and watched as other parents and children stood and made their way through the stygian gloom. Alarms and sirens added to the awful din and the thought struck her that fire might now be an issue. She lifted Amy's head and looked her daughter in the eyes. 'Okay honey, I'm going to need you to hold tight to mummy as we've got to leave the shop now.'

Amy didn't answer her, and Cassandra could see she was in shock, her skin very pale and her eyes blinking rapidly. Without waiting for an answer, she stood and was gratified to see Amy following her immediately.

'Good girl darling, good girl. Now I just want you to put your arm around Mummy's waist and I'll put mine around your shoulders. Okay, good. Now just look straight ahead and we're going to walk over to the stairs and go down to the entrance, okay honey?' She could hear the shaking in her own voice but watched as Amy nodded to show that she had understood. Cassandra took a step on wobbly legs and felt the increase in pressure around her waist. *Good, she's holding on tight.* She focused on the door at the other side of the room that she knew led to the stairs and headed towards it. It struck her that they were very lucky again in that there were no bodies in the direction they were heading. Her child had seen and heard enough today and Cassandra wanted to shield her from any further horrors.

As she approached the doors, she saw that they had been wedged open and could hear people moving beyond them. Entering the stairwell, she held Amy tighter as they were bumped and jostled by people barging past them. An Asian man careened into her and knocked her against the wall causing her to cry out in anger and fear but Amy clung on and they recovered, making their way down the staircase. When they walked out onto the ground floor, the noise increased as the front of the store had been blown open and was completely exposed to the street. Cassandra saw several bodies lying in contorted positions and stopped, turning Amy to face her and picking her up as she had done when she was younger. She used her hand to tuck her daughter's face against her shoulder in an attempt to spare her the trauma of witnessing so many dead. With grim determination, Cassandra continued through the store and out on to Regent Street. The chaos and panic were instant with people screaming, crying, shouting and yelling into mobile telephones.

Sheer instinct kicked in and although she could not find a reason for it, Cassandra opened up her stride to get as far away from the scene as possible. She weaved a path between the dead and the dying, heading for a small square that she knew off Foubert's Place. She just wanted to get her daughter off these streets and somewhere quiet so that she could call Tim and get back home. Looking around her, she shook her head at the terrible destruction and was thankful once again that they'd been spared. A lump came to her throat as she thought about all the parents and children who had been in the store when the attack had happened.

Her arms were tiring and her quads screamed at her in protest. She hadn't carried Amy like this for years, and she herself was not in the best of shape, couldn't even remember the last time she'd been to the gym. But she was nearly there. The streets around her were quieter with a mix of people like her who were racing away from the scene, and others who'd left their homes and offices, staring transfixed at the plumes of smoke over the tops of the buildings. She gave a cry of relief when she saw the hedges that marked the borders of the square and entered through the open gate, staggering with her load towards one of the green wooden benches. She lowered Amy down and then collapsed next to her, breathing heavily, and put her arm around her daughter's shoulders. Amy snuggled in and buried her head against her and Cassandra leaned her own head back and sucked in large gulps of air. Reaching into her coat pocket with her free hand, she pulled out her mobile and entered the passcode. On the 'recents' screen she found Tim's name and stabbed at it, eyes watering as she could now finally believe they had made it.

Her call wouldn't go through and she tried several more times before she remembered that the phone networks were probably overloaded as a result of hundreds of people just like her, trying to get through to loved ones or the emergency services. Sighing, she typed out a quick text just to say they were safe and would make their way home as soon as she'd caught her breath. Putting the phone back in her pocket, she let out a shaky sigh and tears streamed down her face as she thought about how close they had come to being killed. Sniffing loudly, she wiped her face with the back of her hand, leaving a dark streak across her plaster-whitened features. She felt Amy lift her head and looked down to see her daughter looking at her.

'Are you okay Mummy?'

She ruffled the child's hair and attempted a smile. 'Yes darling, of course. Mummy just had some dust in her eyes that's all.' The thought struck Cassandra that Tim was right; they needed to get out of this city. She'd always resisted this consideration, citing their salaries and careers as opportunities that they just wouldn't have elsewhere. He'd pointed to quality of life, fresh air and uninflated prices of everyday essentials. Well, *now* she was ready to listen, would pack their bags and get out of this fucking city *today* if she could.

Her daughter was silent for a moment, a frown of concentration furrowing her features. 'Mummy?'

Steeling herself, Cassandra took a breath. 'Yes Amy, what is it?'

'I think I'm getting too old for toys now, don't you?'

Despite herself, Cassandra laughed and hugged her child harder, kissing the top of her head and allowing the tears of relief to fall freely.

GREEN PARK, LONDON

Djinn removed the high-visibility jacket, helmet and goggles he'd worn to assist him in gaining access to the site. Tossing the items into a large oil-drum as he passed, he straightened his tie and swung his shoulder bag around, removing a pair of glasses from one of the front pouches and placing them on his face. He attracted no attention as most of the workmen were starting to gather around the portacabins at the entrance to the construction site, stunned by the news that was being relayed across the television and radio sets the managers kept in the temporary buildings. He signed out of the logbook, waved his pass and smiled at the security guard. His smile was returned, the gate opened and Djinn walked away from the muddy entrance and onto the street near the tube station.

The mortars he'd fired from the building had clearly had the desired effect. Even as he crossed the busy traffic, Djinn could hear the sirens wailing across the capital and he nodded with satisfaction at his handiwork. He'd chosen the construction site at Green Park after very careful consideration. It had offered him both the range and the line of sight for his mortars to strike within Regent Street and its teeming population of shoppers and tourists. In addition, the stage of construction at the site was such that a lot of heavy machinery noise, drilling and jack-hammers were in constant use and he knew that by positioning his mortar carefully, he could fire the device without anyone realising the sound was anything other than construction equipment being used.

Several weeks before, he'd followed workers from the site as they finished for the day and eventually saw what he had needed. A single man living alone in probably rented accommodation, but who spent a few hours every night in a local pub. Djinn had simply gained access to the man's house when he'd been out and photographed his documentation. He'd noticed that the workers' passes were colour-coded and that the single man and his colleagues were given the briefest of glances from the on-site security once the prominent purple band on their passes had been seen. And his selection had proven to be correct. He'd walked in confidently on the first day of his plan and signed in to the site, displaying his forged pass and mentioning the name of the single man. His confidence and knowledge gained him access with no further questions from the internal security and he'd used the few hours of remaining daylight to conduct a thorough reconnaissance of the site and its multi-storied building.

The fifth floor of the building seemed to suit his needs. Djinn had seen immediately that it would be some time before the construction crews turned their attention to this floor and that the lack of ceiling cover on the north end would provide him with a perfect platform for the mortar. The next day he'd rented a small van under one of his aliases and hiding the components among various pipes and fittings, had brought the mortar and its projectiles onto the site and carried them over several trips, up the stairwell and cached them, hidden from view, near his intended firing platform. He'd looked over the city from his elevated viewpoint and ran through the plan in his head to ensure he had thought of everything. He had found no obvious flaws that were apparent and left the building site with a last look back up at the fifth floor and the conviction that his plan was a sound one.

And it had worked. He'd fired off eight of the lethal projectiles from the disused floor of the site and been descending the stairwell in under two minutes, attracting no undue attention whatsoever. The site, and indeed the other developments around it, had been so full of noise and activity Djinn could probably have fired off a Howitzer and no-one would have been the wiser. He'd left the mortar on the fifth floor, having no further need for the device and content that when found, it would be traced back to a theft from a military training range several years before.

As he walked along the bustling street, he could see people stopping and staring at the screens on their mobile telephones, no doubt keeping abreast of the news of the attack. He paused as he passed an electronics shop and joined the small group of people who were watching the TV screens in the window display. The televisions showed scenes of chaos and carnage. Burning buildings, corpses strewn on the streets, stumbling casualties with eyes wide in fear and shock. The scrolling banner under the images stated merely that another large-scale attack had occurred in London with mass casualties and damage to buildings. A Freephone number was also displayed for those concerned about people who may have been caught up in the attack. Djinn shook his head in mock sympathy, as most of the group were doing for real, but was inwardly very pleased with his accomplishment. This attack would galvanise the authorities into action as a country's government could not sustain this level of violence and hope to remain in power.

Walking away from the shop, Djinn hoped that his assertion was right. That his actions would push the government into making a decision that would bring these atrocities to an end. They really had no choice as they were rapidly losing the confidence of the people. And he hoped that it would be sooner rather than later as he knew with each attack, the likelihood that he'd made a mistake or overlooked a crucial aspect of his operation grew more certain. Regardless, he would never face the inside of a prison cell. Djinn had no intention of being taken alive but didn't want to enter paradise with the thought that he'd failed to achieve his ultimate objective.

Intiqaam;

Revenge.

THAMES HOUSE, MILLBANK, LONDON

Lovat could see that Matthew Chivers was a tired man. As MI5's Director of Operations, he was probably facing the Prime Minister's wrath in their daily meetings. And probably being told to his face that his job was now completely on the line. As he watched, the MI5 officer removed his glasses and rubbed the lenses on a napkin, the tiredness in his eyes now accentuated as he struggled to focus. Lovat looked at the other four individuals in the room who were, like him, waiting for Matthew to convene the emergency meeting he had called. OD caught his eye and nodded, deep in conversation with DSF while across from them Phillip, the MI5 field officer brought in to replace Giles, was pouring coffee into a mug. Of immediate note was the fact that Crispin Faulks, immaculately turned out save for the purple and yellow bruising around his eyes, sat alone and aloof from the others, keeping his attention fixed upon the screen of his phone. A rapping of knuckles on the table grabbed their attention as Matthew Chivers addressed them.

'Gentlemen. Forgive the last-minute nature of this meeting but as I'm sure you will all appreciate time is a luxury we cannot afford at the moment. Please, take a seat and Phillip will brief you all on the latest developments.'

As they took their seats, Lovat glanced at Crispin and caught the MI6 officer looking back at him with undisguised hatred. The look lasted a heartbeat before it was replaced by a neutral expression and a nod, which Lovat ignored before turning his attention to the briefing that Giles' replacement was giving.

'Gentlemen, as the Director of Operations has already stated, I'm going to bring you up to speed with some recent developments that are going to directly affect our operation.' He paused then ran a series of Power-Point slides that showed the locations and effects of the mortar attacks from earlier that week. 'Okay, I'm sure there's nothing else at this point to talk about regarding the effect of this latest atrocity, however what I do have to offer is, finally, a tangible lead.'

Lovat sat a little straighter in his chair and gave the screen his undivided attention as another series of slides were cycled through.

'The mortar we recovered was stolen three years ago from Salisbury Plain and we recovered it from the scene at this building site in Green Park. We assessed that the attacker had to have brought the mortar and bombs in by vehicle and so started trawling all available footage of the site entrance and the area.' Another slide was presented that showed a man of Asian appearance in workmen's clothing exiting a white panel van. '*This,* Gentlemen, is our attacker bringing the mortar into the site. This next slide shows him leaving and this one, entering the site the next day. This last one shows him leaving the site after the attack. It is likely that he was unaware of this camera that caught him as it was positioned some weeks ago by a private security firm. The construction company engaged them to catch the person who had been stealing copper piping from the development but, crucially for us, it was positioned covertly in order not to alert the workforce to its presence.'

Lovat felt the palpable tension in the room as each man memorised every feature of the face on the screen in front of them. He cleared his throat. 'Any identification as yet?'

The MI5 officer shook his head. 'No, but we don't think it's going to be long before we're hot on his heels.' The officer turned and put up another slide. 'This is the van that he rented, using the alias of Mohammed Akhundzada. False driver's license, cloned credit card etc. etc. *However*, what we do have is his journey across London and we're currently examining every piece of camera footage that he is caught on to tie him down to a location.'

Lovat turned his head as DSF spoke. 'Timeframe?'

Phillip shook his head. 'Nothing definite, I'm sorry to say but we have twenty analysts on this, 24/7. My hope is that before the day is out, we are at least confident of his last sighting. Let me demonstrate'

Lovat watched as the MI5 officer switched from the Power-Point presentation to another feed that showed a large-scale map of Central London, punctuated by a series of red dots which Phillip began explaining.

'This is a live feed of the current movement-mapping of the subject. The red spots indicate locations where he was caught on camera. As you can see, we last had him at Green Park Tube Station and the analysts were just accessing their CCTV systems as I came to brief you. As I said, we'll get his last known location by the end of today.'

Matthew Chivers spoke. 'Thank you, Phillip, both for the thorough briefing and some bloody well-needed good news on this. Brigadier, I suggest you make haste and have your chaps on immediate notice to move. Oliver, I suggest your team head down to the analysts and be prepared to react and examine any possible locations that they find.' The Director of Operations rose and began collecting up his papers. 'That is all Gentlemen but please remain in constant contact and apprise Phillip of any updates however small they may be.' Before he made it to the door he was interrupted by Crispin.

'Erm…Matthew, if you like I can have some of our analysts brought in to assist with this and I'm happy also to hunker down in the Ops cell with the SIG team and pitch in where I can.'

The MI5 officer looked over his glasses at Crispin for several seconds before replying. 'Crispin, you have brought three things so far to this operation: Mistrust, obfuscation and suspicion, all of which have collaborated to make me question what it is that you believe your role to be here. So, to that end, no thank you; both to your offer of extra analysts and your personal assistance. In actual fact, I see no reason for your continued presence here and I will be calling on your own people to inform them of this fact. So now, if you don't mind, get out of my fucking building.'

Lovat's eyes widened in surprise, both at hearing the urbane and cultured officer utter such a profanity and at the expression on Crispin's face. The MI6 officer's mouth had dropped open and he was clearly reeling from the unexpected statement. Looking around him, Lovat saw DSF chuckling to himself as he followed Matthew out of the room. Phillip approached OD and Lovat and nodded towards the door.

'Come on. I'll show you down to the analysts and you can sort yourselves out from there.'

Lovat picked up his notebook and with a last glance at the stunned MI6 officer, followed his CO out of the room.

In the silence that followed, Crispin felt something akin to a panic attack coming on. His heart was racing, and he could feel his breathing quicken as well as a sensation of being light-headed. He dropped into a chair and attempted to calm himself. He was in the shit now and no question. Once Matthew Chivers made that call to Crispin's superiors at Vauxhall, his career in the Service was over. He stared at the blank wall in front of him as his mind raced with escape strategies and exit routes that he could employ to extract himself from the situation, but nothing realistic was coming to him. Shaking his head, he knew that it was only a matter of time until the analysts tracked SCIMITAR down to a location and deployed the SF teams to arrest him. His eyes widened and he leapt from the chair, crossing the room in two swift strides and picked up the remote control that Phillip had been using to give the presentation. It was the same type that they used in Vauxhall and with a sense of building excitement, Crispin activated the plasma screen that showed the live-tracking of SCIMITAR's movements,

He cursed when he saw that the map had now updated and the red spots covered several locations near Baker Street. *Where the hell is he going?* Crispin stood back and viewed the wider constraints of the map and punched his fist into his hand in exultation. He knew *exactly* where SCIMITAR was heading and if he was quick, he could stop all this in its tracks and remain the darling of his Service. But he needed to act *now*. Spinning on his heel, he sprinted through the long corridor, aware of the stares that he was attracting from the offices he passed. Running was just something that wasn't done in the hallowed halls of the country's intelligence services.

Crispin cleared security and as soon as he was on the street, called his surveillance and SF contractors and put them on immediate notice to move in the Edgware Rd area. As both teams had been waiting for such a call, their responses were quick and assured. His next call was to his own analysts at Vauxhall and consisted of just one simple request; the address of the ISI safe house on the Edgware Road. Their willingness to help told him that Matthew had not yet made the call to Crispin's superiors as he would have been shut out of any such information if this had happened.

He returned his phone to his pocket and flagged down a taxi to take him back to the flat in Surrey Quays. Crispin needed access to his computer and more pertinently, the secure portal so that he could plan this operation as quickly as possible. As the taxi made its way across the city, he called Nick Brechin and asked for one of his surveillance officers to meet him at the flat and act as his driver while Crispin coordinated the operation. Again, Nick acquiesced with no further questions other than the address and stated that he would text Crispin with the details of his driver and car once he'd identified a suitable individual. Sitting back in the taxi, Crispin let out a deep sigh and allowed his body to flop, relaxing for what felt like the first time in days. He was going to *do* this. By the end of the night his ordeal would be over with nothing to come back and haunt him. Once SCIMITAR was dead, he'd arrange a very quick leak to the press to ensure that the rabid publicity that followed would leave his elders and betters with no option but to embrace it as a stunning success for MI6.

A grin crept over his features and he nodded to himself, thoroughly pleased with his plan and actions. *This is the real Crispin Faulks, not that sorry, bloody hand-wringer from the last few days. THIS is who I am.* Glancing out of the window he wondered how far along the analysts at MI5 and their SIG counterparts were. *No matter.* He had the lead and he didn't intend to lose it to a few geeks and a couple of squaddies.

THAMES HOUSE, MILLBANK, LONDON

Lovat and Nadia hunched over the screen in front of them, the strong light from the computer highlighting their faces. Lovat put his finger on the screen and traced the roads and streets between the red spots that marked the terrorist's, or Zulu One as he'd been designated, progress.

'Where the hell do you think he's going?'

Nadia answered. 'Shit. Could be anywhere. How far behind him are we?'

The Chief Analyst looked over at the screen before replying. 'Just over an hour.'

Nadia turned to Lovat. 'Possible he's heading up to Paddington? Heathrow Express then a flight out of the country?'

The analyst cleared his throat. 'All airports, bus and train stations and ports have his mug-shot already and we've deployed officers to the key hubs just in case.'

Lovat nodded. 'Good, good. I don't know though; something tells me that Zulu One is very familiar with this area. I mean, look at his movements; no hesitation, no wrong turns, this is a very relaxed man.'

Nadia was silent for several seconds before she pointed at the screen. 'Okay, so either he's from, or has been staying in this area for some time.'

They were interrupted by a shout from another analyst sitting on the other side of the room. 'Got Zulu One boarding Bakerloo Line, Northbound, thirty minutes ago.'

The Chief Analyst relayed this information via a secure telephone to the A4 Surveillance team leader who was coordinating the ground operation. He finished his call and turned to Nadia and Lovat. 'Looks like you might be right; he could be heading to Paddington and then Heathrow.'

Lovat nodded. 'Yep, agreed. Let me call my CO as he has an armed team stood by in Uxbridge that we can move towards Paddington.' Lovat swiped out of the secure room and was walking along the corridor towards the stairs. He intended making the call from his secure mobile outside, desperate for fresh air. As he entered the stairwell and began his descent he smiled with surprise when he saw Jenny walking up towards him. He was about to greet her but caught the minute shake of her head and her downward glance at her hands. Following her glance, Lovat saw a small white corner of paper, barely visible, protruding from the side of her fist. He gave a casual nod to show he understood and as they passed, she deftly transferred the paper into his own hand with not a glance of recognition or confirmation. *Good girl.* A perfect brush-contact, the time-old method that

Agents and their Handlers used to pass sensitive documentation. Closing his fist, Lovat continued his descent and entered the main reception area where he put his hands in his pockets for a few seconds while he waited for the queue at the star-trek tubes to clear. With the paper now tucked down into the depths of his pocket he went through the tube and out the other side, feeling the fresh air as it entered through the revolving door that led to the street.

Walking among the hurried crowds, Lovat waited until he'd cleared Thames House by several streets before taking the paper from his pocket and reading it. He whistled as the sensitivity of the information became clear. He was looking at a list of safe houses ascribed to someone called SCIMITAR in the Greater London area. The addresses had obviously been cut from an official report and pasted on to a blank document to mask their provenance but Lovat was under no illusions that he was looking at something produced by Jenny's contacts at Vauxhall. He studied the list once again and found his eyes drawn towards an address on the Edgware Road. *No. It can't be that easy can it?* With a jolt, Lovat suddenly realised who SCIMITAR was. SCIMITAR was the Objective name for an MI6 Target that they'd clearly been operating against for some time. SCIMITAR was the man that in a room in Thames House, a team of analysts were tracking through central London. SCIMITAR was their Zulu One. *Holy shit! All this time that devious bastard Faulks has been running a parallel operation? Why? What the hell is going on here*?

Memorising the Edgware Road address, Lovat grabbed his phone and looking around to ensure he wasn't being overheard, relayed this latest development to OD. His Commanding Officer was silent for several seconds before giving Lovat the go-ahead to run with his instincts. Terminating this call, he immediately redialled and spoke to the Armed Response Team commander in Uxbridge, directing him to get his team to a side street a couple of hundred metres from SCIMITAR's safe house in readiness.

Next, he messaged Nadia and told her to make her way to his location immediately. They had no time to lose as Lovat was pretty sure that Crispin Faulks would not be sitting on his hands with this information. The rage was rising inside him as Lovat considered the impact of the MI6 officer's duplicitous involvement. Many lives could have been saved and further atrocities prevented if that little shit had shared his information with the rest of the Task Force. But he hadn't, and obviously for reasons known only to himself. Lovat wondered how high up the chain that this cover-up extended to. *All the way to the Chief of the Secret Intelligence Service*?

His thoughts were interrupted by a breathless Nadia thumping down beside him on the wall he was propped against. She raised an eyebrow.

'Well?'

Lovat filled her in on all the developments he had just learned and what his intentions were. He watched as her face clouded with anger and she shook her head.

'You were right all along, weren't you? That slimy little bastard has been covering his tracks for some reason and playing us for idiots at the same time. What do you think it is?''

Lovat sighed. 'If I was to guess, based on what we know about him and Jenny's information, I'd say that SCIMITAR could be bad news for Crispin and his Service, based on something that happened some time ago.' He looked her in the eyes and held up two fingers. 'And if I was to make a *second* guess, I would say that it is linked to his Op VIKER activities when abroad.'

'Plan?'

'Let's hook up with the ART in Edgware. They're bringing a couple of shorts for us for personal protection and the Boss has signed off on that. Then I think we tie in with the Box surveillance team and get this SCIMITAR housed and ready for an arrest Op. What do you think?'

Nadia stood and wiped the dry debris from the seat of her jeans. 'I think we've wasted enough time already. Let's go.'

Lovat checked her arm and moved in closer to her. 'Okay, but are you a hundred percent sure you're ready for this, what with your head and ribs still healing?'

She leaned in even closer until their noses were almost touching, staring at Lovat with an intensity that made him uncomfortable. 'Don't even think about keeping me out of this. That little shit nearly killed me and *did* kill Giles. I'm in Lovat, and I'm in until it's over.'

Lovat nodded. 'Okay. Just wanted to be sure. So, let's get this done, shall we?' They walked together towards the Houses of Parliament and Lovat flagged down a cab and directed the driver to the street in Edgware that his Armed Response Team would be waiting to meet them at. He took a quick glance at Nadia who seemed preoccupied with the view from the cab, her jawline set in grim determination.

Good. Because we're going to need a whole bunch of that tonight.

EDGWARE ROAD, LONDON

Djinn rose from his prayer mat and rolled the small carpet up before placing it in his long duffel-bag. He hummed a tune to himself as he packed up what little belongings he had in the room. Zipping the bag closed, he took a final look around the small bedroom to ensure that he had everything and was content that this was the case. He picked the bag up, hoisted the strap onto his shoulder and walked out of the room, descending the stairs and opening the front door. Closing it behind him, Djinn strode down the small path and onto the pavement of the Edgware Road, turning left and joining the throng of commuters hurrying home.

As he walked, he ran over the situation in his head. He was under no illusion that he would now be the sole focus of the country's intelligence and security agencies and was a little surprised that the great MI5 and MI6 had not even been close to him. *Yet.* As he weaved his way around the pedestrians, tutting at their slavish worship of their mobile phones, Djinn felt exhaustion hitting him for the first time.

He reflected that it had been a long couple of years that had brought him this far and was now glad that it was nearly complete. *One final piece to play…*

His mood lifted as he saw the restaurant before him and his stomach growled in Pavlovian response to the thought of delicious food. Opening the door, he could immediately smell the wonderful aromas of roasting lamb and fried spices. Taking a seat at the far end of the room, he slid into the booth seat and kicked his bag under the table. A waiter approached and greeted him with a menu and a carafe of water before retreating to the kitchen. Djinn ignored the menu, retrieving his mobile phone from his pocket and accessing his contacts list before finding the name that he was looking for. He typed out a message then read it over again to make sure that it was clear in its content. There was no room for error or ambiguity. Satisfied with his missive, he pressed the send key and waited for the confirmation that the message had gone. On receiving this affirmation, he took the phone apart and removed both battery and SIM card, discreetly dropping the components onto the floor beneath the table. He wouldn't be needing the phone again.

The waiter arrived and took Djinn's order; *tabbouleh, baba ghanoush* and *shawarma*, three of his favourite dishes. The waiter returned quickly with the *sharab ward,* the refreshing Lebanese rose-flavoured soft-drink and poured from a jug, taking his leave once he'd completed his task. Djinn sipped at the cool liquid and sighed with contentment, a small moment of bliss for which to be grateful. Gazing out of the window, he marvelled once again at the cosmopolitan nature of this part of the city. Almost every country of the Middle East and Near East was represented here, along with African and Asian nations and one could probably get by on a daily basis without using any English whatsoever. It was also what made it easier for Djinn to come and go so easily, blending in within plain sight.

His attention was caught by a man berating a niqab-clad woman as she passed him. Djinn understood the Arabic as the man made clear his displeasure at the woman walking the streets without a chaperone. The woman ignored the challenge and walked around the irate individual who threw a final insult at her receding form: *Sharmuta.* Whore. Shaking his head, Djinn wondered why someone who clearly felt so strongly about Islamic practices would choose to come and live in a country that didn't, and then be outraged by it. He turned his attention to his starters as they arrived, cheered by the anticipation of good food.

Nadia turned the corner and transmitted her message over her covert radio.

'That is a positive ID of Zulu One in restaurant, over.'

The acknowledgement from the A4 surveillance team came loud and clear through her earpiece. As she continued walking, she noticed a small builder's van in rather decrepit condition drive past her and towards the junction, the two overall-clad men inside almost hidden by the pile of old coffee cups, *Sun* newspapers and crumpled McDonalds' packaging. She knew from the commentary coming through on her earpiece that this was callsign Juliet Five, one of the A4 Surveillance team now working to maintain control of the target, or Zulu One as he was designated. As she made her way back to the vehicle, Nadia grinned at the recollection of the Arab man calling her a whore. In another time and place she would have corrected his attitude with a well-placed throat punch, but on the bright side it showed that her cover was good. She gave her location over the radio to Lovat and he replied that he was thirty seconds from her. Turning left down a quieter street she heard a car slow up behind her and looked back to see Lovat pulling up alongside the parked cars. She made her way to the vehicle and climbed in, Lovat pulling off as soon as he saw she was secure. He made the call over the radio to say that he had picked Nadia up and that they were moving to the holding area. She looked over her shoulder through the rear window then quickly shrugged out of the confines of the niqab, rolling it up and throwing it onto the back seat. She mussed her hair and then pulled on her seat belt as Lovat turned to look at her.

'Good job. We've got him now.'

'Thanks. You wouldn't credit it though; just sitting there, chilling out, waiting for his food as though he's got not a care in the world.'

Shaking his head, Lovat indicated and turned the vehicle into a wider thoroughfare. 'Incredible, isn't it? Seems to me that the eviller that these guys are, the easier they find it to live with themselves.'

'Well, after tonight there will be one less evil bastard free to continue with his attacks.'

They drove in silence for several minutes, the quiet broken only by Lovat's acknowledgement of the movements of the Surveillance team as they swapped and alternated positions to retain their control of the target. After some time, Lovat slowed the vehicle and pulled into the large parking lot of a leisure centre, the designated holding area for the teams. There were easily two hundred or so vehicles already present and the cars belonging to the A4 and ART teams were using the lot to cover their presence as well as remaining in a close-response role without over-exposing themselves within the target area. He pulled their car into a vacant bay and brought it to a halt, applying the handbrake and turning the engine off. He turned as Nadia addressed him.

'What do you think he's up to?'

'Zulu One? Not sure. Could be he's moving to another location to continue with his campaign. He's certainly not acting like someone getting the hell out of Dodge.'

'That's what I thought; he's not hurrying to get away. I think you're right; he's moving on to his next location, ramping up for his next attack.'

'Well, he's in for one big surprise if that's the case.'

Nadia nodded her agreement. 'When do you think they'll take him?'

'I reckon they'll let him leave the restaurant then grab him off the street. SCO 19, DSF and our ART are coordinating demarcation lines as we speak.'

'I'd assume he's armed.'

'More than likely and I think that's why they'll wait to get him on the street and avoid giving him the opportunity to take hostages under hard cover.'

They were silent for several moments as a flurry of updates came through on their respective earpieces: Zulu One was on the move. Lovat started the engine as he acknowledged the call, preparing to move the instant the request was given. He looked at Nadia.

'Here we go.'

They remained silent, keeping up with the constant flow of information as the A4 team updated Zulu One's locations as well as their own, ensuring that someone on the team always had 'eyes on' the target. Using a mix of vehicle, foot, cycle and motorbike borne operators, the team's communications over the radio were constant as befitted a comprehensive surveillance operation against a dangerous target. The A4 Team Leader informed the SCO 19 team that the target was now heading down a quieter road that could be a good possible for the lift. Lovat felt his excitement grow. *Here it comes.*

The SCO 19 officer acknowledged this, and Lovat could imagine him now moving his team towards the location, two vans full of armed counter-terrorism police officers backed by Lovat's colleagues, driving slowly down the quiet street. An excited voice came over the net informing them that the target had left the street and slipped down a small alleyway. Lovat and Nadia's earpieces were busy with the A4 callsigns updating on their re-shuffling to attempt to cover the area where the target had entered. Lovat looked at Nadia.

'What do you think?'

She was silent for several moments, considering her response. 'Either this was pre-planned and he's heading towards a specific destination or he's spotted the surveillance and he's drilling.'

Lovat nodded. His initial thought was that Zulu One had identified the fact that he was being followed and was now carrying out a set of actions, or *drilling* as it was referred to, in order to force the surveillance team into revealing themselves. One of the most common ways to achieve this was to go suddenly from a busy street to a quiet one, or from a large road to a small alley. Anyone following you through these points were more than likely surveillance teams desperate not to lose their target. It struck Lovat that someone carrying out these actions had clearly been schooled in the subject as your average *jihadi* didn't have this level of awareness. *Who the hell is this guy*?

He listened as the A4 Team Leader's calm tones informed them that he didn't want any of his team to follow Zulu One into the alley way as there was only one exit from it. He had a tiny camera-drone deployed from a van that was flown to a height out of sound and sight of the target which then followed him and relayed footage of his progress down the alleyway. Further A4 teams positioned themselves discreetly around the area where the alleyway opened back onto the street in anticipation of the target exiting the small thoroughfare.

Nadia wondered why the SCO 19 team hadn't just gone for the target while he was in the confines of the alley but knew that it was probably because of the houses that backed onto it. If Zulu One had managed to elude capture, he could easily have forced entry into one of the houses and taken hostages. Like Lovat, she was also curious about the target's background and his knowledge of anti-surveillance procedures. Leaning back in the seat, she acknowledged the amazing job the A4 team were doing especially now they knew their target was trained. She'd worked with A4 on several occasions and the one thing that she'd noted that gave them an edge over their SRR counterparts was the profile of their surveillance operators. They used every demographic of people available to them. Young and athletic, old and greying, businessmen and women, tracksuit-clad ne'er do wells. Her attention was drawn back to the present when the call came over the net that Zulu One was now out of the alleyway and heading south. A second transmission informed the SCO 19 team that there was a lot of pedestrian activity in the area.

Nadia sighed, frustration replacing the initial adrenalin she'd felt when out on the street. She hated the waiting part of operations, had never gotten used to it no matter how often she'd endured it. She knew from her knowledge of the area that this part of Edgware was mixed residential and commercial premises so found it difficult to even second guess what Zulu One was intending. The calls continued to come through on the net and she grinned as she noticed Lovat fidgeting, clearly, like her, desperate to be more involved in the operation.

'What's the matter? Itching to get amongst it?'

He gave her an apologetic grin. 'Something like that. Never been very good at sitting on the side lines.'

She laughed at his admission. 'Don't worry, I'm exactly the same. I'm sitting here chomping at the bit to be a part of taking this arsehole down.'

'It's got to be soon: No way can they let him run for much longer.'

'I know; guess they're just picking their moment.'

They were hushed by another flurry of transmissions and excited voices reporting on the target's change of direction into a small industrial complex. As it was impossible to follow him in without exposing his team, the A4 commander directed for the drone to continue with its follow of the target. He then requested all callsigns to move to positions close to the complex in readiness. Lovat had the vehicle moving before the end of the transmission and drove out of the car park and back into the streets of

Edgware. A further transmission told them that the target had taken a left within the complex and was walking along a row of commercial units, all closed for the evening.

As Lovat made progress towards the industrial estate, the A4 officer on the motorcycle interrupted the status updates to inform everyone that the target had just approached a premises and was unlocking a roller door. A second, rushed call came from another operator who drove past the location in the opposite direction and confirmed that Zulu One had gone inside the building and was out of sight, but had left the roller doors open. Nadia looked over at Lovat.

'We've got him now, partner.'

Lovat nodded. 'Yep. Seems like it. After last time though they won't take any chances, so they'll be jamming the mobile signal before they go in.'

'Yeah, thought that myself. Is that the estate?' She inclined her head towards a road they had just passed.

'That's it. A4 have got it boxed off internally so I'm going to go static down here in case he escapes and manages to get out somehow.' He spotted a deserted stretch of kerb and parked the vehicle, giving a quick location update to the A4 commander. He and Nadia then remained silent as they listened to the constant feed of information as the combined SCO 19 and SAS team made their way to the estate to prepare for the final phase of the operation.

Nadia wondered what the outcome would be: Killed or captured? If she was a betting woman, she would have put money on the former, Zulu One having proved already his lack of interest in the sanctity of human life. The SF guys also had a score to settle and, as professional as they were, they would also be the only ones in the room when the operation went down and consequently the ones who controlled the narrative of events. Even as she was thinking this, she heard the SCO 19/SF Team arrive and inform the A4 commander that they were about to de-bus and make their way on foot to their forming-up positions.

The A4 commander had just started to acknowledge this when he was interrupted by a new voice that cut across the net.

All callsigns, all callsigns, this is ORION, I say again, ORION. Abort, abort, abort. Operation terminated and all callsigns move to Edgware Road Police Station and await instruction. Move now, now, now.

Lovat stared at Nadia whose wide eyes and opened mouth mirrored his own. Shaking his head, he started the car and pulled out of the space, heading towards the end of the road. *ORION* was the codename for the highest operational authority, in this case the Director of Operations for MI5, Matthew Chivers. Lovat had no idea what the hell could be happening that had necessitated pulling everyone off the ground and leaving the target to run free without even drone Overwatch. Maybe they'd learned that there was another trap waiting but that would only have meant holding back from entering and staying on the ground to constrain the target's movements. As he turned back towards the main Edgware Road and weaved between the parked cars, he pulled over to let an oncoming BMW pass, the driver clearly in a hurry to be somewhere. The black vehicle didn't even attempt to slow down as it made its way past Lovat and out of reflex, he turned to fix the other driver with a glare. Instead, for the second time that evening, Lovat found himself slack-jawed with surprise. The driver in the other vehicle did not even acknowledge Lovat, which was fine because it wasn't the driver of the BMW that had caught Lovat off guard, it was his passenger. There had been no mistaking the sandy-blonde hair, the chiselled features frowning with concentration, but mostly the bruising. *Definitely* the bruising.

Crispin Faulks.

EDGWARE, LONDON

Crispin spoke into his encrypted telephone in terse bursts, knowing that time was paramount if he was to have any hope of salvaging the situation. He'd been half-way to Edgware when he'd got the tip-off from his Ops cell that MI5 had a location fix on SCIMITAR and were closing in on the target fast. Crispin had known he had no sure way of beating his colleagues from north of the river so had swallowed his pride and called his Director of Operations and laid his cards on the table. He was minutes away with a team of SF contractors ready to end this and ensure no Service involvement would ever come to light. While not exactly coercion, it was a strong-arm tactic to play on such a senior officer but Crispin was sure that the reputational risk to the Service would be taken as the first consideration. The DO had been quiet for several seconds but then asked for Crispin's plan and his intended time to reach the target. Crispin had then been put on hold and after another brief period had been told the MI5 operation had been pulled and that Crispin was now cleared to execute his operation.

The conversation had been concluded with only three words from the DO before the senior officer terminated the call. *Final chance, Crispin.*

He knew that Eddie, his driver from Nick Brechin's team was pretty pissed off with him as he'd urged and cajoled him to make better progress through the evening traffic, but Crispin was only reacting to the intense pressure of the situation. *I'm so bloody close! This can end tonight.* Cursing again as they were slowed by an oncoming vehicle a couple of streets from SCIMITAR's location, Crispin exploded once again as Eddie began slowing down.

'Don't fucking encourage him man! Put your foot down and dominate the road! Make him pull over for crying out loud!' He saw the curl of distaste on the contractor's lip but Crispin was beyond caring, the man was being paid to do as he was told and nothing more. They sped past the vehicle and he called out the directions to Eddie, even though the driver had already stated that he knew where the location was. Crispin was back on his telephone and talking to Colin Hamer who informed him that the SF contractors were in position within the estate and ready to go. Crispin smiled with relief and directed Colin to wait, he was seconds away and wanted to be one of the first in the building after the breach team had secured entry. Colin's affirmation was another welcome development for the MI6 officer as he'd anticipated the traditional argument about SF not taking 'passengers' on their assaults. As he terminated the call, he ruminated that it was probably the money that made the difference; the contractor willing to put up with a lot more than serving SF in order to secure their lucrative employment. Crispin wondered if maybe he should be using Colin's crew more than the serving guys if this was any indication of how easy they were to work with. His thoughts were interrupted as they pulled into the industrial estate and drove past the road where the target location was. Crispin did not want to spook SCIMITAR when he was so close to ending it for good.

As they pulled to a halt, Crispin saw two transit vans parked together in the forecourt of an industrial unit to his front and five or six men in cargo pants and varied outdoor-brand jackets strapping on weapon holsters and stuffing vest pouches with magazines, stun grenades and radio equipment. Exiting the vehicle, he identified Colin Hamer from the cigarette dangling from his mouth, an affectation that Crispin remembered well from Cyprus. He made his way over and the SF contractor caught his eye and nodded.

'We're all good here Mr Faulks but there's something I think you should see before you give us the green light.'

Frowning, Crispin followed the team commander to the rear of one of the vans where two men were working with a series of iPads and other electronic equipment. They looked up briefly at the visitors then returned back to their activities. Colin explained.

'We've had LADYBIRD in since our arrival and the footage is crystal clear. Shows Zulu One, alone in a single-roomed building with a bag, just sitting and reading.'

Crispin was curious and looked at the footage being displayed on one of the iPads. He could see SCIMITAR sitting in a chair by a desk, a large bag at his feet, reading a book as though he had not a care in the world. He looked back up at Colin.

'Weapons, IEDs?'

The former SAS man pointed at the screen. 'You can see for yourself, there's nowhere to put them, unless he brought them in his bag. Pretty good for us really as we don't think we need to go in noisy.'

Crispin frowned. 'How are you going to do it then?'

'Well, we keep LADYBIRD on target while we approach and then stack at the door. We jam all mobile frequencies then as long as we have confirmation the target hasn't been into his bag, we'll sneak in under the roller door which is out of his line of sight because of this corner here. Once in, we'll just overwhelm him and grab him before he can reach the bag. If you're happy with that, it makes a lot less of a footprint to have to explain.'

Crispin felt his pulse race as he considered this option. Without realising it, Colin had just handed him the exact thing Crispin had wanted from the start of this fiasco; an opportunity to deal with the situation on his own terms. He patted the contractor on the shoulder and smiled.

'Colin, that is exactly why I came to you in the first place. Someone who can think outside the box, that's what I needed and that is what you've done my friend. Yes, I'm very happy with the plan but I'm going to have to demand one little twist; the only person who enters that building is me.'

Colin pulled the cigarette from his mouth and began shaking his head but was silenced by Crispin raising his hand.

'No, wait. Before you dismiss this out of hand, I have to inform you that there is a sensitive national security aspect to this that, unfortunately I am not at liberty to reveal and that only I can deal with. Now, as you've said, with LADYBIRD present and the jammer controlling the mobiles, I can get in and when SCIMITAR sees me and I identify myself, I know he'll come quietly. As I say, I'm not at liberty to divulge anything further but that is where we are. I'll walk him out and you and your colleagues can search and detain him securely and get us out of the area.'

'This is really risky Boss, but it's your Op, you tell us what you need us to do.'

Once again, Crispin found himself pleased with the can-do attitude of the contractors. *Cash really is king, as the old adage goes.*

'Thank you, Colin. Your professionalism is duly noted, and I'll make sure the DC is made aware of how invaluable your assistance has been to us. Now, I *am* going to need a personal firearm for protection and for the off-chance that the target needs some…coaxing.'

Colin nodded. 'What have you trained on?'

'I've had a couple of pre-deployment sessions with the Sig Sauer P228.'

'Okay, wait here and I'll grab one for you.'

Crispin thanked him and turned his attention back to the screen. SCIMITAR's only movements seemed to be to adjust his position in the chair slightly or to turn the page of his book. *Incredible, but what the hell is he waiting for? Extraction? Support?* His thoughts were interrupted by Colin's return. He held out a heavy, black pistol to Crispin and let the MI6 officer take it.

'Careful now. It's loaded and made ready with one in the chamber and a full magazine. I've not brought you any spare mags as you're not going to need them anyway.'

Crispin nodded his agreement and hefted the weapon in his hand. He'd done very little weapon training, in common with most MI6 officers. The only time they'd ever required a weapon was for the odd posting where movement between locations dictated a personal firearm be issued if requested. Most officers never saw the need, content to utilise the protection of the attached Special Forces teams when moving around. He held the pistol by his side and looked at Colin.

'Okay, how do you want to do this?'

'I'll give you two guys, one in front of you and one behind and they'll get you to the target building and then extract to a position of close cover outside. You then make entry and the rest of it is up to you. We'll ensure there are no surprises from outside and that nobody enters the estate until we're done. Good?'

'Simple and effective Colin. Let's not waste any more time, brief your guys and let's do this.'

Colin called over two of his team and briefed them on their roles and responsibilities. When he'd finished, one of them checked the LADYBIRD monitor to ensure there had been no change to the activity inside the building. Satisfied, Colin tapped Crispin on the shoulder and indicated with his head towards the target direction.

'If you're good to go Boss, we'll go now. Sniper Overwatch on the roof will cover us in.'

Crispin nodded and followed Colin's man as he turned and set off, weapon in the shoulder and ready. The second contractor tailed behind Crispin and they made their way quietly between a pair of buildings, hugging the shadows as they came within sight of the target building. The point man stopped and raised his weapon up, studying the open roller door of the target building through his weapon sight. Crispin heard the tiniest crackle of static and assumed that the sniper above them had given the all-clear for the final approach. This was confirmed when the point man turned and indicated with the blade of his hand to the target entrance. Crispin nodded, his body coursing with adrenalin, eager to finish this tonight.

They set off again, a little faster as the front man advanced in a tactical heel-toe walk, fluid strides and bent knees keeping his upper body stable, weapon up and on aim. As they approached the door, the point man pushed a little to Crispin's left and took a standing position with his weapon aimed directly at the gap between the roller door and the concrete floor. To Crispin's right, the backing contractor did the same, providing the MI6 officer with security to cover his entrance. Bringing the pistol up in front of him, Crispin ducked beneath the roller door and entered the target building.

Lovat brought the car to a halt in a screeching of tyres and sat rigid, staring out of the windscreen. Nadia withdrew her hand from the dashboard where she had braced herself out of reflex.

'What are we doing Lovat?'

Her colleague was silent for a moment before he turned and met her eyes.

'I can't. I can't let that slimy piece of shit go back there, clean up his mess and walk away from this as though nothing's happened.' He ran his hands through his hair and let out a sigh. 'I know I'll be fucked for it but I couldn't live with myself if I just let this happen.' He turned back to face Nadia and was about to tell her that he would drop her off nearer the main road but was taken aback to see her grinning back at him.

'Thank fuck for that Lovat. Was beginning to think I was going to have to do this myself. What are you staring at? You need me to drive?'

Lovat shook his head with a grin of his own. He should have known really. Nadia felt as strong, if not more so, than he did about this situation. He looked over his shoulder through the rear window then spun the vehicle in a tight turn, gunning the accelerator and propelling them back along the route that they had just covered. His mind raced as once again, he found himself weaving between the rows of parked cars on the suburban streets. He didn't really have a plan but what he did know was that he needed to get there as quickly as humanly possible to make sure Crispin bloody Faulks didn't get away with murder.

Nadia pulled her pistol from where she had it tucked into the waistband of her jeans and pulled the slide back a little, looking for the confirmatory gleam of brass that showed her the weapon had a round chambered and was ready to fire. Replacing the pistol, she covered it with her shirt which she kept untucked for that very reason. She grabbed a hold of the hand-strap above her as Lovat powered the vehicle into a left turn and accelerated along the narrow street. She stole a glance at her colleague and saw the intensity of concentration apparent in his tightened features. 'Plan?'

Lovat didn't miss a beat. 'None. We rock up right outside and go straight in. Dominate the room and see where the fuck that takes us.' He paused for a brief second as he raced into another small street. 'Questions?'

She nodded. 'None. Sounds exactly like my kind of plan.'

They remained silent as they sped through the sodium-lit thoroughfares and came closer to the target location. For the first time since they had turned around, Lovat slowed the car as they approached the entrance to the industrial estate. Turning into the complex, he took the immediate left and drove past the target building and brought the car to a halt at the edge of the property's drive. He and Nadia were straight out of the vehicle and sprinting towards the open roller door, weapons up on aim, ready for anything. Reaching the door, they looked at each other and with a nod from Nadia, ducked under the roller and into the room.

Crispin had to hand it to the man, he was absolutely unflappable. Looking over the sights of the pistol at his former Agent, the MI6 officer admired the other's nerve.

'Long time no-see Mahmoud.'

Djinn smiled and folded his arms across his chest as he reclined back in his seat.

'Not strictly true Crispin: I saw you several weeks ago, although it was from some distance away and you were rather preoccupied at the time.'

Crispin smiled. 'Ah yes, the St Albans' incident. Okay, I'll give you that, you had me rattled for a few moments.'

'And yet, here we are, just like the old days. Agent PHANTOM and his Case Officer. Bringing back some pleasant memories Crispin?'

The MI6 officer lowered his pistol and backed up against the wall, leaning his back on it as he studied the former Agent. He was too far away to be of any threat to Crispin and there was nowhere else to go in the empty room. He lowered his voice, not wanting the contractors outside to hear his conversation. 'Okay Mahmoud, why? Why all this killing? Why all these games?'

As he opened his mouth to reply, Mahmoud was shocked to see two individuals enter the room, pistols drawn and advancing towards both him and Crispin. The man barked at Mahmoud.

"Get your fucking hands above your head now! NOW!' Mahmoud complied as the man reached him and expertly frisked him from behind. Satisfied, the man then slid the bag away from under the desk and, keeping the gun trained upon Mahmoud, quickly rummaged around inside. Content that there was nothing to concern him he then kicked the bag across the floor, and it came to rest against the far wall. The man then spoke over his shoulder to his female colleague, still maintaining his intense focus on Mahmoud.

'How you doing Nadia?'

Nadia kept her pistol aimed at Crispin's head and watched as the MI6 officer's expression changed from shock to rage at their intrusion.

'What the hell are you two doing here? This is a closed operation and you have just compromised the entire thing. Get that fucking gun out of my face and get out of this room while you still have a shred of a career to salvage.'

Nadia let him draw a breath before speaking. 'Lay the weapon on the ground and using your right foot, slide it towards me.'

Crispin snarled and took a step towards her. 'Right, I've told you both…'

The shot was deafening and shocking, passing close to the MI6 Officer's head and taking a small chunk out of the breeze-block wall behind him.

In the same calm and controlled manner, Nadia spoke again. 'Lay the weapon on the ground and using your right foot, slide it towards me. I won't ask a third time.'

Wild-eyed and trembling, Crispin bent down and placed his pistol on the concrete floor then stood and complied with her directive, sending the gun skittering towards her. Nadia arrested the weapon's progress by placing her boot on it. Squatting down, she retained her focus and weapon on Crispin while she picked his pistol up off the floor and jammed it into the waistband of her jeans. Standing again, she indicated with the pistol barrel that Crispin should move to the wall nearest Zulu One.

Crispin was sure he was going to vomit as he staggered on unsteady legs towards the wall. He noted SCIMITAR watching him with a bemused smile and wanted to feel angry but the fear in him was all-consuming. *She just bloody shot at me! Another fraction of an inch and she would have killed me! Where the hell are my contractors? How did these two get past them*? Reaching the wall, he looked up at Nadia and she indicated that he sit down. Once he was settled, she looked over at Lovat.

'What now?'

Lovat moved a little distance away from Zulu One and closer to Nadia where they could both comfortably cover their respective charges. He turned his attention to Crispin.

‘Okay shithead, you know this is all over for you but do me a solid would you? Who the fuck *is* this guy to you?’

Crispin dropped his head in his hands and was about to attempt to reason with the military operators when he heard SCIMITAR speak.

‘Pardon my ignorance, but are you saying that you have no idea how myself and Crispin are connected? That you are not MI6?’

Lovat nodded. ‘That’s right. We’re not MI6 and we have no clue what the relationship is between you two but it cost the lives of a good friend and colleague and countless others up and down the country so yeah, we’re kind of fucking curious.’

Mahmoud chuckled softly and looked over at his former Case Officer. ‘Well, well, well Crispin, who would have thought it? You’ve been running this operation; how do you say it…off the books?’

Lovat growled. ‘Listen mate, I’m really interested to know what ties the two of you together but I’m equally comfortable putting a bullet between your eyes if you’re not going to get to the point.’

Mahmoud once again folded his arms across his chest and leaned back in the chair, meeting Lovat’s eyes. ‘Very well my friend then let me introduce myself. I am Mahmoud Malikzada, an ISI intelligence officer from Directorate S and up until a couple of years ago, an Agent for the great MI6. Agent PHANTOM.’

Lovat was impressed, recognising instantly the ring of truth from the man sat across from him. He gave a quick glance towards Nadia who raised her eyebrows to signal her own reaction to the admission. The man continued.

'My role for ISI was as the coordinating officer for Taliban activities in Afghanistan, based upon my previous experience and connections within the country. One day, after an important meeting in Kunar Province, I had just left the location when an American Special Forces team attacked. I actually saw the helicopters descending as I drove my truck as fast as I could away from the compound. I was congratulating myself on escaping just in time when I turned a corner and straight into a roadblock.'

He paused and pointed at a small bottle of water on the desk in front of him. Lovat nodded his permission and Mahmoud sipped the cold liquid before continuing.

'I should have known that it would be there, ready for anyone fleeing the scene but it all happened so fast. Within moments I'd been dragged out of the car, beaten, hooded and bound, thrown into a helicopter then taken to a base and a room with only white walls. I was prepared to have been left there for days or even weeks but I wasn't there all that long, though there was a reason for that which will become apparent. Enter Mr Crispin of the great MI6. He was, as one would expect, charming, respectful and knowledgeable. He knew exactly who I was and what I'd been doing and presented me with a choice; work for him as an Agent and carry on my life as normal, or never set foot outside the prison again. His offer came with a very short time-limit; you see, if I agreed, he would have to let me go immediately so that it would appear I had got away before the roadblock had been set up. If I didn't say yes quickly, then the deal expired there and then.'

He took another sip to slake his thirst then met Lovat's eyes. 'I was a professional intelligence officer and knew there were no routes of escape from my predicament so I agreed to work for MI6. Yes, I knew how dangerous this was but I also knew how *important* I was to them; an undercover agent in Directorate S of the ISI. Pure gold. So, I had conditions of my own: Resettlement for myself and my family in the UK once our work was done. And this was the arrangement between me and MI6. Except that…it didn't quite turn out that way, did it Crispin?'

Crispin groaned theatrically and looked across at SCIMITAR. 'You knew the routine Mahmoud; we promise our agents the world to get them on board then wring them dry of their value before tossing them aside and moving on to the next one. Come on! This is the life, you knew that.'

Mahmoud leaned forward and Lovat could see immediately the coldness in the gaze as he stared at the MI6 Officer. '*That* is exactly what I was expecting. *That,* I could understand, it being the nature of our game. But what you did was unnecessary. Evil and unnecessary and I swore I would make you pay for it.

Nadia held up her free hand. 'Whoa. Hold on a moment. *What* did this piece of shit do?'

There was a moment's silence before Mahmoud spoke, his tone softer and quieter than before. 'I contacted my Case Officer and told him that three very senior Taliban, men who rarely entered Afghanistan were coming to meet me at my compound. Crispin arranged a meeting and I gave him all the information he needed. Names, routes, vehicles, timings. *Everything*. I told him that after this, he would have to make good on his promise to resettle my family and I, as I would be directly suspected and interrogated. This was agreed, and I was briefed that one of your drones would pick up the targets when they left my compound, wait until they were several miles away and then strike the vehicle. I held up my part that day. Texted Crispin regularly with updates on the targets' progress as well as the minute they arrived at my home. Everything was going according to plan, except that there was clearly *another* plan all along. One that I knew nothing about.'

Lovat looked at Crispin. 'What's he talking about? What did you do?'

Crispin wouldn't look up and merely shook his head as his mind raced with confusion. *Where the hell are my contractors? Why haven't they stormed this place and rescued me*? He tried to close his ears to SCIMITAR's voice but it was useless, the man was relentless.

'Mr Crispin had told me the truth about one thing; the drone. He had a drone in the sky thousands of feet above my house, watching as my guests and I broke bread and drank chai. Watching as my beautiful wife and daughter baked that bread and made that chai.' Mahmoud's voice became hoarse and loud, echoing in the empty room. 'Watching as my young sons played and laughed as young boys do. But the drone wasn't just there to watch, was it Crispin? Was not just circling like a giant hawk observing the proceedings. No, it was there for an altogether different purpose.'

Nadia felt a shudder of revulsion as she stared at the broken figure of the MI6 officer sat against the wall. 'Op VIKER.' She said it barely loud enough for anyone to hear but SCIMITAR turned his head towards her.

'I don't know what that is but I'm assuming it refers to assassination by a drone. I woke up in a hospital in Quetta to hear that my beautiful wife and daughter and my wonderful sons had been killed in the strike that I survived. Blown apart and burned like animals by the man that *I* had given the information that facilitated that very strike. A woman and children deliberately targeted and murdered for the sake of three Taliban targets who were probably replaced within the month.'

There was silence in the room for several seconds before Lovat spoke to Mahmoud. 'That's why you came here and carried out your killings? Revenge for what MI6 did to your family?'

Mahmoud nodded and met Lovat's eyes with a sadness apparent. '*Intiqaam*, revenge, for me is an obligation not a choice. It gave me the will to live when all I wanted to do was die and be with my family. But I could never face them in Paradise without having avenged their murders. I also knew that I could never find Crispin, he could be anywhere in the world. But I knew that if I left enough small clues to my identity, MI6 would pick up on them and demand that their errant child cleans up his own mess.'

Nadia shook her head. 'You're telling us that all those people you have killed, all those lives you have ruined, was just to flush him out?'

'What choice did I have? Knock on the gate at Vauxhall Cross and ask if Crispin could come out and play?' Mahmoud studied the woman for several seconds. 'You know better than these two, the obligation I was under. Maybe you do not accept the level of violence I employed to achieve my aim, but I know you understand the obligation.'

There was silence for a moment before Lovat spoke. 'Right, enough talk. We didn't come here to…' He stopped talking as a small circle of red light hovered over his chest. When he realised what it was, he spun towards Nadia to see that she was staring at a similar dot on her own chest. He had just turned to the entrance of the room when four bearded men in civilian clothes entered, their automatic weapons up and pointing at him and Nadia, the red-dot sighting system the source of the small illuminations. The point man of the team spoke quietly but confidently, a Scottish burr to his accent.

'Weapons down on the floor and hands on heads now.'

As Lovat and Nadia complied, two of the team peeled away from their colleagues and with their weapons still up on aim, frisked Lovat and Nadia before kicking the pistols across the floor to the other team member who merely kicked them behind him where they came to rest against the wall.

Lovat's mind was racing as he assimilated the new situation. These guys were clearly SF but all seemed a little older than the usual team composition. He was about to speak when he heard Crispin address the team.

'You took your bloody time, didn't you?' As he looked at the MI6 officer, Lovat noted with disappointment the glow of confidence returning to Crispin's face. This team was obviously here to help him cover his tracks. He watched as Crispin pointed a shaking finger at Nadia.

'And that…bitch shot at me. I felt the bloody bullet just miss me! Where the hell were you?'

The men didn't answer but Crispin wasn't waiting for one. Crossing the gap between him and Nadia, he approached her with a look of determination on his face. 'No matter, you're here now. Keep her covered while I teach her a lesson in behaviour towards an agent of the crown.' As he reached her, he drew back his fist and threw a punch towards her face.

Nadia didn't even think, only reacted. She dodged her head to one side and Crispin's fist sailed through the air where her head had just been. His momentum carried his body forward and off-balance and Nadia spun into him, her back against his chest, knees bent and grabbed his punching arm as it reached its full extension. Yanking on the arm and thrusting her hips back into his, Crispin's momentum, assisted by Nadia's force saw him fly up into the air over Nadia's back, his legs scissoring as he screamed in shock before slamming hard onto the concrete floor. Nadia still had hold of Crispin's wrist and pulled up on the joint straightening the arm before thrusting her knee into the elbow while yanking back on the arm.

The breaking of the bones echoed like a shot a split second before the screams of the MI6 officer filled the room. Crispin threw his head back, mouth wide open and wailed at the agony assailing him but his cries were cut short by Nadia's heel smashing down on his mouth and slamming his head back on to the concrete. She pulled her fist back to deliver the final blow when she was stopped by the shout from the Scottish team leader.

'ENOUGH! Step back now or I'll shoot you where you stand.' Looking over at the man and again, seeing the red dot dancing up and down on her chest, Nadia knew she had no option but to comply. Lowering her fist, she took several steps back and stood, arms by her side. Lovat could see that she remained completely composed and wasn't even breathing heavily. Crispin screamed again as he made his way to a sitting position, cradling his broken arm against his body. He looked utterly demented, his hair standing up in unruly clumps, his mouth a mad rictus of bloodied tissue and broken teeth and his eyes wild with pain and rage.

Blood sputtered from his mouth as he screamed an order at the team leader.

'Kill her you bloody moron! Kill them both now! You've seen what they just did to me. KILL THEM!'

There was a brief silence and then a new voice spoke from the darkness near the door.

'I'm afraid these gentlemen won't be killing anyone Crispin.'

EDGWARE, LONDON

As Lovat watched, two men entered the room from the roller doors. He frowned as he attempted to identify who they were and what they were doing. Both men were immaculately dressed in tailored suits and brogues and the older man, who was carrying a bag, was clearly Asian. The fact that the SF team had not responded when these men entered told Lovat that they had been expected. In fact, they still remained in their positions as before, weapons trained on Lovat and Nadia. The only sound was that of the new arrivals' heels striking the floor as they made their way into the centre of the room. The taller of the two, a pale man with piercing eyes stopped and looked over at Lovat.

'We haven't formally met Warrant Officer Reid. I'm Clarence Temple-Marsh, Deputy Chief of the Secret Intelligence Service.' The man then turned his attention to Nadia. 'Staff Sergeant Ali, also a pleasure to make your acquaintance.'

Lovat's heart sank and his head drooped. They had been *so* close. Had just been getting ready to get Crispin and

SCIMITAR into the car and to the nearest police station. And now it was over. The main man himself had come to help his minion clear up the mess. Lovat lifted his head and caught Nadia's eye and saw that she had made the same assessment. His attention was drawn back to the senior MI6 officer as he addressed the SF team.

'Mac, that will be all for you and your guys. Do a last sweep of the adjoining buildings as you leave and tell our driver we won't be long. Oh, and you can return our SIG colleagues' weapons to them.'

The Scottish team leader nodded. 'As you say Boss. Brian, give them their pistols back.'

Lovat looked on in disbelief as one of the team picked up his and Nadia's weapons and strode over to them, giving them back in turn. As Lovat rammed his into the waistband of his jeans he watched as the last of the SF team exited the building. The strange silence was broken by Crispin.

'What's the play here Clarence? Must admit, I'm feeling a little out of sorts, might need a doctor quite soon.'

Clarence Temple-Marsh looked across the room at his subordinate but did not answer, instead indicating with his arm for Nadia to make her way back to Lovat. Once she had joined her colleague, he spoke to them.

'Things are about to unfold here that may seem very strange and difficult to swallow but trust me, swallow them you must.' He nodded to the Asian gentleman by his side. 'This is Major General Khan of Directorate S, Pakistani ISI and he is here as part of a partnered agreement to bring this horrendous situation to an end.'

The General nodded then turned to look at SCIMITAR. 'Mahmoud. You have been very busy I see.'

Lovat saw SCIMITAR smile before replying. 'Mustafa Khan, it has been a long time old friend. Did you bring what I asked?'

In reply, the General lifted the bag he was carrying and walked over to SCIMITAR, laying it on the floor beside him. As Lovat struggled to comprehend what was happening, he heard Nadia voice the same concern.

'If you don't mind me asking, what the hell is going on here? You're here to clean up this bastard's mess?'

Clarence Temple-Marsh looked at his watch before replying. 'Nadia. You don't mind if I call you by your name, do you? The whole military nomenclature is a little long-winded for me. Nadia, to answer your question, yes; I am here to clean up…my junior officer's mess. But not I think, in the way you imagine.'

Lovat snorted. 'Dress it up any way you want, but you're just here to cover up for your Service and make sure nothing comes back to you.'

'Absolutely correct on both points Lovat however the main thrust of my effort tonight is to *end* this. And that is what I need you both to understand.' He looked at his watch again then met Lovat's eyes. 'As I've said, you *won't* understand this, but it has to happen, and it has to happen this way.' He turned to face the general and gave a discreet nod. The ISI officer addressed SCIMITAR.

'Whenever you are ready Mahmoud.'

Lovat and Nadia watched as SCIMITAR rummaged through the bag that the General had brought. Lovat's breath caught as he saw a suicide vest taken out and laid on the desk, followed by a mobile telephone and several sets of zip ties. He turned back to the senior SIS officer as the man began to speak.

'There will be four people leaving this room tonight and those four people will be the only ones who know exactly what happened here. There will be an alternative narrative supplied to the Police and the media to explain the events and this will satisfy both entities in their craving for closure of this situation.' He nodded towards SCIMITAR. 'This man has held our country to ransom and killed dozens of our citizens in order to extract revenge for something that my Service was responsible for. Even now, he has control of a further target primed for massive loss of life.'

Lovat opened his mouth but was cut short by the SIS man holding up his hand.

'Please, allow me to finish as we are rapidly running out of time. So, your Zulu One, our SCIMITAR and Crispin's former Agent PHANTOM, *aka* Mahmoud Malikzada, contacted his superiors at ISI and offered them and us a way out of our predicament. You see, no matter that Crispin acted independently on his unsanctioned killing sprees, you are right; my Service would be left holding the ball on this one, which I will not accept. And Mr Malikzada here will not end his campaign of terror on the UK streets until his *intiqaam* has been satisfied.'

Crispin could not believe what he was hearing and a hollow feeling began creeping into his stomach. 'Clarence…'

The senior MI6 officer continued to talk as though Crispin did not exist. 'So, Mahmoud provided us all with the solution: We give him Crispin and walk away, and he calls off his final atrocity.'

Crispin raised his voice, fear now apparent as he struggled to stand. 'Clarence...Clarence?'

Again, he was studiously ignored by his superior. 'So, Lovat, Nadia. What happens tonight is *pragmatism*; it's not pretty and it's not perfect but it's the world we live in. I would rather that you were neither privy to nor involved in it but we don't always get what we want, so now you are an integral part of it.'

As the words sunk in, Lovat turned to Nadia and saw she had also realised the significance of the SIS man's statement, her eyes wide with surprise. The General cleared his throat to catch their attention and looked pointedly at his watch. Clarence Temple-Marsh nodded and looked over at SCIMITAR.

'All in your hands now Mahmoud. Thank you for holding to your word and may you find the peace you so desire.'

Mahmoud stood and picked up the zip-ties walking across the floor towards Crispin. As he passed the ISI General, the officer patted his shoulder as he passed. When he reached Crispin, the MI6 officer began panicking and pleading.

'Clarence? What the hell's going on Clarence? Clarence *please*!'

Clarence Temple-Marsh straightened the cuffs of his suit as he looked at the wreck of the man in front of him. 'You know how this ends Crispin; *as ye sow, so shall ye reap*.' With that, Mahmoud grabbed Crispin's arms to screams of agony and bound the hands together with one of the ties. Knocking him to the floor to an even louder series of shrieks, Mahmoud proceeded to secure Crispin's feet with another set of ties he had looped together. Satisfied with his handiwork, he stood and walked back to the desk, picked up the vest and put it on, adjusting straps and buckles. Lovat could not believe what he was seeing and was about to say something when Clarence strode past him.

'Everybody out. NOW!'

Nadia took a final look at Crispin as he cowered and whimpered on the floor, his eyes locked on the activities of SCIMITAR as the man finished his adjustments on the vest and picked up the mobile telephone. She felt no pity for him whatsoever and thought that the Deputy Director's words had been pretty appropriate. Turning on her heel she followed the General out under the roller door and caught up with the group as they made their way to a black

Mercedes people-carrier. Lovat walked past it towards their own car but was stopped by Clarence.

'Leave it. I'll have it taken care of later. Get in here with us.'

All four got into the back of the MPV which still retained a new-car smell and was a little bit more luxurious than Nadia had anticipated. The driver closed the automatic doors and was on the move even before she had fully sat down. They accelerated out of the estate and she was surprised to see a cordon of hazard tape and traffic cones in front of them. Just as they approached the tape, one of the SF team they had encountered earlier jogged out from behind a building and moved a section of the temporary barricade to allow them to pass, closing it after they were through.

Lovat looked back and saw the SF contractor climb into a vehicle and follow them at a discreet distance. A quiet buzzing caught their attention and as they looked on, the ISI General pulled his phone from his pocket and looked at the screen. Returning the device to his pocket he looked over at his British counterpart.

'It is done.'

Clarence Temple-Marsh let out a small sigh of relief just as his own phone buzzed in his pocket. Answering his device, he spoke very little, focusing his attention on the details being provided to him. When he terminated the call, he looked over at Lovat and Nadia.

'The General's message was from SCIMITAR, informing him that he had held up his end of the bargain and called off his final attack. *My* call was from my colleague at SO15 informing me that they'd received an anonymous tip-off telling them about a chlorine-gas IED set to detonate in Bluewater Shopping centre. They are responding now but his assessment is that the caller's knowledge of the device points to it being real.'

Lovat was about to speak when a flash of light, followed a split-second later by a loud bang behind them caused him and Nadia to hunch down in their seats to look out of the rear window. He noticed that the SIS officer and the General didn't so much as flinch, the explosion clearly expected. He turned to face the pair.

'That was it wasn't it? SCIMITAR and Crispin? That's what that was.'

The MI6 officer nodded. 'Yes. I told you that you would struggle to understand but to remember that this was a pragmatic solution to a terrible problem. Consider this Lovat; if we had not met with SCIMITAR's demands, this time tomorrow we'd be watching news footage of hundreds of shoppers choking to death on chlorine gas.'

Nadia cleared her throat. 'I think I can speak for both of us when I say that we won't be shedding any tears for Crispin Faulks. As for SCIMITAR, I would have much preferred to see him sweat out his days in a prison cell for the murders he has committed but I'm pretty sure he had made his mind up never to be taken alive.'

For the first time that evening, the General addressed them directly. 'Mahmoud Malikzada was my finest officer and I have worked with him for over twenty years. He has that great gift that few have; the ability to see five moves ahead of his opponent and always be so far ahead he is impossible to beat. Believe me, this ending tonight was not impromptu; Mahmoud would have lined this up as far back as one year before. And you are correct young lady; he would never have been taken alive.'

There was silence as they negotiated the north London streets, the wails of sirens now reaching them from all directions. Lovat was still stunned at the evening's events and how different they had turned out from his expectations. He looked over at Clarence Temple-Marsh and wondered at how someone could arrive at such a cold-blooded decision and not be the slightest bit phased by it. *Probably not the first time he's done something like this.*

'So, what now? For me and Nadia, I mean?'

The SIS officer leaned forward in his seat, closing the distance between them and meeting Lovat's eyes.

'I would like your word that you will concur with the statement of events that I will provide you with. This is not just to conceal the involvement of my Service in Crispin's illegal actions, but also because the general public could never understand our justification for the way we handled the incident tonight.'

Lovat shook his head. 'Just our word? No threats or Official Secrets Act warnings?'

'What would be the point? If you're going to talk, you'll talk. You're both clearly strong-willed individuals and hollow threats don't tend to have any effect on people such as yourselves, more likely the opposite in my experience. No, just your word. I know you are both professional operators and I would put more weight on that than I would on weak coercion.'

Lovat looked at Nadia and after a second gave a small nod. She returned the gesture and they then faced Clarence once again. Nadia spoke for them both.

'You have our word Sir. We have no issue with what went down tonight. The terrorist is dead and the vile bastard who was responsible for it all in the first place is also scattered to the four winds.'

Clarence nodded and was about to say something when Lovat interrupted.

'However, Sir, there is *one* thing I'd like to request.'

'Go on.'

'I'd like it so that Giles gets the credit for the information that led to the death of SCIMITAR. He was a good man who died and whose memory was sullied by Crispin's attempt to blame him for the St Alban's fiasco.'

The SIS officer considered the request. 'What do you have in mind?''

'A leak to the media that Giles was killed trying to bring down SCIMITAR on his own and a posthumous bravery gong for his wife and kids to remember him by and be proud of.'

'I think we can arrange that with a little effort and I actually agree that it is the least we can do. Bravo, Warrant Officer Reid, that was a very sincere request. Generally, in these situations the request centres around personal gain for the individual.'

Lovat ran his hands through his hair and felt tired for the first time that evening. 'To be fair, I don't really think there is anything you could offer that I'd be interested in Sir.'

Clarence Temple-Marsh raised an eyebrow. 'Rare to meet a man or woman who doesn't exploit personal gain when the opportunity arises, I have to say.'

Nadia thought about the SIS officer's statement for a moment. 'I think tonight we saw the dangers of exploiting personal gain all too clearly, and the repercussions that follow.' She paused and looked out of the window. 'I support Lovat's request fully, but I have one of my own.' Meeting the Deputy Chief's eye, she leaned forward in her seat. 'At the first opportunity I want a bloody giant G and T followed by more of the same!'

JOHNSHAVEN, SCOTLAND

Lovat pointed to a disturbance on the sea surface a hundred metres or so from where they sat on the harbour wall. Nadia placed her pint of cider down and shaded her eyes with her hand while she strained to see what he was indicating. As she watched, a small fin broke the surface of the water and she smiled at her success.

'I've got it! It's literally just breached the surface. How cool!'

Lovat returned the smile and took a drink from his own pint then leaned his head back and luxuriated in the warm sunshine. Nadia continued to watch the porpoises as they swept a school of fish towards the harbour wall, fascinated to see the animals so close. She looked around her at the small coastal village and could well see the attraction in living here, particularly on a beautiful sunny day.

After the official version of events had been released and the press feeding frenzy subsided, they'd both felt in a kind of limbo state as they were obliged to be available for the endless rounds of statements and testimonies. While not onerous, particularly when SIS had included them under their immunity umbrella, both Lovat and Nadia soon tired of being constrained to Bracken Camp.

They had been pleasantly surprised when it became evident that Clarence Temple-Marsh was, indeed, a man of his word. A leaked story to the press created the momentum for the posthumous award of a Queen's Gallantry Medal to Giles, as well as laying the credit for the foiling of further attacks as a result of his efforts. Lovat had been particularly pleased as, while he knew it was no consolation to Giles' family, it would be something that his wife and children could look back upon one day with a sense of pride.

The press led the country in the euphoria that followed the killing of SCIMITAR. The redtops in particular fuelling the jingoistic fervour with which this enemy of the state had been dispatched. Lovat and Nadia watched the whole spectacle unfold as observers, content to be disassociated from any publicity and remain in the shadows where they belonged. Time crept by and they complied with every attendance and interview, growing more listless by the day.

But then, slowly but surely, the requests for their evidence concluded and the need for their presence on camp negated. OD had called them into his office on a Thursday morning and recommended they both take a period of extended leave, enjoy the rare downtime that was being afforded them. And they'd accepted willingly, eager to get as far away from the drudgery of Camp routine as possible. Nadia had loaded her Honda Africa Twin, donned her leathers and was on the continent that afternoon, cruising the winding roads through the Alps and eventually spending a couple of weeks in the Italian Dolomites. Lovat had simply returned to his home, loaded his surfboards on the truck and set off around the wild coast of the north of Scotland, riding the big grey beasts that pounded the slate and sandstone reefs.

When she'd returned to the UK, she took Lovat up on his offer to pop up and see him. She'd never been north of Edinburgh in her life and was stunned by just how beautiful the north-east coast was. Lovat's house had also impressed her and she saw why it was the perfect bolthole for him. They'd also struck gold with the weather, an extended period of high-pressure providing long days of sunshine and blue skies. Which helped when a good part of your day revolved around getting seafood straight from the boat and on to the barbecue and enjoying it with cold cider sat on the harbour wall outside Lovat's house. She took another swig of her drink and turned to face Lovat.

'So. What's next for you? Back out to Libya? Yemen? Somalia?'

He was quiet for a moment before turning to face her, Nadia smiling as she saw her distorted image reflected back at her in his sunglasses.

'This might surprise you but…I'm thinking of calling it a day.'

She pushed her own sunglasses up on to her forehead and stared at him. 'Seriously? You're thinking of pulling the plug? I never expected that. What's brought you to this?'

He removed his Oakleys and met her eyes. 'My 22-year point is approaching and it's crunch time really. I know OD will push me to commission, but I can't; I just don't see myself deskbound as a Captain in SIG.' He took another drink before continuing. 'So, I think it's time for a change.'

Nadia shook her head. 'No way. I *know* you Lovat; you'll go crazy with boredom as a civvy.'

'Maybe, maybe. All I know is that it's time; time I moved on and tried something else. And…I've been told not to say anything but I'm pretty sure after all we've been through, I can make an exception for you.' He smiled as he finished his statement and she laughed and punched him on the arm.

'Aw, see; I knew I'd grow on you. So, spill, what's the big secret?'

'I mentioned my leaving in private to OD, who refused to believe that I was serious. But he must have said something to someone because a couple of days after our conversation I get a phone call from one Clarence Temple-Marsh inviting me to an informal lunch.'

Nadia raised her eyebrows. 'Interesting…and?'

'And he told me that he was aware I was thinking of leaving and asked how I felt about working for his organisation in a private capacity. Very interesting work and *very* well paid to the point where I'd only really need to work a few months of the year to have a comfortable lifestyle.'

He stopped as he heard her laughing and cocked his head to one side, surprised at her reaction.

'That is priceless Lovat, absolutely priceless!' She patted his leg in a feigned maternal manner and shook her head. 'I too, had an informal lunch with one Clarence Temple-Marsh who gave me exactly the same offer. Although my selling point is that his organisation's *male, pale and stale* demographic desperately needs someone with my background to enhance their operational capability.'

It was Lovat's turn to laugh now and shake his own head in disbelief. Once his chuckles had subsided, he looked at Nadia. 'And…?'

She took another drink of the tangy cider before answering. 'And, I'm going to take him up on it, providing it's not all bullshit, which I'm pretty sure it's not.'

'No, it's not bullshit: He's old school, likes to be known as a man of his word.' He grinned at her. 'So, looks like we're going to be stuck together for quite some time, causing trouble and creating havoc with the full backing of the state.'

She laughed and raised her glass, offering a toast. 'Here's to causing trouble and creating havoc.'

Lovat picked his glass up and clinked it against hers then took a large swig of the cold draught. 'I wonder where they'll send us first?'

Nadia swallowed some of her drink before replying. 'You know it won't be anywhere nice.'

Lovat laughed, nodded in agreement. 'Let's be honest though, would you really *want* to go anywhere nice?'

She smiled and shook her head. 'Nah. I'd just get bored and end up causing trouble.'

They looked out to sea in companionable silence until the buzzing from Lovat's phone alerted him to an incoming message. Removing the device from his pocket, he accessed his messages and read the new missive before putting the phone away again. He took a swig of his drink then turned to Nadia just as her phone signalled an incoming message. He waited until she had read it before returning her grin.

'Well, looks like we're not going to get the chance to be bored for long.'

THE END

Thank you for reading and I truly hope you enjoyed this book. Please, if you have enjoyed it, take the time to leave a review and let others know how much you liked it.

Thank you once again.

James

www.jamesemack.com

ONLY THE DEAD

'Only the dead have seen the end of war'

In war-torn Libya, veteran Commando Finn Douglas is forced to commit an appalling act in order to save the lives of his men. Haunted by his actions, he suffers a further blow when he learns that his family has been killed in a terrorist attack in London. Numb with grief and trauma, Finn turns his back on the world of war and killing and flees to an island wilderness to escape his demons.

A team of Military Police are tasked with bringing Finn to justice. But for one of the policemen, the manhunt is a more personal issue; a chance for revenge to right a wrong suffered years before.

When Finn intervenes in a life and death situation, his sanctuary is shattered, and the net tightens. The manhunt becomes a race against time between the forces of law and order and a psychotic mercenary determined to exact his revenge on Finn for thwarting his plans.

For Finn, the world of killing and conflict returns with a vengeance on the blizzard-swept mountains of the island.

Only this time there is nowhere left to run.

Only the Dead is a thriller in the tradition of Gerald Seymour and a stand out debut from a new British author.

FEAR OF THE DARK

An idyllic Scottish village...

A small team of rural Police Officers...

A man who won't talk...

When a violent stranger is arrested and refuses to give his name, it is only the beginning. Digging further into the background of their mysterious prisoner, Police Constable Tess Cameron finds that he is a disgraced former Special Forces soldier with a chequered past.

As the worst storm of winter hits the village and communications and electricity are cut, the severe weather is blamed. Tess, however, feels that something more sinister may be responsible for their isolation.

Because the stranger has friends.

And they want him back.

Whatever it takes.

In the darkest night of winter, Tess and her fellow police officers find themselves facing an elite team of killers determined to rescue their leader. And Tess knows that if they are to survive the night, they have only one choice:

Fight.

First Blood meets *The Bill* in this exciting new thriller from the author of Only the Dead.

Printed in Great Britain
by Amazon